A Morbid Initiation™

Vampire: The Masquerade Fiction from White Wolf

The Clan Novel Series

Clan Novel: Toreador by Stewart Wieck
Clan Novel: Tzimisce by Eric Griffin
Clan Novel: Gangrel by Gherbod Fleming
Clan Novel: Setite by Kathleen Ryan
Clan Novel: Ventrue by Gherbod Fleming
Clan Novel: Lasombra by Richard E. Dansky
Clan Novel: Assamite by Gherbod Fleming
Clan Novel: Ravnos by Kathleen Ryan
Clan Novel: Malkavian by Stewart Wieck
Clan Novel: Giovanni by Justin Achilli
Clan Novel: Brujah by Gherbod Fleming
Clan Novel: Tremere by Eric Griffin
Clan Novel: Nosferatu by Gherbod Fleming

The Clan Tremere Trilogy

Widow's Walk by Eric Griffin
Widow's Weeds by Eric Griffin
Widow's Might by Eric Griffin

The Clan Lasombra Trilogy

Shards by Bruce Baugh
Shadows by Bruce Baugh
Sacrifices by Bruce Baugh

The Dark Ages Clan Novel Series

Dark Ages: Nosferatu by Gherbod Fleming
Dark Ages: Assamite by Stefan Petrucha
Dark Ages: Cappadocian by Andrew Bates

For all these titles and more, visit **www.white-wolf.com/fiction**

A Morbid Initiation ™

Philippe Boulle
First Volume in the Victorian Age Trilogy

Author: Philippe Boulle
Cover Artist: Christopher Shy
Editor: Diane Piron-Gelman
Graphic Designer: Aaron Voss
Cover Designer: Chris McDonough
Art Director: Richard Thomas

1554 LITTON DR
STONE MOUNTAIN, GA
30083
USA

WHITE WOLF
PUBLISHING

ISBN 1-58846-828-3
First Edition: November 2002
Printed in Canada

White Wolf Publishing
1554 Litton Drive
Stone Mountain, GA 30083
www.white-wolf.com/fiction

And after all, what is a lie? 'Tis but
The truth in masquerade.
—Lord Byron, *Don Juan*

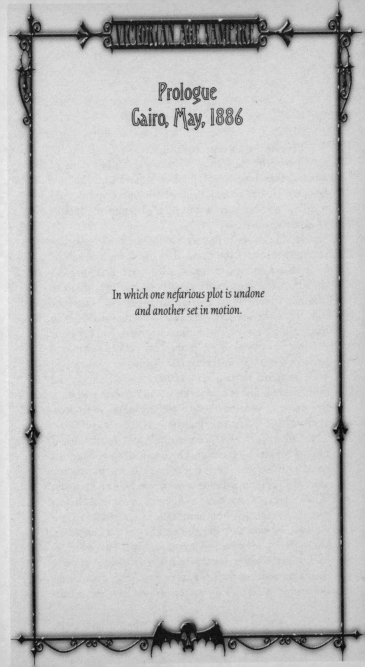

VICTORIAN AGE VAMPIRE

Prologue
Cairo, May, 1886

*In which one nefarious plot is undone
and another set in motion.*

Beckett hadn't expected laughter.

Ritual chants, perhaps. Or the screams of victims of unspeakable acts. Even simple conversation. But not laughter. He had come far enough, though, that he could hardly turn back now because of some madman's unexpected mirth.

He dropped from the stone wall into the garden below and moved toward the house. The place was a shambles, long disused and the victim of at least one fire in the last decade. Once, this had been the home of a wealthy merchant, probably built in the early years of Mameluke rule, if Beckett was any judge of architecture. To hear the locals tell it, though, the last hundred years had not been good to this place—the Ottoman tax collector who had lived in the house in the middle of the last century had been murdered by the son of a farmer who'd been evicted from his land. The official's body was never recovered since the murderer took the liberty of feeding him to street dogs. Beckett liked that image, but the story did not end there. The Arab murderer had been caught by the authorities and flogged before his execution. He supposedly pronounced a curse on those who dwelt in the house of the man who'd evicted his father. The next year, the Mameluke pasha who'd taken possession of the fine manse cut himself on a nail that protruded from one wall. The scratch became infected and ultimately gangrenous. His arm was amputated, but too late, and he died an agonizing death. His two wives both contracted a terrible withering disease shortly thereafter and died within another year. One of Napoleon Bonaparte's aides took up residence there for a few months

A MORBID INITIATION

during the French occupation, but he grew palsied and left it for better lodgings.

From that point on the house stood empty, an oasis of quiet decay in the prosperous Bab al-Khalq district. The high walls that surrounded it on all sides kept out casual observers, but invited squatters and beggars in. None knew how many of these unfortunates lost their lives inside, because few even took note.

Beckett reckoned it was time to rectify that, regardless of the risks—or the laughter. He made his way through the tall grasses that had invaded the inner courtyard toward the smoke-blackened stone entryway. The moon was full and it bathed the area in wan light, but he knew a great many things could be hiding in the deep shadows. Crouching behind what had once been a well, he tried to join them.

Beckett's contact in London, an antiquarian named Halim Bey, had sent him word that the British authorities had acquired a variety of artifacts that might be of interest. Beckett was a scholar and suffered from an insatiable desire to uncover the secrets of the past. Just like Heinrich Schliemann had at Troy and Mycenae and Alphonse Mariette had at Memphis, he sought to peel back the layers of time. That Beckett, like the subjects of his chosen field of research, was what folklore variously called "undead" or "vampire" only made his existence that much more interesting.

Tonight was certainly a case in point. In all likelihood the British archeologists who had collected relics from a tomb just east of Luxor had thought the unique designs hinted at a heretofore unknown dynasty or cult. Beckett, on the other hand, had recognized in the hieroglyphics reproduced from the tomb in the head researcher's notebooks several passages referring to aspects of the vampiric condition: the desire for blood, the fear of the sun, and so forth. This told him that the relics themselves were worth inspecting. Unlike the researcher and his notes, however, these had not returned to England, and so Beckett set off for Egypt. He had not been surprised to find that the artifacts had disappeared by the time he got there. The hieroglyphs also spoke of a variety of rituals and although Beckett was no sorcerer, he understood that ritual magic was no more superstition than vampirism was. It was rare, but it existed.

Some of the mundane pieces in the stolen collection ended up on the black market and from there Beckett had been able to find the seller, a boy named Fahd Benezra. He'd watched Fahd for several nights, and the boy always came back to this abandoned house.

***

Anwar al-Beshi smiled. There was a fissure running through the earthen tile of the home's central room. It had started as a simple nick in the center-most tile, just another random mark of the passage of time in this old dwelling. Then, while he made the first preparations for tonight's rite, it had graduated to a crack.

With the first incantations to the storm and shadow, the crack had grown, spreading first to one and then to many other tiles. When the first slave, the Arab man Fahd, knelt in the northeastern part of the room, making obeisance to a specific place in the western desert, other cracks had appeared, joining their progenitor and becoming the dark, jagged line that now split the room in twain.

"Her blessings upon us." Anwar's voice was a reverent whisper. He nodded to the other slave, the Englishwoman Emma. She stood in the north, aligning herself with the power of the Great Nile itself. Fahd whispered invocations in a language all but dead centuries before the first Arab invader came to the Delta.

A MORBID INITIATION

Emma shed her simple dyed-cotton robe to expose the marks of the Goddess's favor. She took seven deliberate steps southward, the fissure widening with each one. Anwar placed a small golden plate and scalpel at her feet. On the plate was a shriveled, petrified gray mass, whose shape implied something organic. Neither Emma nor Fahd would consider questioning its nature or import—the master treated it with reverence and so blessed it was.

Anwar looked up at his fair-skinned chattel, handed her the scalpel, and nodded. Emma took the thin, sharp blade in her right hand, holding her index finger along its dull edge for stability. She looked up at the stars twinkling down through the ruin of the old house's roof, placed the tip of the blade at the top of her sternum, and pulled down.

The blade ran along her bone, sending jolts of ecstatic agony through her. Red, hot lifeblood welled from the incision, forming like a crimson river in the valley of her milky breasts. It flowed down her stomach, to her pubis and along her left thigh. Blood collected on the underside of her slight belly and in the folds of her sex, before falling in thick droplets to the plate waiting under her.

The first drop hit the withered organ on its tip, others soon covering it in a red sheen. The first wisp of smoke rose from the crack and it smelled of great pestilence.

His broad smile exposing snake-like canines, Anwar al-Beshi laughed anew.

**

Well, that was enough of that.

Crouched in the shadows that gathered amid the ruined remains of the top floor of the home, Beckett had a good view of the ritual going on downstairs. He'd just watched thus far, taking notes and looking for an easy opportunity to gather what he needed to. But now, things seemed to be going too far.

Beckett generally disliked blood sorcerers, but they were an occupational hazard and he hadn't expected the goings-on to be especially bothersome. He'd given up using ghouls long ago, but most of his ilk still fed their blood to a choice few living slaves to serve as majordomos, daylight guardians and attendants. He'd guessed that Fahd was one such slave and it was nice to be proven right—sorcerers were, if anything, more likely to have need of such seconds.

The flow of blood streaming down the nude woman's chest was a bit more problematic. Its rich odor called to the hungry beast that had sat in Beckett's breast ever since he took his last breath. But one did not survive as a vampire for as long as he had without being able to control the urge to feed. And the woman was obviously long gone into the addled servitude and ritual requirements of her bondage—her pale skin was marked with a delicate pattern of scars emanating from her shorn crotch and highlighted by the blood that clung to the white puckers of tissue. She was long past any compassion that might still linger in Beckett's heart.

No, what pushed him to act was the smell. It rose from the cracked tile like a pillar of smoky bile, rotting the very air in the room. Beckett's nostrils flared and the noxious stuff curled into his disused lungs. Undeath had sharpened his senses in countless ways, but now he regretted it. His chest convulsed in a dry heave, trying to expel the pestilence within.

Simultaneously, the vermin began to call to him. Beckett was a thing of the night and had long ago discovered he had a unique empathy for the other beasts who made it their home. Now, he heard the buzzing of flies and gnats emerging from the crack, the scurry of beetles and locusts flocking from miles around, and the scrabbling of rats crawling from under rocks to feed on the carrion to come.

He jumped down.

***

The intruder ruined everything. Anwar was pronouncing the twenty-third of the seventy-five secret names when he barreled in from above. Tall and stocky, he slammed into Anwar and strong-armed Emma to the ground.

"Apologies for the interruption," he said. An Englishman it seemed, fair-skinned and brown-haired. He wore heavy cotton pants, a leather jacket, heavy boots and an infantile smile.

Anwar focused his attention on the man, trying to peel back any and all lies this one might have shrouded around himself. His instincts for such things, sharpened by years of moving unseen through the bazaars of North Africa, told Anwar that this one was a blood-drinker too, a vampire, though unlikely to be a child of the Dark God.

Fahd sensed his master's anger and responded unbidden. Rising silently, he drew a large flat blade from under his robe and moved to attack. Anwar appreciated the effort, of course, but he knew it was futile. The boy got to within two steps of the intruder before the man pivoted on his left foot and struck out with his right hand. Anwar watched in mild fascination as the man's fingers sprouted terrible, animalistic talons, which raked across Fahd's chest. A jet of the boy's blood splashed against the eastern wall an instant before he collapsed.

This foreigner was an excellent killer, and despite everything, Anwar appreciated that.

"You should run," the stranger said. His voice had lost its flippant mirth and came out a rough growl. He held up his hand, now dripping with Fahd's blood, and his lips curled back to reveal thick fangs. "Now."

"If only things were that simple, *khawaga*." Anwar noted with more than a little chagrin that the great fissure had already sealed itself. All that remained was a pattern of hairline fractures in the tiled floor. The ritual was irrevocably ruined and he could feel the effects working upon him already. "In such things, a price must always be paid."

The foreigner must have expected an attack because he kicked out at Anwar with a strength that spoke of potent blood indeed. The sorcerer took the blow to the chest and fell back several yards away, feeling bones break and organs rend within him. Experienced with the mystic ways, he wasn't terribly shocked to see the subtle marks of fate reveal themselves to him.

"Give my regards to the Lady," he said, sure that the stranger had no idea just whom he had served this night. Then, he propped himself up with his weakening arms and his torso, riddled with the dry tumors and bleeding cancers that had emerged when the ritual was ruined, gave way and separated from his shattered pelvis.

The darkness took him then, and Anwar al-Beshi rotted away with a smile on his face.

***

Beckett took some time to survey the ritual chamber. The woman he'd tackled was unconscious but breathing. Assuming she had been tied to the main ritualist, she was probably in for a rough patch. Vampiric blood was highly addictive to the living and when the vampire in question was destroyed it left the mortal bereft and alone. Fahd, who'd led him here, was good and dead, and the ritualist himself was just a pile of ash now.

But that didn't mean the room wasn't of interest. Beckett gathered up what artifacts he could and then examined the walls in detail. The ritualist had decorated it with a complex series of hieroglyphs that seemed to be a continuation of the ones Beckett had lifted from the notebook in London. The central image took up the entirety of the east wall, right where the sorcerer had been performing his rite. It was of a female figure, in the typical twisted profile of hieroglyphs, sitting on a throne. What was interesting about this woman, though, was that instead of a head, she had a black disc on her shoulders. Except for its color, it might be a solar image, because it had long rays reaching out to a variety of smaller figures. These were human males—probably servants—who bore large animal heads on their shoulders. It was these heads that were connected by black rays to the woman's head-disc.

Beckett had never seen this figure before, but some instinct told him it was worth remembering. He was making a sketch of it when the shooting started.

When the bullet dug into his shoulder, Beckett cursed himself for getting distracted. He turned around—the shot hurt, but it would take a lot more than that to stop him—and saw a middle-aged man in the uniform of a British cavalry regiment. He was holding a smoking pistol.

"Get away from my wife!" he said in English.

"Be careful, Colonel Blake," came a second voice, this time with a heavy Egyptian accent. "It is a devil." The Arab with the gift for hyperbole was a religious man, dressed in flowing traditional robes. He was holding a simple torch, which cast flickering light in the room.

This is getting out of hand, Beckett decided. He grabbed the satchel in which he had placed the major artifacts and ran. Blake shot him again as he jumped up and through a high window, but that didn't stop him.

One more strange story from the colonies.

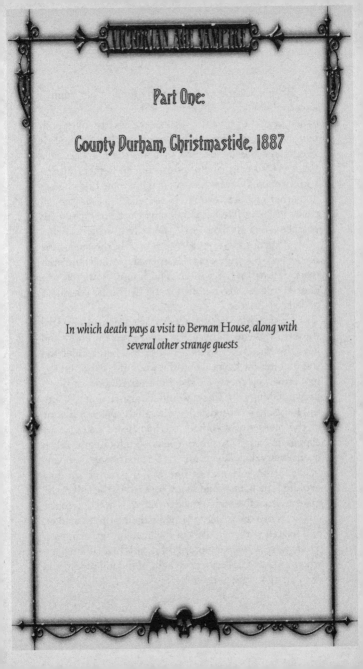

Part One:

Gounty Durham, Christmastide, 1887

*In which death pays a visit to Bernan House, along with
several other strange guests*

Chapter One

Regina had never been overly fond of her family's ancestral home. Bernan House, as the mansion itself was called, was built on a slight rise some twenty miles from Durham proper, near the border of Northumberland. It overlooked the great estate that was the foundation of the family's wealth and position. Tenant farmers raised a variety of crops and livestock, making some fine cheeses and other products. Bernan House and its lands were all that a viscount like her father might need to support his peerage—namely land, title, and plentiful grouse and other game for sport. At this time of year, the lands took on the gray-brown hue of trees stripped bare and farmlands made fallow by the winter. The house, however, was decked in garlands of holly for the Christmas season. A gilded cage indeed.

Approaching her eighteenth year, Regina longed for the days when her father's steward oversaw the estate and kept the house in his stead. Father, Mother, Daniel and she had left for Egypt when she was but a babe and she had grown up there, far away from the moors of north England. Many, she knew, would see assignment to Cairo as a hardship—"an existence with all the pains and none of the pleasures of India," she had heard one grumpy captain in Father's regiment call it—but for Regina it had been a marvelous adventure. At first in the safe company of her brother Daniel or one of her parents, she had explored the bazaars and *souqs*, listened to the call of the muezzin from the Mohammedan minarets that dotted the city, watched the *fellaheen* bringing their crops to market, and looked at the wonders of the ancient Egyptian past. There were perhaps a score of other girls in all of England who had seen Giza under the light of the full moon, and she had met none of them here.

There had been hard times, of course. What had started as assignment to some of the British overseers of the khedive's debts turned into military occupation with the Arabi Revolts by violent nationalists opposed to the longstanding British and French presence in Egypt. Regina was a child then, but she still had memories of Europeans being targeted in the streets before her father's regiment of hussars (and others) had restored order. Throughout her years blooming into a young woman, Cairo's British enclave had grown into a beautiful outpost of the Empire. She'd explored it and many other parts of the great city on the Nile thanks in large part to the complicity of her brother and several of the house servants. Father had given a stern warning about the dangers of the streets and the strange people who might wish to ensnare her. Surely he would have thought her already the slave to some foreign cult had he seen her moving through the *souq* dressed in the robes of a local woman, flanked by her brother and Fallah, whom her father called her maid but she looked to more as a guide.

All that had changed two years ago, when Regina's mother fell ill in Cairo. Lady Emma had never been of the strongest constitution, but her downturn was nevertheless quite sudden. Fifteen-year old Regina had had a long and pleasant conversation with her about a certain lieutenant who had caught her eye on a Monday. By Friday, Emma Blake was bedridden, her hair and brow soaked in sweat and raving about plagues of snakes and toads. Father had already been under pressure to return to England and assume the full responsibilities of his rank as a viscount now that the Arabist threat was ended, and his wife's malady convinced him it was indeed time. That spring, they had set sail for London and ultimately for this dreary estate. All save Daniel, of course, who—

"Daydreaming again, Regina?"

She started at the sound of her father's voice so close at hand. Lord Blake was already dressed for dinner, and looked to all the respected aristocrat and military man. His black hair, shot through with gray, was still cut in a military style, an effect accented by his mustache and the medals pinned to the sash under his dinner jacket. Once a hussar, always a hussar. A smile spread across his face as he beheld his only daughter, and she was quite sure some of it had to do with having successfully entered her drawing room without her noticing. It reminded Regina of the games they had played when she was younger.

"I was thinking of…" Her mouth dried to a nervous, parched cavity. "Yes, daydreaming."

"There is not much day left to dream away, Daughter." Indeed, although it was barely four in the afternoon, the sun, beautifully crimson, was dipping toward the western horizon, and the snow-tinged countryside seen from Regina's window was plunged into elongated shadow and ruddy light. Winter days were very short in County Durham. "Shepherd's delight, it would seem," her father added.

"Yes." She turned to face her father. "Father, I…"

"Hardly the same as the sun between the pyramids in Giza, is it?"

Regina smiled. "No. No it isn't. I miss it still, Father."

"As do I, my dear." He took a seat next to her. "Your grandfather was much better at shouldering the requirements of status and title than I. Do you remember at all any of the balls you attended at Monroe House before we left for Cairo?"

Regina gently shook her head. Monroe House was the family's London residence and although she had fond memories of time spent there, they were the faint recollections of childhood. "Not especially, although Mother has always talked fondly of them."

"Yes, your mother enjoyed those evening affairs a great deal before…" He looked his daughter in the eyes, who nodded her understanding. Some things were better left unspoken. "Well, before."

A MORBID INITIATION

"What about you, Father? Did you enjoy them?"

He smiled. "Some, yes. Your grandparents were the finest hosts in London, some said, and one always had a fine time with the finest people. But your grandfather always said that he was born to the manor and I to the saddle, and I must agree with his judgment. Give me a regiment of fine men at my side and my duty to the Queen in my heart."

"How could you give it all up, Father?"

"Hush, Regina. I have never had a fool for a daughter and I won't have one now. You know full well that the choice was not mine to make. It was only the revolts and the needs of the Empire that kept me in Egypt after my father died. The family needs its lord at home now."

"Yes, Father." She wanted to scream, to lash out at the man who was damning her to balls and parlors and being seen but not heard.

"But enough of this talk of gloom and duty. I am here with happy news for you, Regina." He smiled and looked at his daughter's doubting eyes. "I have received a cable from London that Lieutenant Seward will be joining us in time to see the New Year in."

Regina couldn't suppress a smile of her own, one that brought a chuckle to her father.

"You see, happy news. And happier still. When last I was in London, I met with Seward and he made a request of me, my dear. He asked me for your hand in marriage."

Regina felt a chill run through her, followed by a flush of heat. Marriage! With Seward, the one man who— how to put it?—had made his way into her thoughts again and again.

"We shall discuss the details upon his arrival, my dear, for if the life of an army man's daughter is not easy, the life of his wife is truly Herculean. I wish you to be happy my dear, and I need to know that you would be so at his side—his career is in the colonies, I think."

"Oh, Father! Yes, yes, and again, yes."

"Careful, Regina, do not make any hasty decisions. I have not yet given my assent to this union. Do not be in a rush to spend your life in the heat of Java, Honduras or Lagos."

Could he know, she wondered. Could Father understand that that was exactly what she was in a rush to do? To get away from this large and empty house a stone's throw from the Northumbrian border. To get away from the things expected of a proper young girl and see the places others only dreamed of.

"We shall have plenty of opportunity to discuss matters. I have invited Seward to stay with us through Twelfth Night."

"Yes, Father, of course." She embraced him. "Thank you."

"Yes, yes. Now off to bed with you."

***

James, Lord Blake watched his daughter head for her bedchamber with a happy scurry and it brought to mind the child she had been. The child she no longer was, he realized with a touch of chagrin. What had happened to the little girl with unruly brown locks who had a thousand questions he was happy to answer? The girl who'd hiked up her skirts to run across the decks of the steamship to Alexandria?

The answer was simple, of course: she'd grown into a fine young woman. Unruly locks had become well-tended curls. All the pudginess of childhood was long gone and the fine features of a beauty had emerged, one that not even the dour clothes of the day could conceal. She reminded him of Emma on their wedding day, of the lithe and cheerful beauty who'd stolen his heart and turned a marriage of obligation into something more. To think he'd railed against the fates that compelled his

A MORBID INITIATION

father to select for him a wife based solely on the fact that her dowry and inheritance would make solvent a viscounty just as ancient as it was impoverished. How he had bemoaned that decision! Only to find in Emma Ducheski that rarest of flowers: a true love.

That was before, of course. Before those terrible nights on Hampstead Heath in London. Before poor Lewis—who'd stood as his groomsman on that happy wedding day—met his awful fate. Before the departure for Cairo and the sickness, the scars and the betrayals.

Lord Blake didn't even notice the smile vanish from his face and the cold thing curl up in his gut.

**

Alone in her bed, Regina's dreams and memories came to celebrate with her. Closing her eyes, she returned to that night little more than a year ago. One of her last in Egypt and her first alone with Seward.

It was September and a pleasant heat tinged the Cairene night. In the three months since Father had announced that the family would be returning to England, hardly a day or night had seemed to go by without some new visit or social gathering. Father had been under a great deal of pressure to return to the mother country and take up the duties of a viscount, something that colonial service precluded, but now that he had given in, the task of relocation seemed epic in scale. Sea captains, land agents and military officers paraded through their home in the growing Garden City district of Cairo, and Father was constantly going over their reports. His military mind attacked the task of uprooting himself with vigor, but it seemed to Regina that he was making things more difficult than they needed to be. It was intentional, she knew now, a way for him to delay becoming the man he'd fought long and hard to avoid being—a country lord.

What Regina remembered most, however, was the parade of doctors attending Mother. A "tropical fever," Father called the ailment that kept his wife in bed much of the day and sent her through raving nightmares most of the night. Regina had been shocked by her mother's screams the first time she'd heard them and run to find her father, but the night terrors became a taboo after that. Everyone in the house knew they existed, but Father would only discuss them in the vaguest terms and usually only with stern-looking medical professionals arrived on the latest train from Alexandria or Port Said.

All this meant that he'd had little time for Regina or her feelings about returning to England. Despite the visitors who increasingly insisted on calling her "Lady Regina," she had little interest in the life of a viscount's marriageable daughter. She had enjoyed the freedom of living among the Queen's subjects in Egypt, where the pressures to marry and produce an heir were less severe. Her father had been in no hurry to dowry off his daughter to a colonial social climber, but she feared he would succumb to the pressures of expectation once back in England. In the meantime, she had found herself in the lone company of various house servants.

But this evening, Lieutenant Malcolm Seward was her accompaniment. The young man, perhaps ten years Regina's senior, had served under her father since the military occupation of 1882. Colonel Blake's style had never been so rigid as to discount the value of his junior officers and the two had become as close to friends as possible under the circumstances. That bond only grew tighter when Seward wrestled a manservant with Arabist sympathies to the ground just before he could run Colonel Blake through with a knife. Regina was aware of the high regard in which her father held the young lieutenant and their paths had crossed at several social functions.

And, truth be told, she'd thought of him much at other times. His features—fine blond hair, broad and muscular frame, steel-gray eyes—refused to leave her be. She'd even found herself in an uncharacteristic girlish fit when he arrived at the ball with the daughter of one of Sir Evelyn Baring's aides on his arm. What was that girl's name? Oh, yes.

"I'm surprised you aren't with Paulina this evening, Lieutenant."

Seward, standing on the balcony overlooking the twisting lanes of the Garden City and the Nile beyond it, looked away. "No, not tonight. Her father wouldn't want that."

In her memory, Regina could perfectly read the anger and frustration Seward tried so hard to hold in check. At the time, she'd just thrilled that Paulina might no longer be a concern. She couldn't resist a mild jab. "Oh? Are you not to be trusted, Lieutenant?"

His gaze turned on her and for a second something dark roiled behind his eyes. "Did Paulina say anything to you?"

"Hardly." Regina had barely even seen the girl in the last few months. "I'm sorry, Lieutenant. I did not mean to upset you."

He walked from the balcony's Grecian railing to one of the white stone benches designed for a comfortable view of the river. He sat with his back to the Nile, facing the doors into the house proper. "No," he said, his voice defeated and deflated, "I'm the one who owes you an apology. It's…"

Regina went to him, interposing herself between the bench and doors, kneeling to look him in the eye. The whalebone spine in her corset dug into her sternum. "Please, Malcolm, what happened?"

A thrill of fear went through her. Without realizing it until the deed was done, she'd used his Christian name. Doing so without invitation was to assume an intimacy she only hoped existed between the two of them. He would be well within his rights to be cross.

"The truth, I suppose." He looked into her eyes and she saw his agony, but no anger. "Her father decided I was not a proper match for his daughter. A minor officer, untitled and unlanded, just wasn't what he expected."

"Oh, Malcolm…" Regina hoped she'd kept the relief out of her voice.

"My father purchased my commission with his last pound and I have no land or estate to offer. It was foolish of me to even entertain a girl of Paulina's status."

"She…" Regina found her throat suddenly dry. Her thoughts were her own, but to share them… "She is the one who was a fool."

"What?" His eyes grew soft and Regina feared she'd be lost in them forever. "What did you say?"

"You heard me, darling." And she kissed him.

She'd never kissed a man before and feared she wouldn't know how. Her lips trembled and when he didn't immediately react, she thought she'd damned herself as a foolish child. But then his hands were cupping her face, pulling the two of them closer together into a deep embrace. His lips parted and enveloped hers and she felt heat welling up in her body. The painful corset faded from her awareness and all she could feel was him. She inhaled his scent, felt the tickle of his mustache, tasted the saltiness of his lips tinged with tears she didn't know were hers.

Something told her to remember everything about the moment, and those memories (backed by letters to and from Malcolm) had sustained her for over a year. Now, with her father's happy news, memory gave way to dreams thus far undreamed. Alone in her bedroom at Bernan House she felt his lips part anew and a delicious thrill went through as she felt his slick tongue probe her. She knew these desires were improper, but that very fact made them all the more enticing.

Like a wanton woman from one of the secret books she had found in her mother's study last year, Regina's dream-hand traveled down his chest to the source of his manhood. For his part, her imagined lover explored her body suddenly and fantastically devoid of the corset, petticoats, gowns and garments that had bound her in reality. Delicious heat rose from her naked skin and she felt his ardor grow.

"Darling…" Her raspy whisper was the only real vocalization of the passionate moans of her fantasy. It was enough.

***

Regina preferred Bernan House at night, truth be told. Her head still full of images of Malcolm Seward, she walked the empty hallways of the third floor. It was cold, certainly, but she was well bundled and now too restless to remain in bed. She slipped into one of the upstairs rooms with a view to the north. It had been her grandmother's sewing room, if the enameled workbox and bolts of fabric were any indication, but it probably had not been used in the years since her death seven years before.

Regina wondered what the woman had been like. She'd only known her as an infant. Her only real image of her grandmother was the sepia-toned daguerreotype taken of her and her husband—Regina's grandfather— lying in their graves before they were buried. The Arabi problem had made a return to County Durham impossible for the new Lord Blake and his family, but the funerary cards had arrived by ship some months later, there to complete the black wardrobe the family had adopted in mourning. Black, like the bolt of dyed broadcloth ready for sewing that lay nearby and would for a while to come. Indeed, Mother hadn't been able to use the room since her arrival here, her sickness keeping her mostly in bed, but the room was cleaned and ready for her. Mary, her lady's maid, had prepared it and maintained it without having to be told to.

Regina had passed by an entrance to the servants' quarters below-stairs earlier in her midnight wanderings and Mary had emerged as if on cue, seemingly aware of every movement in the old house. Regina had sent her back to sleep, shushing away complaints that it wasn't proper or some such. Regina had suppressed a smirk, wondering just what Mary—with her concern for propriety—would think of the dreams that had sent her mistress's daughter wandering the halls.

She took a seat in the rocking chair by the window, allowing herself a smile at the thought of shocking Mary. Beyond the thin windows of the house, the Durham countryside had been swallowed by a moonless night. A tapestry of stars spread across the sky, with bands of gray clouds creating a pattern within them. The landscape was a uniform black, like a bottomless sea or some preacher's description of the purgatory between luminous heaven and fiery hell. An expanse of sheer nothingness.

Regina smothered the candle she had been carrying to light her way and stared out into that nothingness. Sitting in a darkness almost as absolute, she strained to find some detail in the lands that were her father's. Some nocturnal bird or scavenger whose movements would betray it, some lonely farmer heading out by lamplight to the fields he would till at first light. A daughter returning from a secret rendezvous with the son of a neighboring family. But she found none of it. The land was dark and empty, devoid of the endless variety she had known in Cairo, devoid of any hint of a life other than that expected of her.

"Oh Malcolm," she whispered to the night.

***

The two men—one tall and thin, the other short

and corpulent—had walked several miles in the dark, through the light snow covering the frozen ground. They'd set out at sunset and it was well past midnight now, when they arrived on the grounds of the great house their wayward cousin inhabited.

The tall man looked to the upstairs window from the darkness of the grounds. He carried no light and needed none thanks to the gifts his servitude brought with it. There, lit by the flickering light of a candle, he saw the young daughter of the house. A beauty, that one.

"Come." The short man whispered, but the tone of command was unmistakable. The tall man responded— the master had charged him to accompany the other man, after all—but he felt his bile rise. If he were to keep his composure, he'd have to find a way to sate the hatred he felt toward this pudgy little fellow.

The girl in the window extinguished the candle. To others that would hide her as well as the darkness hid the two of them, but not to him. She was still there, and he had to admit, she looked delicious.

Yes, she would do nicely.

Chapter Two

"Do you ever dream of escaping, darling girl?"

The question sent fingers of numbness through Regina. She'd had Mary wheel her mother out to the north balcony outside her bedroom to enjoy the unexpected warmth of the noonday sun, but Emma Blake hadn't spoken before she asked that question. Despite the day's comparative warmth—last night's frozen fields would be muddy and wet, now—a woolen blanket seemed to keep her nestled in the wooden, wheeled chair Mary had used to move her mistress from her bedchamber. Beneath it, a simple but heavy dress, covering her from the top of her neck to the tip of her toes, and a matching bonnet completed the envelopment of the sickly woman. Until she spoke, Regina had thought her mother was sleeping.

"Sometimes." Regina looked down at her mother, who seemed as pale and thin as ghost. Tears had welled in the corner of her eyes and that sent dread to Regina's heart. "But what do you mean? Escape from what?"

"From everything. From me, from this house, from… from yourself… from…" She looked out at the estate, unable or unwilling to put into words just what bondage she felt her daughter might wish to escape.

"Oh, mother." Regina sat by her mother, looking into the clouded eyes of the woman she'd once thought of as so strong. "Do not worry about me. Lieutenant Seward arrives soon and he brings happy news. I—"

"Be careful, Regina," her mother interrupted. "Your father has been a good man, but it isn't enough. It's never enough."

"I…" Regina's throat tightened. Despite the sickness and spells that had plagued her over the last two years, Emma had always been a role model for her daughter. Regina looked to her mother as a guide for the ways in which a woman might find partnership, respect and security with a proper husband. To hear her give voice, after twenty years of marriage, to some of the same fears she herself struggled with was more than worrisome. Truth be told, it felt like a betrayal.

"What are all these dark tidings, Emmy?"

Regina turned around toward the room and the unfamiliar voice. Mary was standing to the side of the door, demurely positioned to usher in two visitors. The first, the man who had spoken and now smiled broadly in Regina and Emma Blake's direction, was short and more than a little round. He wore a beard and his black hair was turning gray. Spectacles with small but absurdly thick lenses straddled a slightly crooked nose, giving him the appearance of a mole dressed as a man. Behind him, mostly obscured by a combination of the first man's girth and the shadows of the room, stood a taller man. He gave off the impression of an undertaker, his eyes sunk under a heavy brow and the brim of a tall black hat.

"Uncle!" said Emma. Her voice rose to a semblance of happy energy, better than Regina had heard in months. "Happy Christmas. When did you arrive?"

"Just now, Emmy. We left Durham by coach this morning and came straight here." He waddled slightly as he stepped onto the balcony, and the image of a countryside burrowing creature stayed with Regina. "We could hardly have made another stop before coming to visit my favorite niece."

The other man stepped forward as well. If his portly companion was a mole, then he was a serpent, moving with quiet and deadly grace. His long, thin arms ended in gloved fists clenched around a wooden walking stick. His eyes, pinpricks of reflection in shadow, darted about and Regina had the unsettling impression he was looking for prey. She stood to greet them.

"Uncle Thomas," Emma said. "You remember my daughter Regina. Regina, Mr. Thomas Ducheski, your great-uncle."

"Dear Regina," Thomas the Mole said with a smile of broad, white teeth. "I haven't seen you since Lord Blake's departure for Egypt. You were but a child then."

"No longer." The tall man's voice was as reptilian as his body, a slithering cold thing laced with threat. "Our cousin has grown into a woman."

"Yes, yes." Thomas looked slightly discomforted, but covered it with a chuckle. "Emma, Regina, may I present Mr. Gareth Ducheski, solicitor with offices in Durham and London."

"A pleasure," Emma said without conviction.

Regina held her tongue altogether. Her mother had never spoken very much about her family or her life before she married James Blake, then a dashing lieutenant in the hussars. The Ducheski were merchants and manufacturers, removed from aristocratic circles by their professions and their Slavic origins. They were successful in the age of industry, however, and grew wealthy from warehouses in Newcastle and Liverpool, mines in County Durham, and a growing number of factories across the north of England. Regina knew well that her parents' marriage had been a strategic one—an old title paired with new capital. Marriage as an exchange of goods was hardly the thing of the romantics, however, and it made Regina uncomfortable given the news her father had brought her. Did Malcolm see her as a conveyance for some similar social exchange?

"What brings you to our home, Mr. Ducheski?" Regina directed her question squarely at Thomas, avoiding Gareth's cold, hungry gaze and her own lingering doubts.

"Why, the pleasure of seeing you and your mother, of course." The smile again.

"Now, Uncle Thomas," Emma said, her voice growing tired anew, "My husband and I have never tolerated foolishness in Regina or in those who addressed her. I will not have my own blood's lies undo that policy. The truth, please."

Gareth placed his hand on his smaller relative's shoulder, his long black-clad fingers bent slightly and digging into the wool of the man's jacket. "Yes, cousin Thomas. No need for dissimulation."

"Of course, of course." His smile almost covered his wince. "To be fully up front, there is some familial business to attend to. A matter of your... inheritance, Emma."

"Oh." Emma Blake's eyes closed for several seconds and it seemed to her daughter that she was fighting for consciousness. "I had hoped this could wait for another time. In London, perhaps?"

"That it could wait?" Gareth asked, his incredulity eclipsing his predatory menace. "This is hardly the attitude I'd expected in one such—"

"Now, now," interrupted Thomas. "Please forgive Gareth's brusqueness, my darling niece. He is less used to the niceties of society than you or I."

"Not at all," said Emma. Regina remained silent but was not at all displeased to see the tall, serpentine man put in his place.

"I would have liked nothing more," Thomas continued, "than to discuss all this in the quiet confines of Lady Merritt's garden on Park Lane once you had come south to London for the season, but Aunt Eleanor tells me there is a certain urgency to matters."

"Is Eleanor here?" Emma raised a weak hand to her chest, suppressing a shudder.

"No, she remains at Lion's Green. But she is anxious to hear from you." Lion's Green, Regina knew, was a small property some ways from Bernan House, near the city of Durham proper.

"Of course," Emma said. "We should go inside."

"My, um, my thoughts precisely," Thomas said.

"Mary," Regina said, "will you please get Father and—"

"That won't be necessary, dear," her mother interrupted. "I'm sure there's nothing that needs your father's attention."

"No, certainly not," put in Thomas. "If we could just discuss matters alone?"

"Yes, of course," Emma answered. "Regina, thank you dear. We can continue our conversation later. Mary, could you assist me?"

And with that, Mary was wheeling her mistress inside with Thomas and Gareth Ducheski in tow. Regina was left behind, a child dismissed by adults concerned with serious matters. No tolerance for foolishness, indeed.

***

"Begging your pardon, ma'am," said Mary, "but I trust those people not a whit." Mary's accent gave her judgment the semblance of a pronouncement from some medieval midwife or even, if one overlooked gender, a rural sheriff. "They are a strange lot."

"I know what you mean, Mary." Regina was sitting in one of the downstairs rooms, trying to read through one of the literary supplements she'd received from London. She was not being very successful as thoughts of Malcolm, of Mother, and of her own newly arrived relatives affected her concentration and made her lose track of Mr. Hardy's latest story. Mary's commentary pulled her out of the tales of Wessex once and for all.

"There are stories about them in Durham, ma'am." Mary took a seat. Her slight frame was draped in a simple woman's dress, blue cotton sewn by her own hands late at night when the mistress hadn't needed her. She never quite looked Regina in the eyes—such wouldn't be proper. "Mr. Collinsworth the innkeeper says they were accused of witchcraft years ago."

"Mary, don't tell me you believe such tall tales." Regina smiled, the maid's quaint superstitions doing more than she could know to calm her. If there was one thing she'd never worried about, it was her mother dancing under the moon at a witch's Sabbath. "You'll be telling me to tie foxglove and wolfsbane on her door next."

"I don't know just what to believe when it comes to their lot, ma'am. But the Devil works in strange ways, I know that much. And the Devil has a long history in these lands."

"And God is everywhere, Mary." Regina stood and walked toward the hall. "I'm more concerned with the affairs of Man these days, if you must know."

"If you don't mind me saying, Lady Regina, all is God's affair." Mary moved toward the back staircase, and the hidden world of servants. Before she vanished, she added, "And the Devil's too."

***

He liked the girl's smell, Gareth did. A fine odor, like a lily wilting under a too-strong sun, or peat moss just beginning to ripen on the moor. Sweetness laced with the prospect of decay. A bud in need of picking.

Let Thomas play at liking and loving dear Cousin Emma and her pathetic life of aristocratic normalcy. Let him mournfully bring her the news. Pathetic to carry what should be a great honor as if it were a condemnation.

Sitting in the drawing room chair, his eyes closed and his nostrils flaring, he concentrated on the smell of the girl imbued in the very furniture. He turned his head and brushed his long nose against the satin fabric and the cover placed to protect the chair from the hair oils of gentlemen. He inhaled sharply with an audible sniff and gulped in the air and its odors.

She'd been here much of the afternoon, reading and talking with that prattling, bony maid. The scent told the story of dear Regina—confusion, anger, with an undercurrent of what, anticipation? Yes, and deeper than that another scent, the lingering pungency of sex.

The thought of that fine little thing rutting like a mare played itself in his mind's eye and the scarred vestiges of his manhood unfurled themselves as best they could. Savoring the image, he inhaled anew and played with the perfumes of this wet, young thing. Ah, no. She was no country whore, riding the stable hand in some cheap novelette passed discreetly in parlors and uproariously in taverns. No, her scent had the tinny flavor of dreams and imaginings. This girl's legs parted only in some private fantasy. She dreamed of what she could not have, what she hadn't the courage or gifts to become.

Poor girl. He wondered what it would be like to be as blind as she was, to live like the rest of the world. What would he be if he did not know the pleasure of scent and sound, of the rich unholy ichor that brewed in his veins and opened the benighted world to him? What if he did not share the gifts of his master and his line and was nothing more than another weakling of a man? That would be a very unpleasant thing indeed.

He breathed in her scent again and smiled.

Chapter Three

That night, Regina dreamed of dark things. She was trapped in the dream, sealed away in some forgotten labyrinth, with serpents and beetles crawling across the walls of weathered stone. A great weight was upon her too, as if terrible shackles held her down lest she should become loose in her fury.

And furious she was. Anger as she had never known boiled in her breast, a slavering hatred directed at all those who had wronged her. Against the father who had brought her back to England. Against the mother whose illness had forced that fate on the family. And against Daniel, especially against her brother Daniel, who had had the ability to say no, to flee to the Navy to escape his duties as his father's son. Gnashing against the hard leather strap that passed through her mouth and kept her teeth from clenching, she knew just how ready she'd be to pay her brother's price for freedom. So what if hated-father and coward-mother banished her from their thoughts? What were familial bonds if they ended in shackles or a noose?

Flies, bloated on the meat of corpses, buzzed through her dark prison and laid their eggs in her very flesh. She raged and felt a great scream welling up within her parched throat. A scream terrible enough to shake the foundations of her jail and tear the bonds from her mouth so she could feed the broiling hatred once and for all. Screams that would never end—

And it was screams that woke her, but not her own.

Regina sat bolt upright in the bed, with only the wan light of earliest morning coming through the east window of her bedchamber. For a second all was quiet, and then the shrill screech returned. Mary.

Without even grabbing a housecoat to cover her shift, Regina ran to the hallway, following the maid's cries. They led her down the east wing of the house, toward her mother's apartments. Lady Emma rested in the north wing in the hopes that isolation from the bustle of main house would calm her spells. This morning, at least, there was no calm in the north.

Regina ran along the mezzanine overlooking the main hall, which connected the wings of the house, and took a servant's door directly into her mother's foyer. She found Mary at the threshold of the bedchamber. In between her cries, great wet sobs came upon her as she stared into the room. Regina pushed past her, hoping against hope that her mother was well. She was not.

Emma, Lady Blake lay across her bed not at all as Regina had left her the evening before. Where once she had been wrapped tightly in the downy covers, they were now strewn across the floor. She was naked, save for the shreds of what had one been her silk chemise. Her head lolled over the side of the bed away from the door and her skin was pale in the half-light, so that she looked like nothing so much as some Greek statuary—save that this statuary had been marred by vandals.

Pink puckers of scar tissue covered her flesh like the tattoos of some Pacific warrior or pagan priestess. They formed intricate patterns on her skin and came in a variety of shapes and sizes. Small round points, as if she had repeatedly stabbed herself with a knitting needle, formed a V on her stomach, pointing at the more definite lattice of lines around her most intimate areas. An ugly, glossy line of tissue ran down the middle of her chest above all those marks, a clear testament that someone or something had tried to cleave her in twain along her breastbone. Regina had never seen her mother unclothed before, clearly for reasons that went far beyond propriety.

Regina ran to her mother's side, quickly picking up one of the blankets to cover her nakedness. It was cold and clammy in her hands, soaked with the sweat of a fever, no doubt. She made it around the bed and gasped. Emma Blake's cold, empty eyes stared up at her daughter and smears of something that could only be blood ran from her mouth.

There was no doubt in Regina at that moment: her mother was dead. Nevertheless, she felt for the beating of a heart, and found only a chill expanse of unmoving flesh. A layer of perspiration, like dew on the cool grass of morning, covered Emma's skin. Regina threw the blanket over her and tried to raise her head, which hung like a dead weight. She managed to ease her mother's back into a recline and saw more evidence of a sickly fever, great stains of sweat soaked into the sheets on which she had lain.

"Oh, Mother." Regina leaned in and kissed her lips. They felt clammy as the skin of any fish in the sea, and tasted coppery with blood. She closed Emma's eyes with her fingertips. The corners were caked with the white, salty residue of tears, the result of the fever, perhaps, or great sorrow. "Rest in peace."

Regina felt tears of her own welling inside her, and searched for some activity with which to hold them at bay. She landed on Mary, still sobbing and screeching intermittently, frozen at the threshold of the bedchamber.

"Hush, Mary," Regina said, to no visible effect. The maid stood, crying, looking at the bed. "Mary!"

Still no response. Regina walked back to Mary and waved a hand in her face, but she reacted not at all. Standing where she was, Regina clearly blocked Mary's view of the bed and the body of Emma Blake, yet she still seemed to be looking that way, sorrow and terror playing out on her face. She mouthed the word "no" over and over between her cries.

"Mary! Wake up!" Regina said, grabbing her at the shoulders and giving her a solid shake. She vaguely remembered that such was hardly what one should do with sleepwalkers and others in shock, but that seemed unimportant. She just wanted Mary to be quiet, to stop screaming and to let her mourn her mother. "Quiet!"

Regina slapped her then. It was harder than she had intended, harder than poor Mary deserved, but it did the trick. The maid fell quiet for a second, and then exclaimed, "Milady! Get away from—"

Her eyes focused on Regina for the first time. "Lady Regina... What...? Your mother..."

"I know, Mary. I know." She embraced her then, holding the maid to her and surrendering some tears of her own. "I know."

"Emma."

Regina opened my eyes to see her father standing not three feet away, looking past Mary and her. Dressed in a housecoat, his gray hair standing in strange angles, his mustache unwaxed. No more the royal hussar or viscount—just the mourning husband. "My Emma."

He pushed past his daughter and the maid and went to his wife's bedside. It took Regina a moment to extricate herself from Mary's grip and join him. He was stroking Emma's raven-black hair, whispering some quiet nothings to his companion of many years. Such softness was not typical of Lord Blake, which had made his wife's illness all the harder, since his reaction to adversity was always to fight against it. Regina knew she had benefited from his tendency to leave her to her own devices, but such a display of tenderness coming after her mother's final hour only made her long for it all the more.

Regardless of her desires, the display of affection ended as soon as Regina came close. Standing bolt upright like the cavalryman he was, Blake took charge of the situation. "Mary, stop your bleating and go ready us some breakfast. Snap to it."

"Yes, my lord." She nodded and headed out.

"Regina, go get yourself dressed and we will begin making preparations. When you are ready, find Mrs. Baker and Nelson and have them ready mourning dress. Someone will have to fetch the vicar as well."

Regina had of course seen this behavior from her father many times before, but never in a situation that struck so closely to her heart and his. "But, Papa, I can't…"

"You can and you will!" he thundered. "There are things I must attend to alone, and I will not have you in my way. Now hurry."

James Blake had long taught his daughter to value honesty above all else. *The plain truth is the highest of monarchs*, he would say. So she refused to back down from him at this moment. "No, Father. The marks on her skin, I have to—"

He was upon her in a second, his face red with fury. "Quiet your prattling! I am your father and I will be obeyed in this matter! There will be no talk of savagery and paganism in this house, young lady!"

For the first time in her life, Regina feared her father would strike her. Instead, he laid his hand on her shoulder. She felt him tremble, and although his voice fell to a whisper, there was still steel in his words. "Your mother died of a fever brought from Egypt, nothing else. She will be buried in sanctified soil and I will hear nothing else on the subject." With that he walked back to the bedside, and gathered up the sheets to cover her completely, hiding all signs of the arcane markings across her flesh. He placed her properly on the bed, in a position of quiet repose, and used his thumb to wipe the crusted blood from her lips. "Absolutely nothing else."

Finding her mother had opened a chasm of grief within Regina, and she now saw her father on the other side of it, separated from her. "Yes, father."

With that he turned from her, as if Regina had suddenly ceased to be relevant. She slowly backed out of the room, watching her father attend to his "things." First he wiped the last of the bloody residue from Emma's lips and face with a washcloth and then he went about the room, gathering up the various artisanal items Regina had always associated with her mother. The engraved cartouche of Egyptian hieroglyphs, the lapis-lazuli beads that evoked the shape of blue eyes—he gathered them all into a makeshift sack made with a flap of his housecoat, as if they were poison to him.

"Dirty superstition," he muttered. "Bloody witchcraft."

***

Regina didn't feel much of anything the rest of the night, and into the wan light of the next morning. Under the watchful eyes of Mrs. Baker the housekeeper, the servants ushered in a pall of blackness on Bernan House as the Blake family adopted heavy mourning dress. The boughs of holly and other signs of the season vanished from the house, and Regina wandered into her own dressing room to find Mary gathering up her white and gray dresses to be dyed a deep black. She knew layer upon layer of crinoline would come to engulf her as was proper for a mourning daughter. The Queen herself, in long lament for her dear departed consort Prince Albert, had set the stage of the depths of dreary somberness the bereaved of standing should aim for and in this, it seemed, her father had decided to accept all the requirements of his station.

Standing aside as the servants attended to their lengthy work of banishing all signs of color and joy from her quarters and the rest of Bernan House, Regina took a moment to gaze at the jewelry of her trousseau. One of the great benefits of being the daughter of a colonial military man was the access her family had had to the great bazaars of Cairo and the Far East. Her trousseau was full of exotic jewels in fine settings of filigree and arabesque. The Mohammedan prohibitions on figurative art, she'd observed, made their artisans all the more expressive in the fine geometric patterns of their jewelry. Some would say her trousseau was lacking in cameos and other figurative pieces, but she far preferred what she had. Not that it mattered now—jewels were banished during deep mourning and even a half-year from now, only blackest jet would be proper.

That day, Father Duncan, the town vicar, came to visit and whisper last rites, and he mentioned to Regina and her father that the Bishop of Durham and perhaps even the Archbishop of York would make the journey to Bernan House. If this was meant to hearten her, it did not at all. The visitors who would soon follow would only make her discomfort worse.

***

In the late afternoon, Regina could stand the questions of her own mind no longer and went to the north wing. Malcolm had yet to arrive and her father had adopted a stoicism she thought beyond even him, concentrating on the minutia of mourning and paying no heed to his daughter's trauma.

As the day wore on, and sleep had not come, Regina had wondered if perhaps she had imagined some, if not all, of the terrible scene. For an awful, beautiful moment after she rose herself from an open-eyed daze on the divan of her drawing room, she had even hoped her mother's death was a phantasm created by fatigue and anticipation. But no, the sentiment of loss came crashing down upon her too quickly to be a falsehood. But the scars and strange ritual markings? The blood on her mother's lips? Those she was less certain of. She had to know, to make sure.

The necessities of death had been tended to early on, she supposed, and the north wing of the house was eerily quiet. No maids scurrying, no sounds of the kitchen down below wafting up through ceilings and floors. Instead, only the cloying, dark heat of a house closed against even the slight sun of winter. It was as if the shadows emanated from her mother's bedchamber because the closer she moved to it down the long, broad hall, the scarcer light became. Cracks of sunlight pressed through shutters only to be blocked by drapes. Wan candles and lanterns vanished, replaced by unlit wicks and empty sconces.

When Regina opened the double doors into the bedroom itself, the darkness was complete. She could be looking into the stygian depths, so absolute was the shadow that awaited her. She waited a few moments for her eyes to adjust, but even then she could only make out a few vague shapes thanks to the measly light coming in from the hall behind her. There the rough contour of the four-poster bed that held her mother's corpse, near it the bulk of a large chair, across from that a heavy dresser.

"Enough," she whispered to no one in particular and made her way through the darkness toward the window she knew awaited her at the far wall. She braced herself for contact with some unseen trinket or piece of furniture, but made it to the wall in a few long, easy strides. There, she grabbed the heavy curtains, found the part between the two where a bit of light might make its way in despite the shutters beyond and drew them apart.

"No!" The voice was loud and panicked, half merging with some guttural growl. Regina, startled, stepped away and turned toward the bed, to see her mole-like uncle, Thomas Ducheski, hurtling himself at her from the chair where the shadows had hidden him. "You mustn't!"

The short, round man, moved with astonishing speed, pushing his young niece out of the way and shutting the curtains tight against the single blade of sunlight that had pierced the room. Regina stumbled, knocked aside with a force that hardly seemed possible from such a little man.

"What..? Who?!" Regina's heart was racing.

"It is me," said her uncle. A sudden smell of sulfur and a sharp scratching sound accompanied a flare of light as he lit a long match. He proceeded to light a candle on a nearby dresser, before shaking the match out. "I'm sorry, my dear but you must not open the drapes or shutters."

"And why not?" Regina's voice was hard and accusatory, but she spared a quick look behind the man toward her mother. The candlelight barely reached the bed and the woman laying under its covers. The long shadows gave Emma Blake's corpse an animal aspect, deepening the lines on her face and turning her fine lips into something akin to a snarl. Regina gaped.

"Because…" Thomas too looked back toward the bed and promptly shifted his position to interpose himself between mother and child. "Because it is tradition, Regina. We Ducheski come from the east and we still bear some of the ways of the Slavs. To expose a departed soul to the light of day is to curse it, Regina. Your great aunt Eleanor will explain it all when she arrives this evening."

"I certainly hope so," Regina said as she moved closer to her mother's deathbed. The tricks of the flickering candlelight had passed and Lady Emma looked to be in quiet repose—pale and drawn, but no snarling beast. "I hope so."

***

Thomas was true to his word, at least in terms of the timing of Eleanor Ducheski's arrival at Bernan House. The black four-horse coach arrived just as the horizon swallowed the last red rays of sunlight, the team's hooves and the cab's wheels crunching through the packed earth and gravel of the long drive. Regina—who had been on watch for the possible arrival of her betrothed from the Durham station—watched Morris the coachman greet the horses. Thomas Ducheski emerged from the house as if on cue to receive his relatives, opening the coach's door to help the passengers out.

Regina, watching from a front-facing window on the second floor, tried to make out the details in the twilight. The driver, sitting high in the front of the carriage to man the reins, wore a long overcoat against the winter chill. He wore no hat, but it was too dark to make out any features—Regina had the impression of baldness, but could not be sure.

Gareth Ducheski was the first to disembark from the coach's innards. Regina had no trouble at all recognizing him in the gloom. His tall, thin form, all angles and sharpness, made him unmistakable, as did the harsh way in which he pushed his cousin aside to help the next passenger out. Regina remembered with sudden clarity a moment in Cairo: street dogs fighting for status and the right to pick at a discarded lamb bone, the most dominant of the mangy creatures pinning the other momentarily to remind it of its inferiority.

The woman who emerged from the black coach, Regina concluded, must be Aunt Eleanor, the very mention of whom had had such an effect on her mother the day before her death. Physically, there could be no greater contrast than between her and her nephew Gareth. If he was a serpent—long and sleek—then she was a small, gnarled spider. She walked with the help of a cane and seemed bent over with the weight of years unnumbered and acts unspoken. She moved slowly but with assurance, swatting away Thomas's attempt to interpose himself as the helpful nephew. Her dress was a deep black shell, a simple accessory to the shadows that seemed to cling to her like a second skin. Her face, what Regina could see of it, was a convergence of lines and wrinkles tied together with steel-gray hair in a tight bun.

She had moved only three small steps from the coach when she suddenly looked up—straight at the second floor window where her little niece was watching. Regina felt a chill like a cold blade run down her spine and tension coil in jaw, at the hinge just behind her ears. For a moment

A MORBID INITIATION

she feared she would be sick, but then the old crone looked away and continued toward the front door where Mrs. Baker was surely awaiting them.

Regina headed downstairs. It was time to greet the family, it seemed.

"Other family members will arrive later," Thomas was explaining hurriedly when Regina made it downstairs. The little man was holding up the rear of a party made up of her father, the crone Eleanor and her apparent favorite Gareth. "Aunt Eleanor is here to make initial preparations for the funeral."

"Yes, well," Lord Blake put in as they made their way toward the staircase. "There are some matters to be discussed on that front."

"Later." Eleanor Ducheski's voice was a cold thing, lacking in volume but powerful nonetheless. She sounded like the aggregate of a governess and a military officer, with an accent that spoke of foreign and less-civilized lands. "First, I see Emma. Then we talk."

"Of course, but—"

"Ah!" Eleanor exclaimed looking up from her crouch to see Regina. The old woman's eyes were two black peas set deep in the furrows of her wrinkled flesh. When she spoke, she exposed teeth set at odd angles and discolored by the years. "This is the daughter."

"Um, yes. Mrs. Ducheski, my daughter, Lady Regina." Her father, she noted, was struggling to maintain his composure.

"Pleased to make your acquaintance, madam." Regina bowed down to reach the crone's eye level.

As a response, Eleanor Ducheski walked right up to Regina and began to inspect her as she imagined a butcher might an animal for slaughter. One hand still clutching her cane, she used the other to grasp Regina's waist, then her hips. "Yes, I see."

Ignoring Regina's dumbfounded reaction, she continued her inspection. She felt her niece's bosom under the tight corset, pulled the girl's face forward and, handing her cane to Gareth, used both hands to pull back Regina's lips and inspect her teeth.

"Mrs. Ducheski!" Lord Blake forcibly moved his daughter away from the old woman. Regina, for her part, could only raise her hands to her face where the woman had pinched skin and pulled flesh. "That is…"

"She is truly Emma's daughter, yes? More beautiful than her mother, even."

"Th… Thank you…" Regina stammered out.

"Tsk," the old woman scoffed and started up the stairs. "Beauty makes a woman weak."

***

Regina's stupor lasted through the night and into the early hours of the next morning. The shock of her mother's death and the procession of strange events that happened over the following twenty-four hours—the unexplained scars, the Ducheski traditions, Eleanor's "inspection," and most of all, her father's refusal to address any of it—simply overloaded her heart so that she was barely aware of collapsing in bed that night. It was finding Mary, the poor woman who had actually found Emma that terrible morning, that finally revived Regina's spirit.

In the year Regina had spent at Bernan House— interrupted by the summer season in London—Mary had never struck her as the strongest of women. She seemed rather to be of that breed of house servants who survive the vagaries of their masters' humors by doing their very best to remain invisible. Regina knew that was a commendable skill, one that she was sure had served Mary well, but it had the unfortunate side-effect of making the maid seem more mouse than woman. Her screeching and stammering before Emma Blake's body had hardly seemed out of character. Still, when Regina found her wrapped into a tight ball in the corner of her small quarters, it was enough to shake off the last bit of stupor. This was not right.

Regina's stunned sleep after her dismissal on the staircase lasted only a few hours and gave way to tossing and turning. She felt fevered and flitted between tense consciousness and flashes of dark dreams that mostly fled from her memory as soon as she awoke. Only a few details of the nightmares remained behind as terrible reminders, most prominently twisted images of the crone Eleanor Ducheski. Regina saw her great-aunt's wrinkled and wizened face streaked with blood, her eyes turned black as coal, and her emaciated fingers tipped with nails like talons. *She tried to escape me*, the apparition said, *but she could not. And neither will you, little cousin.* Several times, Regina woke with a start, gasping for air and convinced the old woman's hands were at her throat.

Eventually, she gave up on bed and sleep altogether and returned to her Egyptian habit of early morning wanderings. Regina expected to find Bernan House empty at that hour, but instead she only avoided her maternal cousins by luck. The crone herself was seated in the downstairs library where Regina had intended to nest for a few hours, attended by both Gareth and Thomas Ducheski. Regina peaked in through a door and remained hidden from view, listening to their idle conversation, much as she had done as a girl in Cairo when spying on her parents.

"I had thought the initiation wasn't to be until Michaelmas," said Thomas. "That is months away."

"You need not remind me of the calendar, nephew," Eleanor answered in a voice full of scorn. "All is as it should be."

"But I had just carried the news the day before," he continued. "There was no time—"

Regina was sure she hadn't moved, but she must have made a slight noise at that moment, because Gareth turned in her direction much like a cat who has suddenly detected a mouse. She quickly retreated down the hall into adjoining rooms, and then headed to the second floor by the back stairway. Breathing all together too heavily for her own peace of mind, she crouched at the top of the thin, spiraling stairs and listened for signs of pursuit. After a few minutes of silence she opened the top door and crept into the maids' foyer.

There she found Mary, curled in the darkest corner of the room, muttering quietly. At first, Regina thought she might even be snoring, but as she crept closer to the woman, she could make out words. "The eyes... the eyes... the eyes..." Mary said, over and over.

Regina extended a hand toward her, hoping to comfort or rouse her, but she would have none of it. Mary lashed out with her arm, pushing Regina's away and screaming incoherently. She then flattened herself against the wall, trying to back away from her master's daughter. Her eyes were wild with terror and Regina could see cold sweat beading on her brow even in the half-light of the two candles illuminating the small foyer. Regina was convinced the maid was in some sort of sleepwalking state.

"Mary! Wake up! It's Regina..."

"No! The eyes... No!" And with that she collapsed anew, clutching at her own face with the fury of a child ready to spite itself. Regina rushed to pull her hands away, but Mary still managed to raise several large welts on her cheeks and brow before Regina clamped her hands to the floor. She struggled with the strength of the mad for a few seconds, but thankfully Regina could bring the weight of her body to bear, holding her hands down. And then, as suddenly as it had started, the maid's fit ended.

"Oh, what...?" Mary blinked back a few tears. "Oh, Lady Regina, ma'am, I'm..."

"Shhh," Regina said, trying to console her. "It's all right. What happened to you, Mary?"

"Oh, Lady Regina, I... well... that is..."

"It's all right, Mary. I won't tell my father or anyone else. Please, I only wish to help."

"It's just that, it's as if I've caught your dear mother's humors, milady." The maid continued to babble as Regina guided her to a small bench on the far wall of the foyer, where she might be more comfortable. "Ever since I saw… that is, found her… I can't sleep at night."

"That's to be expected, Mary. You've had quite a shock and it was only the night before last. I can't sleep either."

"Yes, ma'am, that's kind of you to say. But the nights, and most of all the early mornings, have been like pieces of hell itself, if you'll excuse me saying."

Regina nodded quickly to forgive her understandable blasphemy, not wanting to stop her speech now that it was flowing at last. The maid continued unbidden. "The time before dawn is when I get the great bulk of my work done, milady, getting the house ready and all. But now, when those hours come and I wake as I always have, it's like the nightmares wake with me. Oh, ma'am."

"Shhh, I have had dreams as well, Mary. What do you dream of?"

"The most terrible things, ma'am. Like seeing your fine mother again and again, and her night gown all torn and… revealing… that is… I see her naked ma'am, like a harlot, and covered with those terrible marks, like witch's teats."

She braced for the physical retort she expected from a peer who's just heard her mother called a harlot and a witch. Instead, Regina just stroked her loose auburn hair. "Go on, Mary, it's alright."

"And I see eyes, ma'am. Dark and terrible, like wells into the Pit itself!" She sobbed again. "All through the hours before dawn, I see them everywhere, looking at me and *into* me. Like the Devil Himself, I swear it. He's cursed me, I think." She broke into quiet sobs and, although Regina half-hoped she would say more, she couldn't bring herself to impose further suffering on the poor woman.

"It's all right, Mary. You are not cursed." Regina wiped away some more tears from Mary's cheek. "But perhaps you should take some time to yourself. Do you have kin you could stay with? We can certainly do without you for a few days and the rest might do you good."

"Oh, ma'am, yes, I suppose I could stay with my brother Harold. He is a cottager on Gables Heath."

"That's the estate of Sir Milner, yes?" She nodded. "Fine, I will make arrangements for you. Now go get yourself dressed."

"Yes, ma'am. Thank you ma'am." And Mary was gone.

Once she had left, and Regina was alone in the little foyer, she felt tears of her own coming. She hadn't yet cried, and now they came first in quiet crystal beads and then in wracking sobs that shook her to the core. The image of her mother, marked as if by some devilish artist or ancient torturer, returned in staggering detail: her skin, white and bloodless, glowing in the light of the moon, the splash of dried blood across her mouth. Regina collapsed on the ground, tears streaking down her face and her chest convulsing for air. She saw again her mother the next day—was that truly just yesterday?—in that room turned into a dark crypt by shutters and heavy drapes.

In her grief, details of the scene became visible for the first time. Her mother's lips curled back, revealing animalistic teeth in the wan candlelight. But then she had seemed in quiet repose when Regina finally approached, so peaceful and flushed. Her lips a deep red that belied her paleness just that morning.

And what was this talk of initiation? Some deep secret was weighing on Regina's heart, some fact about her mother that had remained hidden for years. A secret that only death could reveal. Mary saw the signs too and could hardly handle the strain. Regina wondered if she could herself.

A vast pit of sorrow opened in Regina's chest, and from it billowed pain and anger. The numbness was gone and now there was agony. This was her mother, the woman who had raised her and loved her like no other. Where others were cold and distant, she was warm and kind. Where others were petty and small, she was wise and caring.

What terrible truths had she hidden beneath her demure clothes and caring smiles? Who was Emma Blake?

Chapter Four

The creature known as Victoria Ash glided more than walked into the dining car of an overnight train from London. The whole conveyance bumped and swayed with the irregularities of the rail, but she seemed not to be bothered at all. Grace in all circumstances had rarely been a problem for Victoria since she stopped breathing.

The car should, by all rights, be closed at this late hour. The train had left London in the afternoon, heading first toward the coast and then turning north toward Durham, from where it would proceed to Newcastle-upon-Tyne and then on into Scotland. Victoria had been carefully ensconced in a large wooden crate at the time of departure, of course, her mind made insensate by the deep, dreamless slumber that took her each day. The wood of the crate and the careful layers of packing within it had protected her alabaster flesh from the rays of the sun, which had an unfortunate effect on her kind. In her more romantic moments, Victoria spoke of missing the delicate touch of sunlight warming her bare skin as she lay in the fields of Aquitaine in the heady days of June or July. The truth was, she was unsure if she could even remember that sensation. What was worse, she didn't know just when she had forgotten it.

The three men at the back of the car were likely responsible for keeping the car open long past its accustomed hours. The tired looking barman who was the only attendant still manning a station carried over another round of sherry and did his best to hide his exhaustion. His three clients were all young gentlemen serving in the hussars, if their waxed mustaches and uniforms were anything to judge by. They were playing cards—casino, she guessed, from the quick play—and laughing about days gone by. Victoria stood in the shadows of the car's forward section and watched them. There were others of her kind who might be interested in the goings on in County Durham, some of whom collected soldiers.

***

"Marriage, eh Seward?" Easton lifted the glass of sherry that the barman finally brought around and toasted his brother in arms. "To the fine lady—what was her name again?"

"Regina." Seward laughed a bit at his large friend's forgetfulness. Drink always did this to Easton, made him a loud, mirthful, clown. Hard to believe this bellowing, smiling drunkard was capable of acts of true savagery and true heroism in combat. "Her name is Lady Regina. Lord Blake's daughter, yes?"

"Don't mind Easton," Pool put in. Thinner and swarthier than the loud lummox Easton, Lieutenant Pool had been Seward's friend for far more years. They'd served together in Egypt under Lord Blake's command. "He's only jealous."

"Ha!" Easton exclaimed. "A wife is a shackle I don't need. They're only good for dragging one about and squeezing out a brat every few years. No thank you!"

"Not all of us," Seward said, "are the second sons of a senile marquis who covers up our every indiscretion. Some of us need to establish ourselves."

"And not all of us," Pool added in support, "are content to know only the pleasures of every whorehouse from Whitechapel to Calcutta!"

"Ha!" Easton bellowed. "Give me a wet whore over every dry lady in Mayfair!"

"You," Seward said, "have been visiting the wrong ladies."

***

Victoria moved forward in the car, her senses sharpening and taking in every detail of the three men.

So this was the fiancé of the daughter Blake, tall and handsome in the pedestrian way of English men. He had a hunger to him, she would give him that, some drive that put him a notch above a generation of well-bred, badly behaved aristocrats.

The others, Easton and Pool, fit more into Victoria's tastes for the bizarre. Easton, the connoisseur of flesh if his friends' jibes were any indication, was a mountain of a man whose heart beat faster than it should, making him ruddy and flushed. His red mustache and mutton chops only added to his barbarian flair and rough edges. A modern-day Viking, this one.

As for Pool, he was shorter than either of his companions, the more proper stature of a cavalryman. A fine scar ran down the side of his cheek and along his neck, tracing a line of fair, hairless flesh in the black beard and swarthy skin of his face. Italian or Spanish blood perhaps, surely on his mother's side with a name like Pool. Had his father married a foreigner or simply diddled with an immigrant maid and had the decency to see to his education? Aristocrats had a tendency to do that—when the bastard child was male.

"May I join you, gentlemen?" The three were satisfyingly surprised by her approach, although shock soon gave way to a wave of hungered emotions Victoria took in with the pleasure of a gourmet tasting a new dish.

From the larger-than-life Easton, a hungry and boring grin of lust. His thoughts, in all likelihood, never strayed beyond his desire to mount this fortuitously arrived female. His only reaction was to shift in his seat to accommodate his swelling member. Typical. She dismissed him.

"Of course, madam." Seward, the soon-to-be-wed young lieutenant, reacted with a propriety that belied his own hungers. He half-stood to welcome the lady and looked about nervously. His hand shot out to catch the rim of his chair as the train swayed in the night, and his eyes took her in with apprehension. He was no chaste choirboy, this one, but he saw danger in a beautiful woman approaching in the night—a risk to his engagement perhaps? Or to some other plan? His apprehension was interesting, the type of emotional flavor she enjoyed, but not tonight.

"A fourth, splendid." Pool, the short illegitimate, looked up at her with an easy smile and began dealing cards. "Whist it is, then."

Victoria sat opposite the man and marveled at his sheer calm. Flickers of emotions played themselves out under his façade—no breathing man could completely hide his feelings from one such as she—but they were only mild reactions. This man had faced enough in his life that the appearance of strange women on night trains was nothing to get excited about. He simply accepted the new circumstances and carried on.

She picked up the cards of her first hand, ordered them with ease, and focused her attention on the little man. Or, more properly, she focused his attention on her. The dark, cold blood in her veins grew hot and she pulled his eyes to her. To her flesh, her eyes, her hair. *Am I not beautiful, Lieutenant Pool?*

He reacted, certainly. She saw admiration, lust, even fascination, bloom in him. His pupils dilated and his neck developed a few stray beads of sweat. His hands shook just a bit. But the fascinating thing was that there was no fear. These new hungers swept over him and he neither thrilled to them nor ran from them. It was clear to Victoria that he simply accepted their presence and carried on.

As Seward put down the first card to her right, she looked across at Pool, her partner. The scar on his neck ran just near the jugular. Whatever wound had caused it must have bled profusely. She felt her sharp teeth extend behind full, moist lips.

She would taste that blood this night.

Chapter Five

Malcolm arrived that day. Taking the train from London and then hiring a hackney carriage from Shincliffe station just south of Durham proper, Easton, Pool and he all arrived in the middle of the afternoon. Seeing him descend from that coach, dressed in the finery of a hussar, Regina felt true joy for the first time in days.

She had been busy much of that day making preparations with father. He agreed with her suggestion of sending Mary to stay with relatives, but only after he spent some time with the poor woman himself. Perhaps too curious for her own good, Regina managed to overhear their conversation much in the same way she had spied upon the Ducheskis in the early hours of the morning, by staying unseen in an adjoining room.

"It is good that you find rest with your own family, Mary," her father said, in the tone of a loving *pater familias*. "You have been a great help to us, and I know my dear wife was very fond of you."

"Thank you, your lordship. I was very fond of her ladyship myself."

"I must warn you, however," he said, steel suddenly running through his voice, "that this is no time for gossip."

"Your… your lordship?"

"I will not have tongues wagging across the shire with spurious tales of my beloved Emma's death, do you understand? The fevers of Egypt took her at last and that is all we can ever know." He must have actually grabbed her then, for her breath caught with shock. "I will tolerate nothing else, Mary. Nothing."

"Yes, your lordship." Her voice cracked with tension, even fear. "Of course."

"Very well, now gather your things and Milton will take you to your family."

Regina slipped away before Mary could excuse herself and sought some quiet corner to think. It had not even been two days since her mother's passing and she already felt the fabric of her life unraveling. Strangers calling themselves kin had descended on the house throughout the course of the day, more Ducheski cousins and other relatives with names stranger still. They came in from Durham and from the port of Newcastle-upon-Tyne. Some stank still of coal dust, attesting to their duties near the mines that dotted the horizon of the county. They even had servants of their own, and by the afternoon the whole north wing of the house was given over to them. Most certainly including the bedchamber in which lay Emma Blake.

Worse still than this plague of invading black-clad locusts, Regina's father, who had seemed like a pillar of strength her entire life, was crumbling along hidden fault lines of lies and secrets. He must have known about the scarring and whatever dark associations had caused it, but he would not discuss them with his daughter. She understood his desire to keep the memory of his wife as untainted as possible, but just like Regina's brother Daniel's decision not to return to Bernan House, this seemed like another subject that would drive father and daughter apart. In fact, James, Lord Blake had barely managed to speak to Regina at all since that terrible dawn discovery. It seemed to her that he was too conscious of betraying the truth he had always told Regina he worshiped, and now could not face the accusations he imagined in her eyes. Beneath it all, the creeping suspicion that her father might possibly bear matching scars and markings wound its way through Regina's thoughts, widening the gap between the two.

So to say that Regina Blake was relieved to see Lieutenant Malcolm Seward arrive would be a great understatement. Although they had shared only one precious evening of solitude, their letters had been like a rescue line for her in her prison of proper English living over the last year. Now, with tragedy and secrecy conspiring against her, she needed his companionship more than ever, and she rushed to him with little concern for propriety or decorum. He and his mates were just entering the main foyer when she raced down the stairs and collided with him in an impromptu embrace.

"Oh, Malcolm! Thank Providence you're here."

"Regina, my darling." He enveloped her in his arms for a brief few seconds. "I've just heard the terrible news this morning. I am at your service."

The previous year, during her father's first parliamentary season in London, wagging tongues had called Regina a "New Woman." She had taken it as a compliment, given her intolerance for fainting weakness in her sex. Seward's appreciation of her as a person of worth, one not to be coddled or discounted, was one of the critical things that forged her own affection for him, and despite a longing to this once be weak, she decided to be strong with him instead. Stepping back from him a step, far enough for a certain propriety but close enough to feel his presence and he to feel hers, she was able to catch her breath.

"Thank you, Lieutenant. My father and I welcome your presence and wish you a merry Christmastide despite the grief we know you share." The pretense of formality surely seemed strained, but Regina noticed it put the other officers at ease and that must have relieved Malcolm. Pretense was an important part of military command, it would seem. "And my heart lightens to have you by my side."

"You are very gracious, Lady Regina." He bowed ever so slightly, although Regina spied a small smile on his face at the pretense. "And may I present to you Lieutenant Easton and Lieutenant Pool, also of the 12th Hussars, and stalwart companions both."

"Milady," they said in unison, bowing as well.

A MORBID INITIATION

She took them in for the first time. Easton was something of an oversized version of the traditional dashing hussar, taller even than Malcolm and red-haired. His mustache was well trimmed and his eyes blue and deep enough to cause a flutter in the hearts of many a countess or heiress, she was sure. Pool was slighter and darker, with finer features despite his thin beard and the scar along his face. His thin lips parted in a slight smile as he looked at Regina, and she had the impression of a corsair from a bolder time.

"Pool was a classmate of mine as a child and served under your father's command as well. Easton is newly attached to the regiment, but has already proved his worth many times over. In fact, I dare say I owe both these men more than I could ever repay after our latest battles in Sudan."

"Were you hurt, Malcolm?" Regina did her best to keep up with the news from Egypt and her father's old regiment, helped at times by reports Lord Blake shared with her. She knew well that the Empire maintained itself through force of arms as well as trade.

"No, or at least not seriously. We faced some harsh moments, however, and Lieutenant Pool managed to outmaneuver some of the insurgents as they were trying to cut us off from reinforcements. All ended as it should."

"Glad to hear it, my boy," came Lord Blake's thundering voice from atop the grand staircase. Regina thrilled to hear that officer's tone in his voice, evidence of a strength she had not seen in him in the past few terrible days and nights.

"Colonel." All three lieutenants snapped to attention, but Regina could see a smile creeping onto Malcolm's face. He had been her father's closest man in Egypt and their reunion was one of true friends more than of a commander and his subordinate. "A pleasure, sir."

From that point on, the day was taken up in happy reunions, earnest condolences and talk of happenings in

Egypt and elsewhere in the colonies. They spent a goodly amount of time discussing the recent declaration of the canal at Suez as a neutral waterway open to ships of all flags, and the implications for the flow of goods and relations with France. The political power of Sir Evelyn Baring, Her Majesty's Consul General of Egypt, had continued to grow and there was talk of ascension to the peerage. The prospect of who would succeed the aging Khedive Taufiq as the nominal Egyptian head of state seemed moot—whoever it was would answer to Baring.

Pool and Easton participated in some of these discussions, but for the most part it was Seward, Lord Blake and Regina chatting away as they had on a few occasions in Cairo. If the two newcomers seemed taken aback by a woman's participation in these discussions of supposedly male matters, they kept their comments to themselves. Regina would have liked to believe they were awed by the vigor of her own personality, but she knew that in all likelihood they were but taking their cue from their superiors in the matter.

A few times, Seward tried to move the conversation onto matters more grave. What had finally happened to Lady Blake? What arrangements were being made? Who were these visitors he had spied upon his arrival? Lord Blake would have none of it. He made cursory answers, but always returned the conversation to politics, economics and military affairs.

The Ducheski kin, for their part, kept well away. They continued to use the north wing as their preserve and while a few of their servants came and went down the halls near the drawing room in which the Blakes and their guests chatted, neither Eleanor, Thomas, nor Gareth made an appearance. All the better, Regina thought.

***

A MORBID INITIATION

That night, Regina found that sleep still would not come. But this time it was not dark images of dread relatives, or the black eyes of poor Mary's delusions, that kept her from Morpheus's arms, but visions of the man who slept in the guest chambers nearby. Closing her eyes, her fantasized memories returned. She felt his arms around her and smelled the subtle perfume of his skin. She thrilled to his hands, paradoxically both rough and gentle, caressing her cheek and his lips finding her own.

Propriety easily gave way to the longings of the night, all the more so because the reality of Regina's days had become so bleak. She welcomed her imaginary Malcolm's caresses, his touch along her neck, her arm and her leg. Unable to sleep, but as if in a dream, she felt heat building within her and writhed with forbidden sensations. To feel his kisses, to return them with the fire that she felt, wiped away all her sorrow and dread.

"Malcolm…" She moaned and imagined his hands exploring her skin. Her own hands acted as his, pushing her shift up her thighs, exposing her sex. He, or she herself, pulled the muslin fabric higher, over her head until it fell off like some discarded skin. She lay back on the bed and felt his imaginary hands run over her stomach and cup her breasts, suddenly tender and aware in the cold air of a country house at winter. She tossed her head back and ran her hands back down between her thighs, like a wanton harlot or a pagan she-thing, like—

Mother.

She froze with the sudden image of her mother's naked form, drawn back over her bed in a final apoplexy of want, the pink lines of arcane scarring attesting to long years of depravity. Regina quickly drew in Mary's ravings of Emma Blake writhing just as she had been, and a sudden chill came over her. Gooseflesh rose on her skin and she felt sweat beading her brow. She trembled and curled onto her side, spasms and tears overcoming her. The sorrow within her opened further to swallow her whole.

A knock.

Suddenly overcome with shame and the fear that it might be her father, Regina ran to the door to make sure it was locked. "Who is it?" she asked through the wood, trying and failing to keep her voice from sounding frantic.

"Darling, it's me." A shudder went through Regina at the sound of Malcolm's voice. What would he think were he to enter and find her naked and flushed? What would he do? Embarrassment and forbidden pleasure fought for control over her. "Let me in," he said.

"No… Father wouldn't allow it." Her stage whisper carried through the door and she turned the lock, which caught with an audible click. "He… he's had more than enough to deal with."

"He is asleep, darling. I must see you."

"Not here, Malcolm. He's bound to wake."

"Where then?"

Regina searched her memory for some safe haven. Milton had yet to return from Gables Heath where he had brought Mary—no doubt Father had asked him to watch over the poor girl for a night before coming back. "The coach house. It will be empty. Meet me there in a quarter-hour. Hurry, before Father wakes."

She heard him walk off with a final invocation that was reduced to a mumble by the wood between them and his haste to leave. She scurried to the bed and slipped on her shift again and then a housecoat and slippers as well. She did her best to cancel out the marks of thrashing and sleep on her, pulling a brush through her hair and dabbing her face with a washcloth at the basin. She tied her hair back with the silk ribbon Malcolm had given her that night on the Nile and pinched her cheeks to bring some color to them.

All these minute tasks of womanhood served to focus Regina's attention somewhat, but she was well aware of a tense heat building within her. Sudden recollections of the desire to which she had so recently abandoned herself bubbled up and caused flashes of heat. She tried her best not to run along the hall and down the stairs—*Quiet, lest you wake Father.*

***

Gareth Ducheski watched Regina Blake from the shadows. Standing stock still in the darkened corner of the upstairs hall not twenty paces from the door to the young lady's bedchamber, he'd listened with some interest to her whispers to her lover. That wastrel of an Englishman had passed directly in front of Gareth without noticing him, so focused was the lieutenant on the passions in his loins. Gareth hated the stink of that man, full of pride and hunger for things he felt the world owed him. A bastard son unless he missed his guess, or perhaps the last child of a poor pseudo-aristocrat who could just barely scrape together the twelve hundred pounds to buy his boy a commission in the cavalry. Pathetic. Gareth only hoped that Her Majesty's Army had taught him to fight, so that he could at least enjoy killing the boy.

The lady behind the thin wall to which Gareth pressed his back, however, was a far more interesting flower. He remembered well the scent of her on the drawing room chair. That scent had drawn him here tonight, the predator's instinct that she would be fruit ripe for the picking.

And how true his instinct had been! He'd arrived not a half-hour ago to the delicious aroma of rising blood and engorging labial folds. His keen hearing had made him privy to her moans and tremors as forbidden thoughts gave way to heated explorations. He could hear the slip of fabric on heated skin, of palms on stimulated flesh, the sudden inhalation of pleasures discovered. He had been mere moments from proceeding to the next phase—seasoning his prize with a dash of fear—when that weak-chinned Lieutenant Seward had come up the stairs on his own illicit journey.

Gareth had waited for the two lovers to exchange their whispers and now, at last, Regina emerged from the room to head downstairs to find her laughable paramour. His prize so close at hand, the shriveled root between his legs leapt to its twisted, painful fullness, but still he waited. They were headed outside, where they would be safely away from prying eyes, where he could play with them more freely.

Lady Regina vanished down the hall stairs and Gareth allowed himself a smile. He would have his fruit tonight. Yes, indeed.

***

Regina made it outside reasonably sure she hadn't woken the house, and trotted across the frozen grounds, clutching her winter cape tightly. It was a cold winter night marked by only a touch of damp, but Regina felt only the heat in her blood as she wound her way down the darkened path toward the abode of Milton the coachman.

She found no lights on at the coach house, but when she tried the door into the simple quarters there, it was unlocked and slipped open without even a creak. As soon as she entered, she saw the faint light of an oil lamp turned low in the corner and spied Malcolm's silhouette near it. He increased the flame slightly and she saw him there, dressed in light clothing, having already stoked the small oven to create some warmth. He was beautiful.

"Darling," she said and ran into his arms. Away from the eyes of propriety, they searched for and found each other's lips in short order and shared the deepest of kisses. His arms curled around her back, lifting her into him as her lips parted to accept his tongue. She clutched at his hair and head, welcoming his warmth. She thrilled to the forbidden nature of their encounter, which made each breath sweeter.

When they finally broke that initial embrace, they collapsed onto Milton's simple bed in the corner of the room. Malcolm lay on his back and she curled next to him. She savored the simple joy of being with him and felt the undercurrent of passion long denied building anew.

"I've missed you, Regina, more than you can know." To hear an admission like that from a man of the world like Malcolm was a little shocking, but heartening as well, for she certainly had felt the same. To read sentiment in letters was one thing, to hear it coming from his very lips was another. It was his honesty that Regina loved most and his understanding that she would not stand for pretense. "The fighting in Sudan has been very difficult. There's been a great deal of blood shed…."

"Shh, my love." She touched his lips with her fingertips and turned to face him. "You are here now."

He smiled. "Yes, yes, of course. I am a fool at times, my darling, to burden you with my troubles at a time such as this. Lady Blake was of the kindest sort and was so good to me and the men in Cairo. I… I'm so, sorry."

"Thank you." She lay with her head on his chest, listening to the beating of that beloved heart for long minutes. To speak more seemed unnecessary. She just wanted the warm safety of his company, the assurance of being with one who understood. Malcolm seemed to feel the same, for he did not speak either for a long time.

It was Regina who finally broke the comfortable silence. "I wish we could still marry, Malcolm."

"We shall, my love," he said, "only later than we had both hoped. It would be wrong to bring so joyous an occasion in conflict with the proper mourning of one so loved as Lady Blake. We must wait."

"I know, but waiting is like a stabbing pain to me, Malcolm. Father is folding in upon himself and the house is full of cousins each more distant and ill-tempered than the last. I feel myself going mad already."

"I cannot account for your cousins, darling, but I know your father to be a good and strong man. He will come through well enough, as will you I'm sure. And I shall not be so far away, my love, for I think assignment in London is in my near future."

"Truly? On what account? I thought you were to stay in Egypt or even India…"

"Ha," he interrupted. "Your father has been gossiping, I see. Yes, there was talk of the East Indies, but I have friends in many regiments and they have let it be known that I could have a post more close at hand if need be. And seeing you, my love, tells me that need is."

"Oh, joy!" She did not wait for his embrace to come, but took it for herself, turning to find his lips anew. She felt him start for a second and then respond, and it was as if the dams of prudence were breaking like some rotted wall before a flood. Her body lay atop his like a blanket, pressed as close as could be without shedding clothing. She felt not only his heart, but his entire body moving and responding to her own.

Such intimate, proximate contact was hardly the purview of proper young women and Regina had only ever been so close to a man in half-remembered dreams, but instinct filled the gap left by inexperience. Her thighs, pressed against his midriff, felt him swell with envy, and they responded as if on their own, writhing to accommodate his manhood. Wanting, needing to feel more, she let her lips descend to her beloved's neck and kissed the salty, stubbly flesh there. A gasp escaped his lips and his hands moved down her back, finding her sides, thighs and rear.

Regina slipped her hands to Malcolm's chest to undo the jacket that tied at his neck. For his part, he reached down and gathered up the skirts of her chemise and housecoat, finding her bare flesh for the first time. All thoughts gone from her head, she bucked slightly, arching her back to push more tender flesh toward his probing fingers. His collar came loose, exposing muscular and downy chest for her hungry mouth. She kissed along his collarbone to the divot at the top of his sternum. Her tongue momentarily tasted cold metal as it passed over an iron bull's-head pendant Malcolm wore, but she spit aside without a second thought.

His hand stroked up her thigh till there was thigh no more, and she gasped in response, blood pumping through her veins so loudly that she did not hear her own exclamation. That was enough to loose his own fiery lust, it seemed, for before she could even react, his strong arms were flipping her over onto her back and he was atop her, her head pressed tightly against the wall of the coachman's quarters. Her skirts were up to her waist and her legs wrapped around him trying to pull him within. She felt his swollen organ pressing through his breeches onto her most sensitive flesh and cries of pain and delight escaped from her throat.

He moved down her neck, opening both housecoat and shift, his hands roughly grabbing her breasts and his mouth licking and biting her flesh. Desire raged within her, and her heart was fit to explode. Then, instead of rising up her body anew, he yanked her lower under him like a hungry animal ready to be sated. At that moment, she wanted nothing more than to be his prize, so when he bent to roughly bite at the flesh of her neck, she pushed herself into his manhood while raising her head to accommodate his bites.

She saw a silhouette at the open door of the coach house.

Chapter Six

Victoria Ash's carriage, hired out near the train station in Durham, made its way down Bernan Lane. The coachman—a mountainous mulatto named Cedric—had accompanied his mistress from London along with her maid Theresa and he kept a careful eye on these two horses as they pulled the vehicle forward in the dark. The moon was up, thank Providence, but Bernan House had none of the gaslights of London to chase away the dark and the winter chill was deadening. They advanced into the blackness of night between two barely seen rows of elms. He only hoped the lane did not take any sudden turns, lest he end up pushing the carriage out of the Northumberland muck. If he had longed for the country life, Cedric would have stayed in Jamaica.

"This is far enough, Cedric." Miss Ash's voice easily carried to his ears, despite the clip-clop of the horse team, the crunch of frozen gravel under steel-banded wheels, and the wood frame between cabin and driver's seat. Cedric suspected that no barrier could truly stop him from hearing his mistress's voice and he was right.

In fact, Victoria had not spoken aloud at all, simply mouthed the words she wished her servant to hear. She was constantly aware of him, and of his unquestioning devotion to her. The carriage slowed and then stopped.

"Wait here," she said—aloud this time—after she descended from the carriage. "If I do not return by dawn, proceed to the house."

"Yes, ma'am."

Victoria did not spare him a backward glance as she proceeded afoot the last few hundred yards toward the grounds of the house proper and its entourage of stables, coach houses and other subordinate buildings. She knew very well Cedric would sit ramrod straight until she called him anew or the day's light emerged from the east. He'd

A MORBID INITIATION

fed from her slit wrist just a few hours ago, so her leash around his heart was tight indeed. More importantly, she'd spied something of interest down the lane and she had little time to waste.

***

Gareth loved the hunt, especially out here in the country. London's alleys and lanes provided him with some sport among those who would not be missed, but the chances of unwelcome witnesses and other distractions limited his opportunities. Even a Limehouse whore might attract the attention of a foolishly curious passerby and that meant a second body to dispose of. Now Gareth certainly had no objections to a second trophy, but such things could easily get out of hand and before long one was looking at massacre rather than murder.

But the country! In the country he could let his prey run and scream and plead. Already delicious Regina was heading for the coach house and from there it was not far to acres of farmlands and fields quiet as the grave. And the fop of a lieutenant was no trouble, because he would make for an interesting motivation for his nubile paramour.

The possibilities played themselves out in Gareth's imagination while he followed Regina at a discreet distance. Perhaps he would cut out Seward's weak heart and show it to the young lady. That had worked very well two years ago with that Welsh couple in Brixton, after all. Would it be too much to actually eat the poor hussar's heart before moving on to Lady Regina? That would be a new twist on matters.

Gareth cursed under his breath when he realized his prize had already entered the coach house. Too distracted by future possibilities, he'd lost track of present necessities. He imagined Aunt Eleanor's raspy voice scolding him.

Concentrate on actions, she would say, *not imaginings*. He hurried toward the darkened coach house—

Only to be stopped a few paces later by a strong hand on his shoulder.

"Excuse me," said a woman's melodious voice, "but perhaps you had better leave them alone."

Gareth had already turned around by the time she completed her sentence, and in fact he had intended to lash out at whoever this interloper was. Instead he found himself looking straight into the deep eyes of a true beauty. Much more so than little Lady Regina, this redheaded woman, in her fine gown and evening shawl, with her hair in perfect little ringlets of crimson, was a rare prize. Like a piece of cold porcelain.

Absently, in some part of his mind not quite so enraptured with this beauty, he wondered just how she had appeared behind him so suddenly, but that didn't seem terribly important. No, all that mattered was scenting this new prize. Gareth called on all the hunter's senses Master Wellig had granted him and inhaled sharply.

He nearly gagged. Her scent was subtly sweet, like a rosewater bath or beeswax candles, but it carried an undercurrent of cold earth. It was the hint of things dead that clings to gravestones and swamps, the remains on a blade no matter how well oiled. It was the master's smell, and that of all his inner circle of unbreathing and unliving acolytes and worthies. This woman—this creature—was a vampire. And a vampire unknown to him could mean only that she was a threat to the master.

That thought broke the spell her gaze had put on Gareth—no lust could be greater than his devotion to the master. He smiled then and in one fluid motion drew his long hunting knife and struck. It took him a second to realize the woman was no longer there.

In the instant it took his blade to travel out, she had circled to his left. She moved so quickly that she appeared even to Gareth's impressive senses more like a mirage shimmering from one place to another than a solid person. Only the faint whisper of robes shifting and gravel being kicked aside told him she was material at all, until he felt a quick knock at is right hand and a sharp pain in his gut. He looked down to see his own knife sticking out of his stomach.

"Get to bed, boy," the vampiress said, now standing a good ten paces away. "It is late."

Gareth collapsed. He smelled his own blood on the air.

***

Victoria could feel sharp canines pressing out of her palate and longed for the taste of blood. The ghoul, surely one of the inbred degenerates who infested these parts, would survive if she left him be. He had fed on his master's vitae copiously and it would heal the stab wound she had inflicted given a bit of rest. It would be easy to slit an artery right now and drink deep of him, sending him into a well-deserved grave and sating her own hunger for the time being. Yes it would be very easy—

No. He was the thrall of another of her kind and vampires rarely took well to spiteful assassinations of well-trained slaves. No, he would be on his way and she could deal with the repercussions of hurt feelings. Let the little ghoul stew in his evident hate, she had better things to do. Like head for the coach house where Emma Blake's child was hiding.

Victoria walked to the isolated house near the stables at a more moderate pace than she had used with the ghoul. With every step, she focused her keen senses on the house. She could hear whispered conversation easily, but the night air carried other sensations. Passion. Desire. Fear. They blended into a heady soup that delighted Victoria.

Getting within a few yards of the house, she concentrated a little further. The emotional waves lapped up against her with a salty caress and she responded. The hot blood that sat in her cold, dead veins began to circulate, creating a current that caught those same waves and sent them back stronger. She felt the paramours' desires becoming overwhelming, cracking through the carefully constructed dikes of propriety and decorum.

She pushed the door open and found them in a deep embrace. The heart of the moment came in tall breakers, smashing against her and returning to the two young lovers as a spray of carnal want. For the first time in nearly ten years, Victoria took a sudden, involuntary breath. She felt her skin, normally cold as marble, grow flushed and then paradoxically pucker with goose bumps.

She absentmindedly undid her shawl and let it drop to the floor, but she could not take her eyes off the beautiful, unrestrained display on the bed across the small room. This young lieutenant whom she had so casually dismissed on the train from London seemed transformed by the presence of the beauty who had her bare legs wrapped about him.

Victoria shifted just slightly to the left so as to better see the girl's features. Another inhalation. Emma had been a rare flower in her nights in London, but young Regina was exceptional. A prize above prizes.

Look to me, Victoria mouthed to the girl. And she did.

***

Regina's sudden scream broke the spell of her and Malcolm's passion and he understood almost instantly that they had been seen. He quickly rose off the bed and covered her by throwing over her the blanket they had lain upon. Not the best pretense of virtue, but it would have to do, and Regina clutched it to herself as if it were as infallible as a nun's habit.

A MORBID INITIATION

Malcolm sought no cover but instead stood between the bed and the door as his beloved's protector. How could a man go from hungry animal to stalwart gentlemen in naught but a heartbeat, Regina wondered.

"Who is there?" he demanded. The figure was in the dark of night and barely visible. "Show yourself!"

Regina did not quite see the newcomer's entrance, for Malcolm blocked her from the door, so she had to read the surprise and awe in the sudden softness of his posture. What had been a military man's *garde-à-vous* became a boy's surprise. He took a step back and to the side and Regina saw, in the low light of the single oil lamp, the most beautiful creature she had ever known stride slowly into the coach house.

The woman was taller than Regina, with hair of a red that spoke of Irish or Scots blood. In another woman, such ruddy locks might have marred her beauty, but not with her. Indeed, that hair was short and expertly curled to frame her fine, rich features. She wore a gown in the style of Regina's mother's or grandmother's day, but it seemed not at all outdated on her, with its flowing skirts beneath a tight bodice that itself rose to a low, open collar. Her breasts, white porcelain orbs, were exposed practically—but not quite—to the aureoles. A choker of black or emerald was at her throat, centered on a cameo of ivory or bone that held the image of a black rose. But all this was merely a fine frame for the twin masterpieces that were her eyes. It seemed to Regina that they caught the wan light and reflected it back a hundred-fold, sparkling between blue and green.

She knew she could lose herself in those eyes.

"Forgive me," the woman said in a lilting voice Regina associated with singers of operetta, "but I seem to have lost my way. I'm sorry for interrupting your sleep."

This beautiful stranger must have known, even if she had not been watching for more than a second, that sleep was not what she had interrupted. Regina felt a pang of guilt, but it faded before it could take hold. Indeed, the fires that this mysterious lady's arrival should have quenched with icy shame, instead returned to the young aristocrat. The red-haired woman looked straight at her, half-naked below a thin coarse blanket and she felt her heart pound. Her right leg, still mostly exposed to the air, moved up and Regina delighted to the friction. She could not look away.

"I am looking for Bernan House," the mysterious woman said, without a hint of the fire she was stoking. "I wish to pay my respects."

"I… I will show you," said Malcolm.

"That would be very gracious of you, sir."

She looked away from Regina to take Malcolm in and his betrothed felt a sudden shiver run through her as the extent of her current position finally came to her. As had long been her custom, Regina covered her shame with words and questions. "Who… who are you, madam?"

"Forgive me," she said with a smile. "I am Miss Victoria Ash. I was a friend of your mother's in London and came as soon as I heard of her tragic fate."

"Yes, Miss Ash, this way." Malcolm grabbed his jacket and led her out the door and toward the house, leaving Regina to make her own way. It took Regina until she was fully clothed to let go of the pique that had grabbed her at being discarded thus and realize the full consequences of being caught in such a condition. This could very easily mean her ruin, and still she felt more jealous than mortified. It took her until she was at the house to realize she was as jealous of Malcolm for taking Miss Ash from her, as she was of Miss Ash for taking Malcolm.

Chapter Seven

Regina slept deeply that night, carried by vague sensations of illicit pleasure and continued memory of those luminous eyes. Once again, details of her dreams faded with the light of day, but she recalled at least one sensation of stabbing ecstasy that echoed still when she woke.

After such troubled days and nights, sleep didn't release Regina easily once it had finally taken her. Indeed, she woke much later than was her custom—past midday even, and when she sat up the blood rushed from her head quickly enough to bring her close to a faint. She stroked her throat, where she felt the echoes of some pain—surely the result of Malcolm's wild bites the night before—and stumbled to the mirror to examine the telltale marks. Once there, however, she found her neck almost unblemished. Only a few small marks remained, and she felt they would fade quickly under the cover of the high collars of mourning dress.

The routine of morning toiletries and dressing, with the housemaid Elizabeth taking what was usually Mary's place, once again allowed Regina to shake off the lingering haze of the night. Certainly, her love for Malcolm was true and real, and passion for a true love was not something she felt especially ashamed of, but there was a difference between passion felt and passion acted upon. To go from an illicit kiss to a full imitation of a Whitechapel bawdy girl… it seemed inconceivable in the light of day. And yet, it had felt so right the night before, so obvious. There had been no decision to make, no choice of virtue or vice, simply a response to instinct and emotion. *What*, Regina thought, *would Mother make of all this?*

Elizabeth helped to adjust the black crinoline over black wool of the dress the young lady had chosen for the morning, or more properly for the afternoon. Regina watched in the mirror as the maid dressed her. She had never thought of herself as one of those girls concerned with having the most stylish of attire. Raised in Egypt, it was difficult to keep track of the royal whims that defined London fashion and she was happy to be saved that extra pressure. Neither did she consider herself a homely girl, but she had been satisfied with the beauty God gave her and not sought to adorn it overmuch. Still, looking at herself in the mirror, and at the cut of this most appropriate of dresses, a cut seemingly designed to suppress and conceal every curve of her physique, she could not help but compare herself to the image of Miss Ash from the previous night: her gown, somehow balanced on the razor's edge between style and scandal; her hair, not a strand out of place; her skin, whiter than fine china. Regina was a dowdy farm girl in comparison.

"Thank you, Elizabeth," she said to break the spell. "I must get downstairs before Father organizes a search party for his only daughter."

***

"I will not stand for this!" Lord Blake's face was red with passion and he stood bolt upright from the chair in the sitting room. "She was my wife and she deserves better!"

Eleanor Ducheski, small in the chair facing him, remained seated. Her keeper Gareth, however, took a step forward, seemingly ready to fight Blake off in his own house. "She was indeed your darling wife these past years," the old crone said, "but she was born our kin."

"That gives you no right—"

"Please," Eleanor raised her hand. "Sit."

And he did. From Regina's vantage point on the divan by the window, it seemed as if her father had been struck a blow, so hard did he fall back into his chair.

"You know, do you not, that the Ducheski family has important traditions about the burial of the dead? I believe this was all made clear in those days when the marriage of dear Emma was discussed, yes?"

"Yes," he said, with markedly reduced, but not altogether absent, energy. "I understand that, Mrs. Ducheski, but there are other considerations here. Burial in the cathedral's graveyard is our right and I will see Emma granted that respect."

"There are," Gareth put in, "certain complications in that regard, no? An undertaker would have to deal with cousin Emma's corpse, and he would see certain things..."

"What are you implying!?"

"Shush, child," Eleanor said to Gareth before turning to Blake, newly irate, in the chair facing her. "My nephew implies nothing. But there are people hereabouts who tell scandalous stories about dear Emma. Some of your churchwardens might listen if they examined the body for burial. Uncomfortable questions would be asked."

"There is *nothing* to be uncomfortable about." Lord Blake stole a glance at Regina then, no doubt urging her to keep quiet.

"What is true and what is told are different things. We can explain to the churchmen that other burial traditions are required, and the matter will never be raised. It is a good solution, for your reputation and Emma's memory."

The conversation had gone on like this for nearly an hour. Regina had found her father in the sitting room discussing her mother's funeral with Thomas Ducheski and looked to join the discussion. Eleanor and Gareth arrived soon thereafter and Regina surmised that this conversation had already begun at some earlier time. Soon enough the battle lines were drawn between Lord Blake's wish for a proper English burial in the familial crypt on the grounds of Durham Cathedral and the Ducheski matron's insistence on the obscure traditions of her family. Most importantly, she insisted upon burial in a familial crypt at Lion's Green, an obscure property a short ride east from Bernan House that Regina had assumed was church land. Thus far, Regina had remained apart form the heat of dispute, content to observe and leave to her father the job of setting things as he wished them. But enough was becoming enough.

"Mother's memory," she said, perhaps louder than she had intended, "would be served by following the wishes of the husband and daughter who loved her, Mrs. Ducheski. Not by hewing to those of a fair-weather aunt absent from her life but ghoulishly transfixed by her death."

Before Regina could brace herself, Gareth Ducheski had covered half the distance between them in a couple of strides. He fixed her with the look of an executioner set to his gruesome task.

"Gareth!" The crone's cracked voice stopped him in his tracks and he stepped back. His gaze never left his intended victim, however, and Regina saw his fist clench once, twice. She had the distinct impression of an attack delayed, not avoided.

Eleanor too looked her young niece straight in the eye. "Do not lecture me on the duties of family, young miss. I know more of the responsibilities of the blood than you can ever imagine. Did your mother tell you the story of her family, of the Ducheski?"

"No."

"We have been in England only a few centuries, my dear, but we have been a family for far longer. The lands we were born to, in what is now Hungary, were overrun by Magyars and Turks and others of even worse ilk. We were nobles in those lands, like your father is here, but without the pretense of Parliament and your House of Commons. We *ruled*."

"So, why didn't you stay in Hungary?"

"Do you not listen, child? The land was beset by fools and weaklings. The people's spirit was broken and hewn to the Church of Rome or the Mohammedan Turks. We found shelter in England and moved here. We were forced to pay a heavy price, to give up our birthrights of land and power. Our hosts craved the moneys we carried with us, and felt sure that the lost Ducheski would vanish into nothingness so far from their homeland."

She swallowed then, making a sound like a sheet of dry velum or parchment being torn. "They underestimated us. Nobility is not only in the land, girl, it is in the blood. By staying true to our ways, we have stayed strong. They would not give us land, so we built commerce and industry. Go, girl, go to the mines here or the shipyards of Newcastle or the rail yards and you will see your cousins at work. Our fine Norman hosts left us a pittance and we built from it a revolution of industry. Your dear grandfather, the viscount, the aristocrat, the lord of this fine manor, was all but poor and destitute. He paired your father with Emma to gain hold of her inheritance.

"For him, she was a dirty common girl who happened to have the money he and his son needed, an inconvenient purse filled with gold to replace his own squandered fortunes. Do not tell me of love and family, girl."

Regina realized abruptly that Eleanor had risen out of her chair while she spoke, and had walked right up to her young niece. To Regina it seemed as if that wizened face suddenly appeared a few inches from hers. The old woman's breath was hot and smelled of some meaty spice.

"Come, Gareth," she said, and left.

Shaking off the strange lethargy induced by Eleanor's diatribe, Regina made to go after her supposed great-aunt, but stopped when she glanced at her father. All the life and vigor she'd always associated with him were gone, and he sat sunken in the chair. He seemed gaunt and dark circles rested under his eyes. "Father," she said gently. "Are you well?"

For a moment he said nothing. His head rocked gently as if seeking some solid purchase atop his stooped shoulders. Finally, his gaze locked upon his daughter with some solidity and he spoke. "No, I think not."

"Shall I call for a doctor?"

"No, no. I just need some rest. Have Nelson bring me a brandy if you will, and I will sit here for a spell and gather my strength. These last days have been… trying."

She obeyed him immediately, but calling to the manservant took time and she was all too aware that her Aunt Eleanor and Cousin Gareth were all the while retreating into the safe haven of the northern wing of the house. There was little drink left in the decanter in the cabinet, but it was enough for a single glass. She gave it to her father, who mumbled a thanks and seemed ready to doze already, and then she dashed off to intercept her Ducheski kin. She was not finished interrogating the old woman.

It was not Eleanor, but her nephew Thomas whom Regina found in the hall to the north stairs. His back was to the wall and he was facing the hard stares of Malcolm Seward's two companions, Lieutenants Easton and Pool. Their conversation ceased as soon as Regina approached, but she could tell it was not a discussion between friends. Indeed, angry words were being exchanged when she entered the hall, a question of precedence or right of access apparently.

"What right do you have to be here?" Thomas had been asking when Regina came into view. Although they all stopped their arguing, she was in no mood to let angry words lie and she picked up, as best she could, the train of the conversation.

"They are here, dear uncle, as guests of my father and myself, the lord and lady of the house. You would do well to remember that." Regina had had enough of her cousins' presumption of position in this house. Lieutenant Pool looked especially satisfied by her defense of his position and smirked at the dreary little man he had cornered.

"Yes… yes, of course." Thomas ignored Pool's glare and looked at Regina. "I was actually looking for you, niece. I… I would like to speak to you about your mother's, um, arrangements." The silence hung and he nodded toward Easton. "In private, perhaps? I hope we can resolve the…"

Regina hesitated, still wanting to run after her elderly aunt. But still, Thomas, who had seemed truly affectionate with her mother, could prove very useful in swaying things her way. "I suppose. Lieutenants, will you excuse us?"

Pool registered a touch of shock that he was being dismissed so, but recovered quickly and bowed slightly with a soft "Certainly." Easton followed suit, doubtless taking his cue from his fellow. She directed Thomas into a small drawing room overlooking the north grounds.

"Thank you, Lady Regina." He sat, looking distinctly uncomfortable in the full summer sun coming from the windows.

"You were dear to my mother, uncle, so I owe her to show you every kindness. But I must say that your aunt and kin have done very little to alleviate this house's grief. Or to show proper respect to my father, Lord Blake."

"I apologize for that most sincerely. We are of a rougher culture than your father and our ways can seem coarse to outsiders…"

"Did you ask for me simply to launch a broadside of platitudes, uncle?"

"No. No, of course not. Please forgive me." He coughed slightly and turned his back fully to the window. "I hope simply that we can find a way to accommodate both our traditions without further upsetting… anyone." In that moment of hesitation he glanced around and

Regina wondered just whom he was referring to. Eleanor? Did the hag hold that much power over poor Thomas?

"Go on."

"Yes, yes. Your darling mother, who was very dear to me as well, deserves I think, to be honored by both her family of birth and that in which she found such love."

"You should perhaps inform your aunt of that love, uncle. She seems to believe Father was somehow saddled with an unwelcome bride."

"Yes, I fear that is a legacy of her relations with his lordship your grandfather, whom I believe you never knew. But you are quite right that she needs to understand that you and Lord Blake truly loved our dear Emma and have only her best interests at heart." He rose then and settled into a small chair, dusty from some neglect, away from the window.

"What I propose," he continued, "is that we invite Father Duncan, the vicar of this very parish, to perform a proper ceremony here at Bernan House. Your mother could then be buried at the familial crypt near Lion's Green according to our own traditions."

"I doubt a simple private service would satisfy my father."

"I'm sure that Father Duncan would be glad to remember dear Emma in his Sunday sermon, perhaps even whisper such a mention to the bishop at Auckland Castle. Surely that would assuage your father's desire to see his beloved wife remembered by the parish, no?"

In fact, it did.

Regina brought Thomas Ducheski's suggestion to her father once he awoke from his uncharacteristic afternoon slumber and he accepted it. She had expected some further objection, but her father seemed worn out and he quickly acquiesced to the compromise.

"Perhaps it's better this way," he said mostly to himself, which was the most he had alluded to his wife's condition thus far. Regina feared the act of denial he had dedicated himself to was the root of his weariness. "Call for Father Duncan, will you Regina?"

***

It was dusk when the priest arrived for the impromptu service. He had known Emma, Lady Blake only a little, but to Regina's mind, he did well. He directed the household servants to set up chairs in the north study, just down the stairs from the departed's bedchamber, and to use black linens to add the proper air of mourning. The mirror and glassware cabinet were removed—the latter with much grunting by one of the groundsmen and Milton the coachman, who'd returned that morning from Gables Heath—and the room draped with floral arrangements taken from the small greenhouse Regina's grandmother had once kept. Thomas, for his part, took charge of the bedchamber itself. Her uncle, it seemed, was well versed in the funerary arts and had arranged Lady Blake's bedroom quite properly for viewing of her body by the assembled mourners.

There were, however, few of those. Regina and her father, of course, along with Malcolm Seward and his regimental brothers Lieutenants Easton and Seward. The servants found time away from their chores to attend and Father Duncan came accompanied with a few of the local luminaries, such as the sole local solicitor. Mr. Whitby, the tenant of three large tracts of the estate—one used for farming, two exploited for coal mining—also attended the simple service, held at six o'clock that night. Of the Ducheski kin, only Thomas and Eleanor attended the service itself.

Victoria Ash was the last to enter the study-cum-chapel. Regina had not seen her at all that day and part of her had hoped she had left Bernan House. She felt the blood rushing to her cheeks as the redheaded beauty entered, the remembered shame of their last meeting competing with an uncomfortable thrill at seeing her anew. Miss Ash wore nothing so risqué as her attire of the previous evening, having chosen an elegant black gown for the somber occasion. She made her way to Lord Blake, who sat silently at the front of the room, and made her condolences.

"My greatest sympathies, Lord Blake. Lady Blake was a great friend to me."

"Yes… she was a friend to many people." He hesitated a second before asking, "My apologies, but have we met?"

"No, I think not. I made Lady Blake's acquaintance last year in London at a small gathering at the home of Lady Winthrope, whom I believe your wife corresponded with during her time in Egypt." Miss Ash and Father exchanged a few more pleasantries before she asked, "May I ask your leave to sit next to your daughter, Lady Regina?"

Regina's throat caught with tension. Lady Winthrope she recognized as a insufferable baroness who had spent some time in Cairo. There had been a whining brat of a son, if she remembered correctly, but she had not seen him in ten years, so she assumed he had grown into a whining dandy of a man. That Victoria moved in such circles did not engender confidence in her discretion, and she could easily ruin Regina here and now, at the most devastating time possible. It would take only a simple word to her father, within earshot of cousins, priests and other wagging tongues.

"Oh, I suppose. Have you met my daughter?"

"No, I have not had the honor." She smiled and Regina relaxed a touch. "I arrived late last night and she was fast asleep by that time, I'm sure. Lady Blake spoke very well of her daughter, however, and I had always hoped to meet her."

"By all means."

As Victoria made her way to a seat near hers, Regina tried to distract herself by scanning the small assemblage. She wished with all her heart that Daniel, her brother,

86   A MORBID INITIATION

could be here. His quarrel with their father should not prevent his last chance to see their mother. But then, she did not even know where he was or how to reach him. A midshipman in the Her Majesty's Navy, he could well be off the coast of Borneo or landed in Australia, for all she knew.

Regina also noted that Mary was missing. The woman had gone to her family for rest, but Regina found it vexing that she had not made the return journey to pay her respects to the lady she'd served. Had word perhaps not reached her of the hurried service? Or maybe the shock of finding Lady Blake like that was enough to keep her away from an event sure to involve seeing that same body anew. Either scenario was possible and understandable, but Regina still found herself angry at the woman.

"Lady Regina," Miss Ash said quietly from her place, "a pleasure to meet you at last. I hope you will consider me a friend as your mother did, and unburden yourself of your grief somewhat. Any confidences are safe with me."

Regina relaxed at that and thanked her stars for Miss Ash's discretion. Further conversation on the topic had to be put off, though, as her mother's body was brought to rest in the makeshift chapel and the simple and poignant service began.

To Regina's mind, the vicar led the odd congregation in prayer and remembered her mother well. Although she had been ill for much of the time since the family's return from Cairo, Father Duncan managed to evoke many of the things Regina loved about her mother: her kindness, her vitality, her quick and fetching smile. He also used the recollections of some of his lay aides—whom he had consulted before arriving—to reminisce about Emma's childhood in the region and recounted a few scenes of life in the nearby village that were new to Regina. Morris, she noted, smiled and nodded at the story of young Emma lost in the fields when she had taken a fancy to stories of explorers and decided to emulate them.

It was full and true night by the time the prayers were done and the men carried Emma Blake, resting on a stretcher constructed earlier that day and draped in black cotton and lace, out to the waiting carriage-cum-hearse. The attendance followed, using a small number of cabs and other conveyances to travel in slow procession up Bernan Lane and along the county road toward the Ducheski crypt at Lion's Green.

Regina rode with her father, Malcolm and Father Duncan, Morris atop guiding the horses. The other servants used a simpler coach, while the two lieutenants accompanied Miss Ash in her own carriage. The Ducheski kin, who all now came out of the woodwork, had their own conveyances. Eleanor and Thomas, Regina noted, rode with the body itself.

The journey to Lion's Green, the small estate that was home to the Ducheski familial crypts, took two hours. The party traveled silently along the rough county paths and the better-maintained roads that carried commercial traffic to Durham proper and other major settlements. Regina had never been to Lion's Green, sitting as it did as a sliver of land between large estates. She wondered idly just what the property's origins were. Land had long-since stopped being the exclusive purview of the nobility, but the estate was said to have a medieval pedigree. When had it slipped into the hands of foreigners and merchants like the Ducheski family? Mary's tales of witchcraft and curses bubbled back up into Regina's memory. Could it be that no one else *wanted* the land?

When the procession approached its destination under moonlit skies, Regina became convinced that the final scenario was likely indeed. A stone arch sprouted from the crumbling, moss-covered remains of a wall centuries old that marked their entry into the domain of her mother's kin. The carriage lanterns briefly lit the stones and revealed a large carved lion's head engraved from the arch's keystone. It reminded her of the reports and sketches of the lions' gate at Mycenae, excavated early in the century by Heinrich Schliemann.

"'Shall he in Argos dwell?'" she said, quoting Aeschylus, and bringing a wistful, fleeting smile to her father's lips. He had always supported her fascination with the classics.

Regina tried to get a sense of the terrain, but the darkness swallowed almost everything. Slightly to the left of the road and ahead, behind the heath that seemed to dominate that part of the landscape, rose the tower of Lion's Green proper. Like a huge dungeon for a castle long-since destroyed, it was a monolith of blackness against the scarcely lighter hue of the night sky. Firelight flickered from the top, indicating medieval crenellations and matching murder holes.

"Charming," she said.

The procession took a right turn away from the great tower and proceeded through gardens, which were lit here and there with the lanterns of pedestrians making their way in the same direction as Emma Blake's corpse. Straining to make out the details in the gloom, Regina caught silhouettes of enormous hedgerows and classical fountains. She saw what might have been strange spiny fruits hanging from the bent boughs of trees oddly leaved for the time of year. A low rock wall that ran alongside the road became progressively more choked with thorny vines and soon Regina lost track of it amidst hedges and darkness. Bare trees grew so close together that their limbs wound about one another and their trunks leaned in toward the path, threatening the fleshy trespassers in their domain. Regina had no difficulty whatsoever imagining inquisitors and witch-finders of some bygone age condemning the inhabitants here to the pyre for heresy and deviltry.

They were waiting for the funeral party at the end of the path. If Regina had felt before that the Ducheski clan descended on Bernan House like an invading army, she now felt like a lone soldier deep in the enemy's motherland. Dozens of people of all ages and descriptions lined the sides of the path into the clan graveyard. She could see entire families, babes in arms and crones alike, looking at the passing procession with what could only be described as reverence.

"Good Lord," said Malcolm, "look at them all."

One of the onlookers raised an arm in some parody of a salute, and Regina gasped. The man's hand, ungloved and oversized, had been the victim of an industrial accident or a ravaging disease. The fingers, if they could actually be called that, curled around one another like tangled roots and were tipped by black, animalistic nails. Regina scanned the crowd, averting her eyes from this unfortunate, only to find that he was hardly the only malformed Ducheski cousin.

Thomas, Eleanor and Gareth had seemed a little odd, but the assembled crowd positively teemed with victims of some strange affliction. Here, a woman looked up from under a hooded overcoat and smiled a snaggletoothed grin out the right side of a face that seemed to have slid down her skull. There, a boy knelt on a crutch, careful not to put weight on the mangled leg that ended in a club foot. Eye patches, canes, crutches and slings seemed as necessary in this throng as gowns and fine suits at a high ball in London.

The crowd was thickest right at the gates to the cemetery, where the procession halted. Several of the healthier, or at least sturdier, men approached and took up Emma Blake on a makeshift palanquin. Others opened the doors of the carriages, ushering the guests into their macabre midst. Regina stuck to Malcolm's side. She could feel the tension running through him. A smell like freshly tilled soil clung to the crowd and Regina had the sudden urge to run as far away as she could from this place.

She didn't, instead fixing on a single face in the mass of malformed mourners: a slight girl with wisps of black hair falling over her eyes. The girl smiled at the gaze and Regina returned it, glad for this one island of human warmth in a sea of bizarre rituals and worrisome portents. When Malcolm and she passed the girl, lame and clutching a crutch made of gnarled wood, Regina took her hand and slowed her pace so they could walk together. The unlikely pair walked near the back of the procession through the forest of graves, each covered with a patina of night frost.

The graveyard was, like all such places, built on hill and the crowd wound its way through the tombstone-studded slopes like a procession of ants. Small groups carrying lanterns split off from the main line, until the field of tombs was bathed in a diffused yellow light. Most of the stones were simple markers, all engraved with characters of the Cyrillic alphabet used in Russia and other Slavic lands.

"There are no crosses," Regina whispered. Graveyards maintained by the Anglican Church were usually devoid of heavy adornments, of course, but she had expected this one to be different. It was her impression that the Ducheskis, at least the first immigrants to County Durham, had been followers of the Orthodox Church. Having seen images of Moscow and St. Petersburg, she understood that the Eastern faith had a distinct attraction to symbols and other icons.

"They're bad luck," said the girl at Regina's side.

"Bad…" Regina stopped and knelt to look the girl in the eyes. "I'm Regina, but you can call me Ginny. What's your name."

"Anna," the girl said. "Just Anna."

"Well, Anna Justana, who told you that crosses were bad luck? They are the symbol of our Savior, how could they be bad luck?"

"Nah-hunh," she said, shaking her head emphatically

and sending her locks to and fro. "The Savior's symbol is the..." She paused and closed her eyes, struggling to wrap her young tongue around a complex word. "The emelent... elemenfal..."

She gave a small grunt of frustration and hobbled rather skillfully on her crutch over to one of the seemingly unmarked gravestones. She brushed off the frost and traced along a geometric pattern carved in the stone. "The circle-square-triangle. That's the Savior's sign."

Regina looked at the pattern, a large triangle intersected by several circles and squares. She scanned some of the other gravestones and saw hints of similar patterns and sigils in them. The symbols were varied—a large obelisk marked the peak of a small hill over which they passed and bore a serpent eating its own tail—but most were more geometric in nature. The circle-square-triangle trinity repeated itself in a variety of configurations, along with other shapes and curves. Mary's talk of witchcraft seemed less and less idle conjecture.

Emma Blake's final resting place turned out to be a great crypt built into the top of the graveyard's tallest hill. Regina was the last of the funeral party to get there, thanks to her discussion with little Anna. The construction reminded her of the dwellings of medieval and ancient men still being uncovered in some of the archeological literature, stone and earthen huts built in such a way that grass and moss might climb over them to swallow them whole. With the broad door set deep into the soil, it seemed to her that her mother was being carried directly into the underworld.

Very few of the assembled Ducheski kin continued on into the crypt proper. Regina, her father, and Malcolm forced themselves forward through the crowd of suddenly immobile cousins, determined to see this strange procession through to the end. Father Duncan did not join them, or at least he failed to make his way through the throngs. Anna, Regina noticed, did not follow either.

Once inside, Regina revised her opinion. This was no simple familial crypt but an outright mausoleum, with tombs on each wall and several rooms. Her mother lay in the middle of a central chamber accessible through a tight hallway. Regina took her position along the left wall, just shy of a sconce that held one of the torches lighting the chamber. She noted that there were other passageways leading from the chamber and wondered just how far this structure went. Was this the opening of some immense catacomb?

Eleanor Ducheski stood at the front of the chamber, with Emma Blake's body lain in front of her. She cleared her throat and then began to speak in what Regina imagined was Hungarian. The words had a musical quality to them she associated with the east, although they were tainted by their provenance from such a withered set of lungs. She felt she was hearing a prolonged death rattle.

"She is commending Emma's soul to the protection of the soil," Thomas Ducheski whispered. Regina had not seen him approach but appreciated the translation. Surrounded by kin she did not know, participating in a ritual in a language she did not understand, bereft of any familiar religious symbols or practices, Regina Blake felt more a foreigner in this dark corner of County Durham than she ever had in Cairo.

Eleanor continued to speak while those who had carried the palanquin through the graveyard lifted the granite lid of one of the three square vaults set into the floor of the room like a triangular altar. Regina had expected her mother to be entombed in one of the smaller wall-chambers—surely the major graves in the floor were reserved for whichever dubious worthies had once been paragons of the strange brood. The tomb being readied was separated from her by the other two and so she examined them, but found they were covered in symbols she did not recognize. The wall-graves bore Cyrillic script, most likely the names of the dead, but the three rising from the granite floor did not.

"It is something akin to your own talk of ashes to ashes and dust to dust," said Thomas in his stage whisper. "Emma will be allowed to return to that state in that vault."

"And then?"

"Then her remains will be placed in one of the wall receptacles."

Although the prospect of her darling mother rotting away slowly until she was but desiccated flesh and fragile bone was a ghoulish one, it did explain what was occurring and managed to somehow put Regina at ease. It was, after all, what would have happened to her remains in a more traditional burial, although her bones would not have had to suffer the ignominy of being replaced elsewhere. Regina returned her attention to Eleanor.

The palanquin bearers had taken up Emma Blake's body anew and were positioning it above the looming tomb. Despite this, Regina couldn't help but take note of a man standing behind Eleanor. She could have sworn that he had not been there when the old woman had begun her Slavic invocations, and his bearing convinced her he had not been among the mourners who came from the graveyard. Indeed, he was a refined man, with well-trimmed black hair and a suit that seemed well-tailored and even stylish under a heavy black cloak. He was tall and his features were hawkish and sharp, as if some unseen sculptor had chiseled his flesh with a rough tool. When the bearers lowered Emma into her tomb, he nodded once, turned and headed down one of the darkened tunnels in the back of the crypt. Regina strained to catch a hint of where he was headed, but lost him in the gloom. By the time she returned her attention, the palanquin bearers had deposited their charge and were taking up the slab of a lid to close the vault. She barely had a passing second to see her mother lying peacefully, her arms crossed and eyes closed, before they sealed her away forever.

***

"I am returning to London straight away, I'm afraid." Victoria Ash was standing near her carriage, her servant readying the horses for travel. The rest of the Blake party were milling about, but Regina had found herself slightly apart from them and noted Victoria's rush to leave.

"I… Thank you for coming…" Why couldn't she speak? She sounded like such a silly girl, even to herself.

"Please, it was the least I could do." Victoria clasped Regina's gloved hand in hers and the younger girl felt a shiver of excitement run up her limbs, altogether different from the cold air of night. "Your mother… your mother was dear to me. Just as you are."

Victoria slipped one of her hands into her fur-lined coat and withdrew a small, ecru visiting card. She handed it to Regina. It read:

> Miss Victoria Ash
> 49 Charlotte Place

"Please come visit me when in London," Victoria said. "You are always welcome."

Regina felt herself melting despite the cold night. In a desperate quest to recover her poise, she began to protest. "But, Miss Ash, I…"

"Now, please, my dear. I know we have just met, but I see in you all the greatest qualities of dear Emma." She looked over her shoulder. "It saddens me that we have had to meet under such gruesome circumstances, and in such company."

Regina swallowed and struggled to regain her composure. Victoria was still holding her hands, and her mind refused to focus.

"Do you know much about them?" Regina finally asked, perhaps too loudly. "Mother's family, I mean?"

"Only that I wish to be far from them and I hope you will keep your distance as well." She finally released Regina and climbed into the carriage, still speaking. "I regret leaving your mother to their dubious care, but some things are beyond our power to change."

"I suppose…"

Victoria's coachman closed the door behind her and climbed to his position. She sat facing forward and extended a delicate, porcelain arm out the window to gently cup Regina's upward-turned face. "Do be careful, my dear."

As the carriage pulled away, Regina mouthed silently, "I will." She was only dimly aware of the single tear running down her cheek .

Chapter Eight

The Blake party returned in the wee small hours of the morning to Bernan House and all proceeded to bed with only perfunctory goodnights. At some point on the ride back, Malcolm had realized it was now the new year, that Lady Blake was lain to rest right around the very moment 1887 had become 1888. Neither Regina nor her father saw that as anything to truly celebrate.

Regina hoped for a second night of oblivious sleep—she certainly felt exhausted enough—but found that the gloom of having entombed her mother followed her into her slumber. It was a melancholy sort of dream, bereft of the horror and passion her previous imaginings had entailed. Instead of monstrous eyes or Malcolm, she saw her mother silhouetted at her bedside. It was dark in her dream, and only the pale moonlight through the window allowed Regina to see Emma Blake at all. Despite the gloom, she clearly saw crimson tears streaking her mother's pale cheeks, something that seemed all the more odd because she rarely remembered colors in her dreams.

"Mother…?" she asked in the dream.

"Shh, my beautiful girl." The apparition stroked Regina's arm. Her flesh was cold as the grave. "I've just come to say goodbye, and… and that I'm so sorry. It wasn't supposed to be like this, little angel."

"Mother… don't go…"

"I have to. It's… it's all for the best… Now, go back to sleep, my love."

"No… I…" but the dream-world spun and faded as oblivion enveloped Regina again. It felt like she was falling….

"No!" She sat bolt upright in the bed and found wan dawn light coming in through the muslin curtains. She was now fully and truly awake, but the echoes of the dream were still strong enough to make her sorrow acute. She sat there and shivered, aware of everything she longed for but could not have: her mother, a final goodbye, an explanation.

That morning, Regina had Bernan House largely to herself. Lord Blake, Malcolm Seward and the other two lieutenants slept late, practicing the military tendency to get sleep when one can. Regina wished she could join them, but the dream images of her mother would not leave her alone. Victoria Ash had left Lion's Green straight for Durham and a night train bound for London. As for Regina's beloved Ducheski cousins, they had all abandoned the house for lodgings in and around Lion's Green. After a few days of feeling as if her father and she were under occupation by some strange garrison of Slavs, the contrast of the empty house was striking indeed.

Even the servants were scarce. Mary presumably remained with her family—*How could she have missed the funeral?* Regina wondered—and the others remained largely unseen. Elizabeth emerged as Regina made her way downstairs, but the maid was clearly exhausted and Regina sent her back to her bed. It was early, and Regina wished to be alone.

Oh Mother, she thought, *what happened to you?*

She wandered to the same study in which her father and Aunt Eleanor had quarreled, curled herself into the biggest chair there, and let the thoughts come. She had done all too little clear thinking over the past few days and now memories replayed themselves in new orders and with new meanings. Mother's conversation with Thomas on the eve of her death. What had she been unready for? What was this "initiation" Thomas had mentioned? The dark, sour fact of her mother's corpse, naked and bearing the marks of some torture or pagan act. Mary's near catatonia and her absence from the funeral. The funeral itself, so full of strange relatives and odd symbolism. And Miss Ash's warning.

It was the Ducheskis' fault. Regina was sure of it. Whatever news Thomas had brought her mother had upset her and sent her fragile health into fatal collapse. Lord Blake had returned the family to Bernan House to shield his wife from the vexing humors of the Nile Delta, but other humors had found her there. And what of the markings on her flesh? The strange traditions of the Ducheski had to be at the root of it all. What had her father called it that terrible night?

Witchcraft.

Regina decided then and there that she would know the full truth. And more so, she would hold accountable those who had condemned her mother to such a decline. No matter what. She felt no hesitation, and dismissed altogether the sensible notion that bringing entire families of unseen aggressors to justice was no easy task. Her mother was gone and she could not conceive of a world in which no one could be held responsible.

***

The rooms that had been Emma Blake's bedchambers, and the place of her death, seemed to have died themselves. The site of love, sorrow, horror and confusion over the last days, they now revealed themselves to Regina as rather plain, even shabby. Bernan House was a fine residence, but the Blakes had not been numerous for several generations and the rooms of the north wing all showed evidence of a certain disuse. There were chairs in her mother's dressing room she was sure hadn't welcomed a sitter since before her own birth almost eighteen years ago.

Mother's sickness hadn't added to the life of the room, and in the aftermath of her death it had only been turned upside down by her bizarre cousins and the necessities of mourning. The bed seemed to sag as if shattered under the weigh of sorrow it had borne, the drapes hung slightly askew and a faint crack ran through the mirror over the dresser.

Regina moved from lantern to candle, adding as much light as she could to the room, but still gloom clung to every surface. No light whatsoever came from the window and the air was stuffy and heavy, so she moved to the drapes and pulled them back. It reminded her of the day after her mother's death, and the image of Emma's face suddenly curled into a snarl by the play of shadows came to her so suddenly that she shook. The heavy drapes, made of rough canvas, felt coarse in her hands as she clung to them. Finally she drew them open, pushed the wooden shutters out and let in some air.

After a few deep breaths, she turned toward the bedside. Perhaps her mother—

She stopped mid-stride. *Canvas?*

Regina turned on her heels and returned to the window. Bernan House had thin muslin drapes to provide shade and shutters to provide a tighter seal against harsh weather. She'd never noticed heavy canvas before. Regina used an oil lamp to illuminate the mysterious curtains so she could examine them. They were heavy and rough canvas, akin to that used in sailing ships, and seemed designed to block out every bit of light.

They were also a hasty addition to the room. The original muslin drapes were still hanging in the corners of the window, behind the heavy curtain of light-proof material. The latter blinds were attached above her head and along the sides of the sill, and it was only by using curtain ties that they could even be opened at all for any length of time.

She yanked at the fabric and found it was held firm by heavy iron nails driven deep into the wooden window-frame. *When could this have been done? And by whom?* The Ducheski cousins or servants seemed likely candidates, but Regina remembered the lack of light the night she had come to see her mother's body and found Thomas

Ducheski there. The drapes had already been in place, but none of the servants had yet arrived. Could a little man like Thomas really do such work? The nails were almost a half-inch thick and driven deeply into the wood.

After some more effort, Regina managed to find a single loose nail, set into a section of the wood that was beginning to rot. She used one of her mother's combs as a makeshift pick and pulled the iron spike out of the frame. When she pulled back that small section of the drapes from the frame, chills ran down her spine.

There, written into the wood of the frame but obscured by the canvas, was a series of eerily familiar symbols. Strange processions of squares, circles, stars, pentacles and shapes she could not quite identify. They were the same symbols she'd seen in the strangely un-Christian graveyard at Lion's Green.

Witchcraft.

***

Regina returned to her own bedroom to find Elizabeth, kneeling by her bed and working with a brush. The maid looked up when she entered. "Oh my, Lady Regina. Are you well?"

"Um, yes, of course. I haven't been sleeping very well, though."

"But you aren't sick? I saw the bloodstains and I was worried, milady."

"Bloodstains?"

"Yes, ma'am. On the carpet here by your bed. I think they'll all come out, but I was more worried about you than a silly rug. Should I get Morris to fetch Dr. Fricker in town?"

"Um, no." Regina went over and clearly saw three red-brown drops on the carpet. Had she bled them without realizing it? She had certainly been distracted enough. "No, I'm well enough. Thank you. You can help me dress for town once you are done, however. I'd like to go see Mary."

***

"So you think she actually saw Lady Blake die?" Malcolm sat across from Regina in the coach as Morris guided it along the road that led to Gables Heath. He'd abandoned the uniform he wore for the funeral and wore a dark winter suit along with a black armband, in mourning for his beloved's mother.

"I'm not entirely sure what she saw, but I have an instinct that it's important." Regina tried to pitch her voice low in the hopes that Morris wouldn't overhear too much from his driver's seat above Malcolm's head. The thin wood and canvas of the cab's frame provided an incomplete sound barrier at best. "She was completely hysterical when I found her, darling. Like she had seen the face of the Devil himself."

"Yes, I understand. But she had just found her mistress dead in bed, and in a condition readymade to shock the sensibilities of a housemaid who hasn't seen much of the world, if I understand correctly. It seems natural that she should be upset."

"Yes, I know, but you didn't see her. It was as if she were paralyzed in some way. Mary may not be the strongest woman I've known, but she verged on a palsy when I found her. Perhaps she remembers something of Mother's final hours now that she has calmed down."

Malcolm didn't speak for several minutes, but Regina could see him struggling for words. "What is it, darling?" she asked.

He swallowed and looked down. "Are you sure you want to hear what she may recall, dearest?"

Of course, she wanted to scream, but the words died in her throat. The memories of her mother's corpse, both sprawled in her deathbed as she had found her, and quiet in her crypt as she had last seen her, swelled in Regina's mind's eye. Did she really want to know a painful truth? "I… I have to, Malcolm. I have to know."

"Then you will," he said.

In the early afternoon of January first, they arrived at the small cottage rented by Harold Bolme, to which Morris had brought Mary. The day had warmed considerably, the sun burning off the chill of the night. Morris leaped from his seat high atop the coach to open the door for his mistress, but Regina was already alighting on her own. She had no patience to wait any longer.

"Hello!" she cried out. "Is anyone at home?"

No answer, although she should perhaps have expected as much. Harold and his family were likely working in the manor house down the lane or in shops in town, as most cottagers would in order to pay Sir Milner his rent. Mary might even be with them. Regina proceeded to the cottage door and rapped on the hardwood. There was no answer, although Regina felt an unease like a tingling crawling under her skin. She reached for the doorknob and felt the tension building in her arm, rendered heavy and sluggish by the simple act of approaching this humble threshold.

"Regina…" Malcolm evidently felt that same apprehension, because he stepped up and seemed ready to pull her back from the door. "Perhaps we should call on the manor house."

She felt the reason in those words and the relief at not having to open this door, and that only redoubled her desire to push it in and confront whatever her instinct was so hell-bent on avoiding. She turned the knob and pushed the door in and was greeted by a cacophony of senses.

First, sound: A terrible buzzing that washed over her and sharpened the tension already building in her muscles. It was like the heaviness in the air just before a storm or the anticipation as the roll of thunder rumbles across the countryside an instant before the downpour.

Then, scent: And here was the torrent of horror, an odor of foul offal and rotted meat, of maturing larvae and other carrion. Once, in Cairo, Regina had found herself in a darkened alley during one of her impromptu escapades. In a corner that likely never saw the sun, but certainly felt its heat, she had seen a strange mass covered in bristled fur. Leaning down, she had touched it, only to gape in horror as the veneer of bloated skin and coat fell from the ripe carcass of this long-dead goat to reveal innards colonized by a mass of white maggots. The odor had practically leapt at her, forcing its way down her throat until she was kneeling in the muck, vomiting and choking. The smell in the cottage was worse.

Through stinging, teary eyes, Regina scanned the room. There were five corpses: three adults and two children, including an infant reduced to a slurry of skin and fat in the gangrenous arms of his mother. That woman had her head thrown back, revealing a long ragged gash across her neck which teemed with maggots and the flies that infested the small dwelling.

Malcolm's voice penetrated the buzzing swarm. "Darling, you must…"

"No!" Regina exclaimed, tasting bile in her throat. "I have to see. I *have* to." She clutched a kerchief across her mouth and nose and looked further.

The elder child had been a boy, and he too had a jagged wound at his neck. His father—Harold Bolme, presumably—lay slumped against the cottage hearth where Regina imagined he had faced his attackers, perhaps with one of the pokers as a weapon. If so, it had been turned against him—the black iron implement lay imbedded in the pulpy mass that had once been the man's head.

Mary was the worse. At first, Regina did not recognized the defiled body as hers. Indeed, the naked female form was arranged in some dark crucifixion on the back wall with the other victims scattered about. She was upside down, one leg pointed straight up and held with a heavy nail, the other bent so that the sole rested on the first leg's knee. Her arms were stretched out on either side, also seemingly nailed to the wall, and her head was missing from her bloody neck.

Missing was perhaps not the word, though, because Mary's head—bloated by rot and its visage twisted with the horror of her fate—stared blind-eyed from the nook of her body's crotch. It seemed like a stray object placed haphazardly in a convenient resting place.

Regina turned to flee the room and saw that the front door had swung partially closed. A pattern of lines marked the inside and she recognized a larger, bolder version of the markings in her mother's rooms. Square and circle, elemental forces, locked together in a way she could not quite understand.

For a brief moment she felt it would be best to stay in this abattoir rather than push through that branded threshold again. Leaving seemed impossible, as unreasonable as entering in the first place. More horrors must lie outside.

At that moment, Mary's head slipped off her own pelvis to hit the ground like an overripe apple. Regina ran through the door and threw herself into the cool snow outside.

She continued to vomit long after her stomach purged itself of all its contents.

Chapter Nine

The day after the discovery of Mary's gruesome fate, Regina, Malcolm and his two regimental comrades sneaked into the Lion's Green graveyard. Regina wished she had gone straight from the cottage to the grave, following her instinct that her mother's death was part of some larger devilish scheme. She tried to explain that to Malcolm on the carriage ride back to Bernan House.

"Mary must have witnessed the act itself."

"But what act, precisely?" he'd asked.

"Mother's murder, of course." She'd become agitated, the nausea of the discovered bodies passing with every yard she put between herself and the makeshift slaughterhouse. "They must arranged her death, darling, with poison or by suffocation. It can't be a coincidence."

"What of these strange sigils, though? You say there are some in Lady Blake's bedchamber as well?"

"Yes, yes. I honestly don't know what they signify. Mary had mentioned accusations of witchcraft at Lion's Green, and perhaps they aren't so far from the truth."

"But would these Ducheski folk truly murder their own kin? To what end?"

Regina didn't have an answer. She gazed out at the cold winter countryside as Malcolm sped the carriage toward Bernan House, the landscape devoid of any of the joys of the holy season. All she had was an instinct that the Ducheski kin had trapped her mother in some sort of snare, like bloated spiders feeding on a stray butterfly. "Passion, maybe? Or jealousy that she had married Father and left their ways behind?"

"Then a single cousin would be behind it," Malcolm said, "and the strange funeral would be simple coincidence, or established tradition? The murder of Mary and her brother's family there to cover up a single act."

"Possibly," Regina said, "but what about the sudden appearance of the Ducheski kin and their preparations? It was as if they were waiting for Mother to die, Malcolm. Like vultures."

"Then you are speaking of some grand plot on the part of your relatives, and that requires a motive. Certainly something more than simple jealousy." His eyes closed in concentration and Regina loved him all the more for it. She'd ungenerously expected him to dismiss her conjectures as woman's fancy, but instead he was puzzling it out. His military mind was attacking a new enemy.

"Did your mother have property of her own?" he asked.

"Other than her trousseau of jewels, no. She came to Father with a large dowry if I understand correctly, but all that became his."

"So this is not a matter of inheritance, then." His eyes popped open. "Unless…"

"Yes?"

"What has become of your brother Daniel?"

Regina looked out the window for a good minute before answering. Even now, after all the events, it was a sensitive topic for her. He, certainly, should have been there to bid Mother farewell. "He refused to return to England with Father and instead joined the Navy. At last report he was in the Lagos colony."

"And Colonel Blake's view on all this?" Malcolm was getting excited and it infuriated Regina.

"He was displeased." *Displeased*, Regina thought, *in the same way the Lord was displeased with Sodom and Gomorrah* .

"Did your father disinherit Daniel?"

"I…" Regina stopped because she had never even considered the matter. Daniel was certainly *persona non grata* in Lord Blake's eyes, but to have gone so far as to strip him of his inheritance? "I don't know."

"Because," Malcolm continued, "if he did, then that would leave you as a legal heir for the time being. And the death of Lady Blake would have the effect of at least postponing any further male heirs."

"I doubt very much Mother was in a condition to bear more children. And if we marry, then *you* would become heir, darling."

"True, true." Malcolm blinked a few times at the realization that Regina's statement could be construed as motive on his part. "But if our union was part of this plot, then surely Lady Blake's death would have been better timed after we were wed. Now, it has the effect of—"

"Postponing our nuptials!" Regina said. "And the same period of long mourning prevents Father from remarrying, thus giving our interlopers plenty of time to get their claws on our lands and titles."

"Yes, yes, but if we follow this cold logic to its extreme it means further assassinations. Lord Blake would leave his fortune to you and your eventual husband, but that might be challenged by a far-off cousin. Do you have paternal cousins?"

"Yes, certainly, although I see them only rarely. Grandfather Blake had three sons and two daughters, Father being the eldest of the five. I have Luke who is actually my elder and a solicitor, Anne who is married to a third cousin of the Duke of Kent,…"

"Yes, so there would be plenty of Blakes to inherit Bernan House. So the plot would have to be all the more complex, perhaps forcing a marriage on you…"

Regina felt the romantic exclamation die in her throat. Her beloved had just theorized about some other suitor replacing him in her future, and despite the pangs of jealousy she knew it was a real possibility. Lest she wish to forfeit her own social position—and at times she did indeed!—her father would be the final arbiter of any potential bridegroom. In the happy days before Mother's death, Regina had had the fortune to have Malcolm come forward and find a warm reception. Now, in the darker days when Lord Blake was a widower and thinking more strategically about the family position, he might hope for a better catch than a young lieutenant with little more than a military record to back his name. There would be several young dukes or the heirs of aging counts eager to add Bernan House to their lands. Thinking of the entirety of her own adult life as a commodity to be entered on a ledger was not something Regina liked doing, but such were the realities of the world.

"We must go immediately to Lion's Green, darling," she said, shaking away her distaste with an urge for action. "We will confront them and ensure that Mother gets a proper burial."

"Not alone, my dear," Malcolm answered. "First we must gather those dedicated to our cause if we are to investigate matters further. Lieutenants Pool and Easton will stand with us and I think it best to discuss matters with the colonel. It is his wife and family we are discussing, after all. Surely he will stand with us."

***

"Absolutely not!" Lord Blake slammed the flat of his hand on his mahogany desk and stood bolt upright. "I forbid it!"

"But Father," Regina said, struggling to keep the whine of a spoiled daughter out of her voice. "We think they were involved in Mother's death. We want to find out more."

"I have to admit, Colonel," Seward added, "that there are several strange things afoot these days. It seems worth taking a look when your kin are not expecting us."

Blake sat down again and his leather chair creaked in response. "They are no kin of mine," he said, just loud enough to be heard.

"But they are mine." Regina went around the desk

to kneel by her father. His rage seemingly spent, he seemed like a man worn down by the years. Perhaps he was. "If they wish me harm, I want to know it and put a stop to it."

"No," Colonel Blake said quietly. "You can't. It's not worth it."

"But—"

"Please, daughter!" Force returned to his voice like a thunderclap but it faded just a quickly. "Please, stay away from those folk now that this is over. It's best that way."

"I will," she said. It was a lie and everyone in the room knew it.

***

Without even discussing it, they all agreed that it would be best to approach Lion's Green by daylight. The Ducheski had a distinctly nocturnal proclivity if the past few days were to be believed, and Regina felt more comfortable with the warmth of the sun on her back— even the pale, diffuse sun of an overcast North English winter.

They took the largest carriage out at first light that morning, heading west along the same road they'd covered in the funeral cortege. There had been a light snow that night, so the wheels crunched and slid along the packed earth and gravel, but Morris kept their course true. The coachman had insisted on coming, having glimpsed the horrors in the cottage on Gables Heath the previous night, but Malcolm and Regina both agreed it would be best for him to remain with the horses and carriage when they entered the Ducheski estate proper. The two lovers, along with Lieutenants Pool and Easton, sat in the coach making what preparations they could. The men were armed, as soldiers with colonial experience are wont to be. Malcolm and Pool both had heavy revolvers along with their cavalry sabers, while Easton had forgone the blade in favor of a scattergun or blunderbuss. They clearly understood that this was not to be a social visit.

The dawn came late that time of year and it was approaching midmorning when they reached Lion's Green. The light of day transformed the strange estate, but did not make it any more welcoming. Regina's memories from her mother's funeral were of a monolithic tower looming over dark, shadowy grounds; of a graveyard full of heavy, gray, frost-covered stones that went on as far as the eye could see.

The truth was somewhat more humble. For one thing, Regina could see how the estate might earn its colorful appellation in the summer months. Frost-covered lawns, bare-limbed trees and bowed hedges evoked the lush gardens that would eventually spread out across the landscape beyond the low medieval wall. In the winter chill, the skeletal trees and brown, half-frozen soil looked sickly and worn. Like the rest of the county, Lion's Green would be dormant until spring.

The tower still loomed, but it looked much less like a gargantuan sentinel than it did a relic of the distant past. How many wars, plagues, purges, winter storms, and famines had this tower seen in its centuries? There were signs of the wear of passing years in the uneven stones and missing crenellations of the tower proper, as well as the crumbled archways and tumbledown buildings that surrounded it. Regina imagined it had once all been part of a fortress of some sort.

Even the graveyard was not as she remembered it. It was not so much a vast necropolis as a crowded, claustrophobic depository of shabby tombstones. Gray frostbitten slabs and ill-balanced obelisks created a crazy-quilt of angles and designs. The geometric sigils and engraved Cyrillic script that marked every single stone only added to the labyrinthine effect. Instead of feeling small before a grand mausoleum, Regina felt she was about to head into the maze of some especially deranged Minos. She only hoped there was no Minotaur awaiting her.

"This way," said Pool, "before someone comes." The slim lieutenant slipped past the iron gates that hung askew on hinges in the low stone wall around the cacophony of graves. He headed immediately to his left, downslope into the shallow gully between the gentle hills of the graveyard. The others followed.

They'd agreed their first priority would be to check on Lady Blake's interment. None of them were especially pleased with the bizarre burial rites of the Slavic family, and the strange sigils and other arcane happenings hinted that something truly perverse might be afoot. Emma Blake had been desecrated enough as it was. Regina was determined to make sure she was at least safe in her final repose.

The low path Pool forged kept them out of sight of observers on the tower and there were also far fewer graves here, down low. Regina remembered walking over hill and dale to get to the familial crypt, but looking left and right, she had a hard time seeing how she could navigate through the tightly packed markers and tombstones of the high ground even in the day, much less at night.

The reason there were few graves this low, however, was clear. The gully served as drainage for the area and although the winter chill had set in, the ground here was muddy and wet—the legacy of a warm winter. A thin layer of ice remained, but the morning sun was turning it into more slurry. The grass made squishing, sucking noises once the frost gave way and pools of frigid, brackish water seeped up around their boots. Further into the graveyard, the gully turned to outright mud and although it wasn't terribly deep, Regina had the chilling feeling of the earth trying to drag her down. Her woolen cape kept the cool air at bay, but did little to stave off the numbing mud.

They rounded the second hill and Malcolm, who by then had taken the lead, suddenly came to a halt.

A MORBID INITIATION

"Careful," he whispered as he crouched. "There's someone up there."

Regina's stomach knotted with tension and she felt tiny tendrils of panic working their way into her spine. Crouching in the cold muck seemed insupportable. She picked up her skirts and waddled forward, low to the ground. "Come on," she whispered to Malcolm, who had drawn his pistol, "we have to see who it is." Most likely, he wanted to object, and knowing that, Regina simply continued on so he'd have no choice but to follow.

They found another funeral, this one downright perfunctory. Two men, one of them a hunchback, were in workman's clothes digging soil out of the slope not ten feet up from the gully proper. On the ground near them was a white bundle of a corpse, a small body wrapped in linens that formed a makeshift burial shroud. It seemed that this cousin was bound for a shallow, perhaps even unmarked grave. Standing just a slight bit higher up the hill, supervising the digging, was Thomas Ducheski.

The hunchback and the other worker were making slow work of the cold, wet earth. Their shovelfuls of muddy soil either tumbled down into the gully or right back into the hole they had dug. The hunchback was singing an asonorous tune as he worked, but neither his colleague nor their overseer seemed inclined to join in.

"Like diggin' in cold shit," the bent-spined man said. Regina, observing from just beyond the bend, could almost feel the wet pustules of his spit projecting as he spoke. "Give 'er a try, then."

The other worker climbed out of the shallow pit, bent over and picked up the shrouded corpse. He waited for the hunchback to get out of the way and then dropped the slight body into the grave. Either the wet soil was not solid enough, or the gravedigger had dropped his charge against the side wall instead of the bottom of the tomb. The leeward part of the shallow grave crumbled like a wet, clotted mess and the body tumbled down the hill. It shed its shroud after a few rotations, finally stopping naked and exposed, one misshapen arm caught on a rock and its left leg twisted under the torso in a way impossible in life.

Regina recognized the thing. It was Anna, the lame girl who'd spoken to her at the burial. Unable to contain her shock at seeing the one Ducheski for whom she held the slightest warm feeling brought low, Regina let out a gasp.

The second gravedigger, who'd tossed the body in, had started down the hill as soon as little Anna had rolled out of her grave. Now, he was at the bottom of the gully and started at the sudden feminine sound of shock. He looked up, locked gazes with Regina and let out a sound like a hound left out in the rain: "Hunnnhhh."

Only a few days before, that sound might have frozen Regina in place, or if not the sound then the sight of the gravedigger's sunken cheeks, snaggletoothed maw and mismatched eyes—one milky white, the other dull brown. He looked like some unfortunate creature made up of discarded parts.

"Hunnhhh!" he groaned again, pointing first at Regina, and then signaling to his cohorts by the gravesite.

The horrors of the last few days, however, had left Regina unable to accept any more fear or hesitation. She felt if she stopped, even for a second, she could go mad, and so she forged ahead. "What happened to that poor child!?" she demanded, to the mute gravedigger and to his more vociferous companions. The mute raised his arm in response, drawing back as if either to guard himself or to cuff this impudent girl.

Regina heard the hard *click* of a revolver being cocked. "That'll be quite enough out of you," Malcolm said. He'd come out from behind the bend and had his weapon pointed right at the brute's face. "You two on the hill, come down here at once."

"Hurry it up," said Pool, who emerged to add his weapon to the fray. "Right now, please." Easton said nothing, but his scattergun meant he didn't have to. He simply pointed it at the two men up the hill.

Thomas Ducheski and the hunchback gravedigger obeyed. The latter eyed the interlopers with outright hostility, cursing under his breath. Thomas, however, approached Regina with apologetic concern.

"My niece," he said, "please forgive my man. He is dumb and incapable of any harm."

"We'll be the judge of that," Malcolm said, never moving his pistol from its bearing on the mute's mangled face.

"He is but a child, really, no more dangerous than an infant."

"Answer my question. What happened to this girl?" Regina pointed at Anna's corpse. She could see rough sutures binding up a long gash through her stomach. The thread was black catgut. Other smaller cuts, forming geometric patterns were visible on her left wrist—the one not jammed in the nook of a rock.

"An tragic accident," Thomas said, looking at the mud slowly swallowing his booted feet. "Kicked by a mule."

"The wound on her stomach…"

"An attempt at life-saving surgery. Unfortunately for naught." He looked around. "But you shouldn't be here, dear niece. These are private lands that…"

He kept talking but Regina wasn't listening any more. He was lying about the girl, of course. She didn't quite see how to get him to tell the truth other than by simply demanding it, however, and she feared that even at gunpoint it would do no good. In the end her ruminations were moot—chaos broke out before she could formulate a strategy.

The mute was the first to move, issuing a terrifying gurgle and surging forward into Malcolm and Regina. He must have noted that his captors' attention had wandered to Thomas Ducheski's fabrications, because he timed his attack perfectly.

Regina tumbled to the cold, wet earth. She heard screams and gunshots and more screams still. She looked down the gully to see Thomas and the hunchback each scurrying away in slightly different directions. Pool fired just as Thomas crested one of the low hills and Regina clearly saw a mist of blood rise from where the heavy lead bullet struck him. In the head, she thought.

She turned at the sound of another grunt, that of the mute bodily tossing Malcolm aside. The man might have been an infant, but he was a very strong infant, and Regina's beloved slammed into the ground with a resounding thump. His sidearm flew from his grasp and discharged from the impact, sending a stray bullet through the head of poor Anna, already more than desecrated enough. Regina and he had other concerns right at that moment, however.

"Hunnh!" The mute loomed over them with renewed aggression, his massive arms held high to strike, his gloved hands clenched into hammer-like fists.

Then came a sound like a thunderclap. Gore shot out through the mute's forehead. His face, once snaggletoothed, now looked like a ripe, red fruit split open. He stood stock still for a second, then tumbled to the ground, revealing Easton holding his smoking scattergun.

Regina rushed to Anna's side, and the men formed into a rough skirmisher formation. The acrid smell of gunpowder did a poor job of masking the scent of blood and offal.

"We have to find that hunchback!" It was Pool. The gunshots in the closed little gully, especially the explosion from Easton's blunderbuss, had done a good job deafening them all and they had to yell to be heard. "Before he raises the alarm!"

Regina grabbed the discarded burial shroud, stained at places with the mute's blood, and knelt beside poor Anna. Malcolm's bullet had punched a hole the size of a half crown into her cheek, shattering the girl's jaw before coming out the top of her skull. There was no blood. Regina looked at the girl's wrist and saw more of the sigils she'd come to associate with these dark days in County Durham. "Be with God," she whispered and roughly draped the shroud over the girl's corpse.

With that she took off toward the largest crypt and her mother's resting place. By the time they noticed her running, it was too late to stop her and the men had little choice but to follow. When they reached the doors leading into the underground catacombs, they could all hear a loud bell ringing in the tower that dominated the property. They took it as a sign their hearing was improving and promptly pushed in the heavy, iron-banded doors.

Regina never considered that it might be a bad idea to do so. She'd come too far and seen too much to be put off by the desecration of a tomb she was half convinced was dark witchery anyway. The door opened with an audible hiss and warm, dank air blew out from it into the cool winter noonday. It smelled faintly of curdled milk.

She ran down the cramped passageway of the crypt, the men in pursuit. After a few turns she had to stop, because the light from outside would not follow her deeper in. The crypt was as dark as any medieval oubliette. Pool struck a match and then lit three tallow candles he had brought with him. They guttered and ran, but they gave some light. Regina took one gladly, along with a few matches for good measure. They all proceeded to the main chamber.

The stone vault was just as they remembered it, a white sarcophagus seemingly carved from the very rock of the floor, with a matching heavy lid inlaid with a variety of Cyrillic letters and other sigils and pictograms. Various combinations of the square-circle-triangle were there as well. The simpler grave markers on the walls seemed to crowd in on Regina and the darkened passageways to deeper crypts still gaped open like the gullets of stygian beasts. This was hell, she decided, and she would liberate her mother from it.

She placed her candle on the ground, her hands on the edge of the stone lid and pushed.

"Darling," Malcolm said, somewhat hesitantly. "Perhaps we should wait… Lady Blake will not be in any condition to be seen…"

The only answer Regina gave was to lean further into her task. She was rewarded when the crypt lid slid sideways a touch. Soon all three men were bent to the task as well, Pool and Easton on one side, Malcolm with Regina on the other. Each group pushing in opposite directions and on opposite ends of the slab, they hoped to rotate it.

"One… Two… *Three!*" At Malcolm's command they all pushed. With the sound of stone grating on stone, the slab turned. It must have been unevenly weighted, or it caught on some irregularity of the tomb itself, because the front end, on which Regina and Malcolm were pushing, shot out much further than the bottom. The point of rotation was a good two thirds of the way down the lid and once askew it could not balance. In mid-push, it tilted and then slipped off the tomb, first hitting the floor on its thin side and then falling over and away so that the top of the lid faced the floor and the inside was exposed. It made a terrible crashing noise and both Pool and Easton yelled as they scurried out of the way of the errant piece of marble. Neither Regina nor Malcolm noticed any of it.

The tomb was empty.

"M… Mother?" Regina's voice was small and hopeless. She leaned into the tomb as if hoping to find some sign of Lady Blake's presence. There was nothing. No corpse, no bones, no burial shroud, nothing.

"You have… to leave…"

The voice was ragged and wet, as if the speaker was in the process of drowning or suffering from pneumonia. Surrounded by the dead on land most unholy, Regina's mind leapt to thoughts of specters and ghosts. "Mother… is that you…?"

"Sorry, your ladyship," Pool said. "Thought I'd gotten him." He was pointing his revolver toward the passage through which they'd entered, more specifically at Thomas Ducheski therein. The man was leaning uneasily against the tight walls of the crypt and his right hand clasped a rag at the point where his throat met his left shoulder. There was a great deal of blood.

"Please," he said with a gurgle, "there isn't much time. If you run now"—another wet breath—"you can still make it off the grounds in time." He coughed then, sending bloody spittle down his chin.

"Where is she, damn you!" Regina was out of the crypt and facing her uncle before any of the menfolk reacted. She grabbed him roughly and despite being slighter than he by a good hundred pounds, she still pushed and shook him. His hand came loose and she could see a fresh, pink bloom of scar tissue at the base of his throat. "Damn you all! Tell me!"

"I think you had better answer her ladyship," Malcolm said as he stepped forward and placed the muzzle of his revolver against the man's cheek. "Good Christians don't take well to grave robbery and empty tombs."

"Maybe you should fill it then," said Gareth Ducheski from behind them.

Regina's mind went through the steps of analyzing the new sound—*That is Gareth; he is deeper in the crypt; he must have come through another passage, like the tall man at the funeral.* Malcolm was significantly quicker to react. He pivoted smoothly and surely would have fired as soon as he saw the hated Gareth.

Instead, a gust of dank wind blew through the crypt, extinguishing the candles and plunging the room into absolute darkness.

"He... he can see in the darkness... He's coming..." It was Thomas, whispering and still right in front of her. Regina didn't stop to complain that people simply did not see in the absence of light, or for that matter, that pistol wounds did not scar over in a few minutes. The hairs on the small of her back and the nape of neck rose like opening blooms and she threw herself to the ground. She felt a mass slip right by her.

"It's not sporting to tell them our little secrets, uncle." Gareth, right there. There was a gurgling and Regina could well imagine her cousin choking Thomas Ducheski right there in the dark. "You never valued the family gifts enough."

Regina scurried toward where she thought she'd left a candle. She needed light if she was to do anything, even run out of the damnable place as the coiled fear in her gut screamed at her to do. Pool must have been thinking along the same lines, because he struck at match and washed the room in wan light.

Gareth was indeed throttling his uncle Thomas, but he flinched at the sudden light and dropped the man. Regina was still getting her bearings when Easton moved, coming up to their attacker and raising his scattergun. Regina thought she'd owe the man her life twice over, but it was not meant to be. Instead, Gareth turned with astonishing speed and snatched the weapon from him. Yanked out of the lieutenant's grip, the gun went off, filling the crypt with the sound of a thousand hammer blows, a blue flash and the smell of burnt power.

It only seemed to enrage Gareth who held the weapon by its smoking barrel and used it to club Easton to the ground. There was no sound save for the terrible ringing now in Regina's ears, but the towering lieutenant slumped to the ground very unhealthily.

The match light was fading and the darkness curled into the room again. Regina scurried in a desperate quest for anything to keep the shadow at bay. Any advantage to gain over this mad kinsman. Any clue that would explain what was behind the horror her life had become.

The match light died.

Constricting coils of panic wrapped themselves around Regina's windpipe. She wanted to run, but had lost track of which way was out. She wanted to scream, but couldn't hear her own voice. Instead she crawled as best she could toward the vault that had somehow surrendered her mother. She felt the hard, thick shape of the overturned lid and realized she'd ended up on the other side of the crypt. Further from the exit.

Light. It was slight at first, like the first tongue of flame when an old-fashioned tinderbox catches light. It had the wan, washed-out quality of gaslight, more green than yellow or white. Whatever it was, it was growing brighter.

Regina sat up to look over the edge of the vault, toward the source of the light. There she saw the two Ducheski men struggling and catching fire. Her mind, long past overloading, could not make sense of it. Thomas was gripping his nephew's throat and chest and green-tinted flames seemed to be burning there. Gareth, for his part, was thrashing and struggling. Regina watched as he pushed Thomas away, but his coat and shirt were already alight and the smell of burnt hair filled the crypt.

Gareth must have been in terrible agony, something that bothered Regina not at all, she realized. Still, instead of running about madly, he raised Easton's scattergun, which he still held by it barrel, and swung at Thomas. The wooden butt connect with the older man's temple and Regina heard the faraway sound of a hollow fruit splitting open. She knelt back down, hoping against hope that the horror would end.

She starred at the irregular white marble of the vault-lid's underside for what seemed like a long while. She should run, she knew. There was more than enough light to see by and it would be their only chance of escape. Surely Malcolm and the others were already doing so—

She felt the texture of the marble under her fingers. She could see it clearly now, the expanse of cold stone… and rough grooves in it. Grooves as if left by the fingers of one desperately trying to claw her way out a premature tomb—one somehow strong enough to leave gashes in marble.

At some point she must have stopped screaming, but she would be unable to remember when, later on. It might have been when Malcolm dragged her out of the tomb, past Gareth Ducheski, who was thrashing to extinguish the flames that were turning him into a monstrous bonfire. Or when Pool brought Easton out behind them, the larger man limping. Or as they cut through the gully again and passed the corpse of poor Anna, although that might just have started her shrill cry again.

It was probably sometime after they made it through the lion-headed gate and into the waiting coach. Milton headed off at a hard gallop while the oblivion of sleep and shock reached up and swallowed Regina whole.

***

Eleanor Ducheski was more tired than she had been in decades. Her bones ached as if she were a diminutive Atlas, carrying the world on her tiny shoulders. And, she supposed, that wasn't so far from the truth. After all, the family's fate rested with her and her charge, and the family was her world.

Weak philosophizing, that, she thought, scolding herself. *Fatigue is making you into a silly girl with a martyr's complex.*

She sat back in the plush felt on the train's seat. The softness of it relieved her somewhat. A creature comfort to be certain, but she did enjoy the pleasures of such luxury compartments on express trains. Wealthy passengers were a valuable resource and the porters, conductors and ticket men never questioned eccentric requests backed by pounds sterling. So this old woman and her entourage of strangely misshapen nieces and nephews wished to occupy a wagon's worth of compartments for the trip to London? Not a problem. They wished to have the windows sealed against the light of day, despite the heat that would result? So long as the payment was prompt, it was just one more endearing eccentricity.

Eleanor laid her hand against the heavy trunk set on the floor of the compartment. It was a large rectangular container, banded with metal strips and securely sealed with a large padlock.

"Sleep well, Cousin Emma," she said to no one in particular.

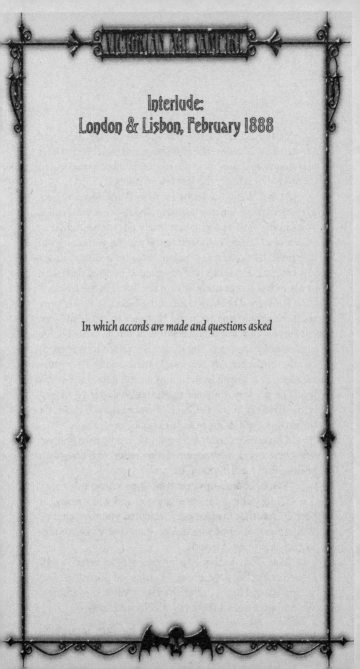

Interlude:
London & Lisbon, February 1888

In which accords are made and questions asked

"Is she ready, then?" Edward Bainbridge, who had breathed his last some thirty-eight years before, took a long and luxurious draught of the tea that had been steeping in its pot at his side for the last few minutes.

Anton Wellig, older by far than Bainbridge, winced. Elevation into the mysteries of the blood—what some called vampirism—had brought him many advantages, chief of which was the ability to scoff at the passing years and even centuries. It had, however, taken away his ability to ingest any common foodstuffs and beverages. Unliving flesh such as his would accept nothing save the blood of the living.

Wellig had been a magus of the blood, so much more than the simple *vampyr* of old Hungary and Bohemia, for centuries and knew aberrations such as Bainbridge occasionally appeared. But to actually watch it happen, to clearly see the true sip and swallow that so clearly put the lie to every feigning imitation of mortal gourmandise his kind practiced was disquieting. Anton Wellig, High Regent of the Chantry at Lion's Green, did not enjoy disquiet. Or impertinent questions from his Londoner lessers.

"Of course. I said she would be ready, thus she is." Was there ever a more succinct summation of their order's philosophy? *I will it, thus it is.*

"Yes, of course. *Ego expeto hic, ergo usu venit.*"

"Quite. The question is, are you and yours ready for her? Or has that mad king emasculated you that much?" Wellig meant the jibe with malice, but expected Bainbridge to take it as a jest. He did.

"Ha! That is hardly a proper way to refer to His Excellency Lord Mithras, Prince of London and Westminster, High Lord of the Baronies of England and Wales, Master of all the Empire's Undead and—"

"May he rot in his own private hell."

Anton turned slightly and looked at the newcomer. He'd heard the creak of the man's leather boots on the wooden floors outside the drawing room of Bainbridge's mansion, of course, but he'd wondered when the new arrival would make his presence known. The fellow had opened the door as he spoke and strode in like a man habituated to leadership, even domination of all those around him. He was that, indeed.

"Lord Valerius," Bainbridge said, "I do not believe you've had the pleasure of meeting my colleague from County Durham. May I present Mr. Anton Wellig. Mr. Wellig, Lord Valerius, once prince-regent of the city, and a longtime friend to our order."

Wellig didn't rise or extend his hand. He did look pointedly at Bainbridge. "None of us have any more need for friendship than we do for tea."

Valerius took the third seat in the drawing room, near the window. The scene outside was astonishingly bucolic for Bloomsbury, the benefit of the ample grounds Bainbridge's mortal associates had acquired for him. It was hardly as prestigious as the manors in St. James that better-placed vampires enjoyed, but it suited the Tremere representative well, being close to his regular haunt at the British Museum. To Wellig's much older eyes it was a galling symbol of the crumbs thrice-damned Prince Mithras threw to Bainbridge, calling it "recognition." He did, however, approve of the medieval statuary Bainbridge had placed in his gardens.

"Where is this young creature Dr. Bainbridge has been so anxious for me to meet?" Valerius wore clothes just slightly out-of-date, more appropriate to Regency flourish than Victorian reserve—although he wore pantaloons and not the tights of an earlier age. His ruddy, Saxon hair was well trimmed and had none of the unruly nature of Wellig's own black curls. To mortal eyes, perhaps he looked a tad eccentric, but his perfect physique, the beautiful cut of his face and his hard, cold eyes surely made up for that. Even

Wellig, much inured to the unnatural charisma some gained from the blood, had to remind himself that this creature was little more than a disgraced princeling hungry for vengeance, so much did he exude the aura of the confident, strong ruler. "If the stories he has whispered are even half-true…"

"They are." Wellig was in no mood for the dainty niceties of this misbegotten parlor-room chat. He had fought his way out of life as a serf to a Magyar whoreson when England was little more than a minor kingdom with delusions of grandeur, trying to catch up to the Spanish, Portuguese and Dutch who had gone out and conquered whole continents. He had stolen the secrets of the very stars, read the secret texts, and trafficked with spirits more fiendish than any blood drinker in this room. He had earned enlightenment, immortal unlife and ultimately the regency of Lion's Green with the industriousness of his thaumaturgic study and the ruthless elimination of those who stood in his way. He would not see the opportunities of this supposed age of industry squandered by aristocratic dandies and genteel wastrels, whether they breathed or no.

"She is ready," he continued. "All we are missing is the substance you committed to bring us. Do you have it?"

Valerius moved nothing but his eyes, which fixed on Wellig. The regent of Lion's Green realized in that instant that he had made a mistake. Without any change that he could have precisely described, Wellig watched the former prince-regent metamorphose. Where once there had been an attractive, even dashing man, there was now a rock-solid object. All the tiny tics of humanity—even feigned humanity—suddenly and completely vanished. No blinks or breaths, or moistening of lips. No dilation of the pupils or shifting of toes in uncomfortable boots or even the slight reaction of the fine hairs of the skin to the movements of the air. Valerius the man was gone and Valerius the immortal was exposed.

"I would see this creature first," Lord Valerius said in a voice that echoed the centuries he'd spent under the night sky.

"Yes," Wellig said. "Certainly." He was reasonably sure that the words were his own, not merely an echoed response to Valerius's will. But if one was overwhelmed, could one tell? "Dr. Bainbridge?"

"Yes, yes. Quite." Bainbridge reached for a satin tassel and pulled it, sending a signal to one of his servants.

A minute later the door opened and in came the lady in question. A black-haired beauty dressed in a simple muslin country dress and a woolen shawl, she walked with her head downturned and trembled slightly.

"Oh, my. Yes," Valerius said, and the spell was lifted. Suddenly animate anew, he rose gracefully from his chair and made his way to the woman. He ignored the aged crone who had appeared behind her, whom he took for some servant or another. He put his gray-gloved right hand under her chin and raised her delicate head to look at him. Her eyes were a fine hue of blue, the left with a yellow-brown flaw. "Beautiful."

He gazed directly into those eyes and parted the thin veil of her will. She was new to the blood, a creature who'd last breathed not a hundred nights ago. He had heard firsthand the dire news of a certain William leading Norman conquerors to the English shore. He was gentle and precise, changing nothing as he sifted through her memories and desires, her fears and hopes. She felt nothing except the certainty of his interest and even that he took the liberty of erasing like an instructor at Eton would a chalkboard.

"Yes, I see some of the nature of your attempt," he said once he'd done his explorations, "and she is certainly quite fetching, but you underestimate just what we face. One does not maze a bull in crepe paper."

"In the right hands," Bainbridge put in, "a simple cape of silk can trap a bull better than steel. Ask the Spanish." Valerius answered only with a dubious look.

"In fact," Wellig said, "you're right to be dubious. Our trap is hardly set yet, because we are missing the ingredient you claimed to be able to provide. So I must repeat my earlier questions: do you have it?"

Valerius reached into the breast pocket of his jacket and produced a small apothecary bottle of amber glass. It was stoppered up in wax and contained a black substance. "I do indeed."

Bainbridge almost leaped for the bottle, he moved so quickly to snatch at it. Wellig, however, was faster and brought a hand down to restrain his younger colleague in the arts of blood magic. He waited for Valerius to hand him the bottle containing the blood of a creature who had been old when Aeneas the Trojan rallied barbarians along the Tiber River into building a city on seven hills.

Oh, what sorcery he would wield.

***

Wintertime, Beckett decided, was hardly the best choice of seasons in which to visit London. Certainly cold had long since stopped being a major impediment to him, and regardless of that he had faced far colder nights in his journeys in Norway and Sweden at the beginning of the century. Perhaps the tapestry of history would eventually bear out the apocalyptic set of runes he'd discovered in the land of the midnight sun (speaking of apocalypses to his kind!) but for the time being they remained one more curious piece to the puzzle of how, or why, a parasitic, predatory species like his ever came to be.

He barely acknowledged the sluice of half-frozen grime a passing growler cab sent up onto the pavement, but he did take time to flex the ring finger of his right hand. A full year had passed before the power of his inhuman blood had allowed him to regrow it from the frozen, broken stump the winter nights on the glacial plains had made of it. His sometimes-companion Anatole had hosted a country fete in honor of his returned digit, he recalled.

And still, London compared poorly. At least in Norway there was the stark beauty of the arctic and the cold howl of wind over lands unsuited to breathing men. Here, there was just the wet, damp dreariness of a winter not quite cold enough to be worth the name. The snow seemed stained brown long before it fell to earth, and it melted into a brackish mess that then refroze in the treads in dirt roads and in the matted straw strewn over the cobbles of better streets. The straw was there to deaden the sound of iron-shod carriage wheels, but in this weather it only added to the mess. By the light of the sun or through the passage of the human masses, the ice would melt only to freeze anew, expanding in the cracks and forcing cobbles up and out of alignment. Anatole, who had spent most of the impressive span of his vampiric centuries as either a pilgrim, a priest, or a mystic, and so was inclined toward symbolism and portents, would doubtless call the displaced stone blocks and the wisps of snow on sheets of clouded ice signs of the madness that lay at the heart of any human enterprise the size of London, much less the Empire. (Anatole was very fond of the story of Babel.)

For Beckett it was simpler. The great metropolis smelled like a dung heap or a sulfur-works depending on which way the wind was blowing, and he found it much preferable if said wind did not carry freezing droplets with it. The only thing winter in London had to recommend it were its long nights.

Despite all his internal grumbling, London it was. The 1795 edition of La Colombe's *Le moine de Caïn* had appeared in the estate of a recently departed duke fascinated by the French Revolution (in the same way a soldier is fascinated by his enemies, Beckett supposed). The pamphlet presented itself as the revelations given to an enslaved friar, the titular "monk of Cain," by an unliving monster inhabiting the form of a priest. It was sometimes taken as an allegory for the excesses of the clergy, but Beckett and other experts saw it as basically what it purported to be. The author (La Colombe, i.e. "the dove," was an obvious *nom de plume* used to evoke the Holy Spirit) had likely been a mortal addicted to a vampire's blood, freed from his slavery—but not his longings—by the destruction of his inhuman master. The revelations were relatively trite in and of themselves, but they included details of events from the long-ago past that were obviously drawn from some very rare manuscripts indeed. Beckett hoped a full reading of the text might give him hints as to where the author had derived these borrowed details, so that he too might consult those sources.

It had gone relatively, but not perfectly, well. There had been an argument, as there often was. And then a fight, as there often was. And then, ultimately, the destruction of not one, but two of the other bidders for the pamphlet. That was less customary. Oh, Beckett had brought his fair share of vampires to their doom in his century and half of existence, but this was a little different. The first bidder had been very much like Beckett, an independent with only dubious permission to even be wandering the streets of London at night and no one to raise a fuss for her passing. The second, though, was under the protection of a vampire prominent in London's night society. His destruction would draw attention and Beckett, as the perpetrator, was unlikely to benefit from that attention. The traditional laws of their kind were that only the prince, the preeminent vampire in a region, could authorize the wanton destruction of a fellow blood drinker. If half the stories Beckett had heard were true, Prince Mithras was unlikely to overlook such a serious matter.

The key was to flee London as quickly as possible, before anything drastic could happen. Flight was fortunately one of the areas of expertise of Halim Bey, the vampire who had passed on word of the pamphlet's discovery to Beckett in the first place. An Egyptian, Halim was a dealer in antiquities among the living and the undead of the Empire's great capital. Beckett was reasonably certain that the portly Arab had some deeper agenda inamicable to the interests of Mithras and the rest of the British vampires who formed part of his clientele, but that could only recommend him at this point. Indeed, one of the reasons Beckett was so sure Halim was not just a loyal peon in the night society was because he maintained very reliable means to transport goods without alerting those who spent their unliving existences monitoring such things. He only hoped that Halim would be just as able to transport a fugitive vampire as a contraband sarcophagus. He entered the shop, causing a series of small bells above the door to tinkle.

The "shop" was a storefront tucked off the Borough High Street, in the crowded mass of the working poor south of the Thames. It was unremarkable, save perhaps for the simple worlds "Karnak Import and Export Co." painted on the glass of the door. Not the most reputable of addresses, but that was part of the attraction for a vampire of Halim's ilk, one with a reputation for dealing with those his more genteel cousins avoided. Dusky-skinned, with an accent full of rolling Rs and throaty pronunciations, he still dressed as a gentleman and paid obeisance to those in charge. He stood as a bridge between the world of proper vampiric society (a contradiction in terms if Beckett had ever heard one) and the looser underworld that existed beyond the notice of the well-blooded. He was certainly not the only such bridge, nor even the most important, but when it came to artifacts from Egypt or the Fertile Crescent, Halim Bey was your man—or your monster.

Beckett waited amidst the crowd of antiquities on display. Two sarcophagi were in prominent positions, seemingly a wedded pair—a king and his queen, perhaps. Each was inlaid with gold and other metals and stones, evoking the still-growing legends of wealth beyond measure available in the tombs of pharaohs. They were fakes, of course, but at least they were well made ones.

"From a craftsman in Cairo," Halim Bey said, appearing from behind a beaded curtain. "His family have been forgers since Saladin ruled the city, or so he claims." The Arab vampire flashed a quick smile.

"Beautiful, regardless of its origins."

"I had not taken you for an aesthete, Mr. Beckett." Halim reached down into the counter that separated the display room and the backstore. He produced a large, leather-bound book. "I have commissioned the same man—working with his two sons, I believe—to create for me a series of pieces based on some of my clients' special sensibilities. I have here some of the sketches, if you'd like to see if anything interests you...."

Halim opened the book so that the sketches faced Beckett. They were beautiful, indeed. But the merchant was right, Beckett had little interest in beauty for its own sake. Looking at the watercolor images of canopic jars, jewel-encrusted cartouches, and supposed fragments of hieroglyphics from lost tombs, he brought the conversation to the matter at hand. "I need transport, Halim Bey."

"I take it the auction was not altogether civil?" Halim flipped the book again, showing off a hieroglyphic design of three men presenting the solar disc to the god Horus. "I had warned you that was a possibility."

"Yes," Beckett grunted. Halim was making clear he already had the upper hand. As if Beckett didn't realize this. "I still need transport. To the continent."

Halim Bey stroked his fine beard with one hand and made the sounds of a man pondering many options. Beckett felt certain the antiquarian had everything planned out already—he'd been dealing with Halim for five years and had never found him unprepared. This was just a show, and an opportunity to flip a few more pages in the unnamed forger's sketchbook in the hopes of eliciting another sale. Halim Bey was many things, but most of all he was an entrepreneur.

As it happened, his strategy worked.

"Stop," Beckett said when Halim was about to turn the page anew. He didn't say it loudly or even forcefully, but it surprised him—he hadn't been paying more than passing attention to the sketches. The one that caught his eye was another hieroglyph, this time a cartouche accompanied by a larger series of illustrations. The cartouche contained a series of sigils Beckett was vaguely familiar with, something about "one thousand visages" or some such. The larger illustration showed a female dressed as a queen sitting on a throne, surrounded by smaller human figures. The larger woman had, instead of a human head, a perfect disc of black. The smaller figures, who all seemed to be workers, had serpent heads and carried large animal heads on their backs. It seemed that they were bringing these heads—or just faces?—to their void-headed queen.

Beckett had seen such a scene before, inscribed across the wall of the Cairene temple he'd broken into two years ago. He'd been following leads whispered by Halim Bey at that time too. Beckett did not believe in coincidences.

"What the hell is this, Halim?" Using his right hand, he grabbed the merchant by his silk necktie and pulled him forward. "What's going on?"

"That," Halim answered without a hint of trepidation, "is a representation of Kemintiri, the thousand-faced daughter of Set. She is a very minor figure in the legends of Egypt, but of rather more significance to the vampires who claim lineage from the Lord of Storms."

Halim Bey, Beckett knew, was referring to the so-called Followers of Set. This lineage of vampires was little-known and little-trusted by most European blood-drinkers. Beckett fancied himself a scholar in the early nights of the world, and knew that according to several sources, these Setites denied the most common story of the origin of vampirism, the progeniture of Caine, the biblical first murderer. (The additional trailing E was, as far as Beckett could tell, a leftover from a time of less rigorous orthography that had become a preference in vampiric circles; such idiosyncrasies were rampant among the undead.) They claimed descent from the Egyptian storm-god Set, whom many of them worshipped not only as a patriarch, but also as a godhead espousing a morality far different from anything in the Judeo-Christian tradition.

Despite his time in Egypt, a land thought to be rife with this line, Beckett had known only a few Setites and they had never been very forthcoming with the details of their faith. Vampires of all ilks existed on a base of secrecy, of course, if for no other reason than to ensure their survival in a hostile world, but Setites took it further. Whereas many other vampires touted their ancestry—to the point of fabrication in many cases—to inflate their own status, the Setites hid such facts from all who did not share their blood. It was Beckett's feeling that even an ancient who walked in the shadows of the pharaohs and watched the pyramids' construction would present himself as a simple trader in antiquities, not long of the blood, something he kept in mind whenever dealing with Halim Bey.

For Halim Bey was one of those few Followers of Set Beckett did know.

"But we were talking about transport, my friend," the trader said, "and I believe I know a merchant captain heading to Lisbon who would be amenable to additional cargo. I doubt I can do much with my neck squeezed to the point of ligature, however."

Beckett released the Arab's tie and scoffed. "Fine. We need to talk about this Kemintiri, though."

"We will, my friend. We will."

***

The steamship *Bartholomew Thomas* left London on the morning of February 26th. The first leg of its journey to the East Indies would bring it to Alexandria, with scheduled stops in Lisbon, Gibraltar, and on Cyprus. Aboard were a bevy of Her Majesty's servants, including a goodly complement of military men returning to active service in Egypt and an even greater number of civil servants traveling there to take up posts in the colonial bureaucracy. *Bartholomew Thomas* would be heading to Port Said after several days in Alexandria, from there through the Suez Canal, down the Red Sea and on toward India.

Lieutenant Malcolm Seward, recently of the 12th Hussars, veteran of hard campaigns in the Sudan, was not aboard, although he did have the good grace to travel to the Isle of Dogs to see the ship off.

"It is bound to be a dreary journey anyway." The speaker was Lieutenant Anthony (né Antoni, in his mother's native Catalan) Pool, also formerly of the 12th Hussars. He had come with Seward to see the ship off and to say a final farewell to their erstwhile companion, Lieutenant Ernest Easton. The latter was somewhere on the deck of the *Bartholomew Thomas* as she steamed into the Thames channel.

"I'll miss him, Tony." Seward turned from the sight of the slowly departing vessel. "I'll miss the lot of them."

"Come now, old boy," Pool said, slapping his once-regimental brother on the back. "Easton had his business and our own to attend to in good Sir Evelyn's corner of the Empire. Leave Egypt to him, for now. This is London!"

"I'm a soldier, Pool. London is a place for merchants and politicians, not for me."

"My goodness, Seward. You sound more like your future father-in-law with every passing moment. Soon enough you'll be making speeches about being born to the saddle, not the manor!"

Seward couldn't suppress a laugh. He'd heard Colonel Blake make that assertion too many times to count, and often at mind-boggling length. "You're right, my friend. I made this choice—enough moaning!"

"That's the spirit." The two walked up the dock toward the waiting four-wheeled growler cab, continuing their conversation as they dodged stevedores moving on to the next ship to be loaded or unloaded and wives still looking out toward their departing husbands. "The hussars were just a steppingstone, remember. Your future is among your brothers."

"I hope you're right." Seward waited until they were safely inside the carriage before giving voice the question that weighed on his mind. "Has the date been set?"

"Ha!" Pool exclaimed. "A second ago you were lamenting your old life in Egypt and now you want to rush head-first into initiation. You are a man of quick moods, my friend. I like that!"

"Let us say I'm anxious to see that my confidence in this shadowy association is not a piece of foolery. I had always imagined my career would be made in the regiment."

"Now you wound me, Malcolm." Pool's smile belied his wounded words. "Do you have a hidden grange or duchy you have failed to mention? A chest of spade guineas or Spanish doubloons, perhaps? No, I thought not. So how do you expect to rise through the ranks of the nobles and the rich who wear the ranks of senior officers?"

"Well, I had hoped to make enough in the colonies to eventually buy a colonel's commission...."

"Come now, you would not be sitting here with me if you thought that was possible. I am the bastard of a truculent baronet with a taste for Barcelonan whores and you are the last son of a gentleman farmer who emptied the family coffers to scrounge together the money for your commission and then lost his land and title in a game of dice. We are not the types who simply rise with the military cream."

"All too true."

"Indeed, those of us with a soldier's heart and a commoner's purse, even if we manage to purchase a minor commission, still end up under the heel of some captain or colonel whose only qualification is his title."

"Colonel Blake was always more than qualified."

"Yes, yes, of course. Lord Blake was one of the fine exceptions, but you'll note that neither of us are in the man's

A MORBID INITIATION

good graces after the debacle last January. Or has the good man decided to let you back into his daughter's life as of yet?"

Seward turned away from Pool and looked out of the growler, which was making its way off the West India Docks and into Limehouse. He bit back his anger and took in the dubious sights: the Chinese men in silk clothing and queues bringing foodstuffs and other packages from the docks, a makeshift poulter with caged chickens stacked precariously on a cart, the discreet and not-so-discreet doors to opium parlors and the hazy-eyed patrons stumbling to and from them, the stink of too many people crammed into too little space, the momentary flash of a Chinese woman's face—a prostitute surely—behind a small barred window. Did they really have the feet of babes, he wondered? It was a whole other world east of The City, just as alien as the great cacophony of Cairo outside the British enclave.

"No," Seward said at last. "He allows my sister Joanna to write to her, but that is all."

"There, you see how these types are. And you'll also note that since he went to half-pay, Lord Blake has left the regiment to a fool of a baronet, Sir Harry the Hare."

Seward smiled at the appellation. "Yes, our cowardly colonel hardly made a grand showing in the Sudan."

"There, you see? That is why we have formed our brotherhood, to ensure that the soldiers capable of defending the Empire actually rise to the positions from which they can do so. And we have allies and patrons in many places, my friend."

"Then why the secrecy? For all I truly know, this brotherhood includes only you and our Cairo-bound friend Easton."

"You do have a flair for the dramatic, Seward! You make us sound like an anarchist cabal. We are a private fraternity, that is all. A private club of like-minded soldiers who believe in the Empire and that you have a great future ahead of you."

"Yes, well…"

"My goodness, enough! We're heading to the club on Pall Mall this instant. Your questions will have answers soon enough."

"And initiation?"

"One step at a time, my good man. That, like anything of importance in the capital, will happen after Easter, once Parliament is in session and the social season has begun."

"Regina will be in London then, I think. I tell you, Tony, if her father is not reconciled to me by then, I'm quite tempted to snatch her from him and take the train to Gretna Green." He did not have to explain that Gretna Green was a town just over the Scottish border that made its reputation from exploiting the differences in matrimonial laws in the two countries—Scots were significantly less insistent on niceties such as parental approval or the age of consent than their English neighbors.

Pool gave him a wry smile. "Have you been indulging in laudanum? I thought you were a soldier, not a fool of a poet. You know as well as I that the colonel would arrange for a very unpleasant annulment of any such marriage and take care to end your career."

"But—"

"No buts." Pool suddenly became very serious. "In fact, consider this your first step toward initiation. No contact with the girl—no letters passed by your sister, no covert telegrams, nothing—until the colonel approves or the club releases you from this stricture."

Seward swallowed and looked out at the streets again. They were in Whitechapel now, cramped and crowded as Limehouse, but with different faces. The poor here were simply of the laboring classes. The workhouses side-by-side with the pothouses and whorehouses. He noticed one discreet panel set into the door of a building like any other, the calligraphed Hebrew script indicating that this was a Jewish place of worship. Such was the fate of outsiders in this metropolis—even to find God, they had to trudge through the gutters.

"Agreed," he said.

***

In the hold of the *Bartholomew Thomas*, within a heavy crate which the manifest insisted contained a seventeenth-century cabinet inlaid with brass, Beckett did not move at all. The sun was up outside, and like all of his kind, it forced him into a deep slumber. He did not feel the rock of the ship as it headed down the Thames toward the sea. The next two nights, he woke to the rock of a vessel at sea and remained still.

Upon waking the third night, however, he realized immediately he was no longer in the ship's hold. What was worse, the lid to his crate was gone and he looked up at the crisscrossing beams of a spacious ceiling. He heard, far off, the lilting melody of Portuguese. He was at his port of destination and he was still alive (or as close to it as he had been in many, many years). Beyond that, he was very likely in a great deal of trouble.

"My apologies for the rude awakening." The voice was slick, well mannered and slightly accented. Not the heavy guttural Arabic flavor of Halim's speech, but something lighter and more poetic. Persian, perhaps. "Welcome to Lisbon, Mr. Beckett."

Beckett sat up from the confines of the earth-filled pine crate.

"It was necessary that I verify that I had received the proper information from my associate Halim Bey." The speaker was sitting on a folding officer's chair set up in the middle of what appeared to be a large warehouse. A matching wooden table held tea-cups that Beckett's keen sense of smell told him contained something altogether different than tea. A low growl crawled out of his guts.

"Please, Mr. Beckett. Help yourself to some sustenance." The man, dressed in a cream-colored linen suit that contrasted nicely with the deep chocolate skin of his bald pate, waved at the china cups.

Beckett was out of the crate before he'd even formulated the thought, and three long strides brought him to the table. He grabbed the nearest cup and downed the thickening liquid within.

"Blood, you mean?" Beckett understood the need for subtlety in the name of survival, but he'd had little taste for the patina of civility many vampires put on the realities of their existence. "Correct?"

The dark-skinned man smiled and raised his green tinted glasses. "Yes, of course. Blood." His eyes were flecked with gold. "Of virgins sacrificed on the altar of the Devil with knives made of the bones of still more virgins, if you care to be overly florid about it."

Beckett stared the man down for a full minute. He was shorter than Beckett and slighter too, but not by much (not that such things meant overmuch to immortal vampires who could call upon the blood in them to accomplish feats of devilish strength and speed). What struck Beckett the most was the man's composure. He was completely comfortable in this situation. A less-than-calm vampire was looming over him, one who had survived one hundred and fifty-odd years of strife. Even if the seated vampire—and Beckett was sure he was that, he'd yet to take a single breath—had positioned a legion of guardians around the warehouse, there was very little they could do to stop Beckett from inflicting considerable harm on their employer. Either the little bald man with a taste for colonial chic was extremely potent in his own right or he was confident to the point of foolery.

Or he knew something Beckett didn't.

"Please, have a seat, Mr. Beckett." The man gestured to another folding chair, currently folded and leaning against a nearby crate.

Beckett took it, along with the second cup of blood. "Lisbon, hunh?"

"Yes, quite. This storage facility is quite near the port. If you listen carefully, you'll hear the reveille at the British warship docked nearby in a few hours."

Beckett didn't say anything at first. The angry, bestial part of him that longed for ever more of the crimson vitae he'd just swallowed also had a penchant for violence. Images of separating this fine gentleman's head from his torso and of ripping Halim Bey's heart from the portly vampire's chest played themselves out in his mind's eye. Calm and poise when rising from slumber were not things Beckett was known for. It took almost a full minute before he felt ready to speak without risking immediate violence.

"I had hoped Halim would have seen fit to deposit me somewhere away from Her Majesty's armed might." Mithras and several others in London's undead brood had their tendrils in the military to one degree or another. It was not likely that some general call to hunt Beckett across the Empire had gone out, but he'd seen unlikelier things come to pass.

"Understandable. And Halim Bey and associates are doing their best to prepare the second leg of your journey. I requested, however, that we have some time to talk before you move on."

Requested? This could just as easily be a blind, of course, but that suggested the bald newcomer was not an agent of Halim's, but an equal. A superior even. Another Follower of Set, then—they tended toward golden-hued eyes, Beckett had heard. "So who are you?"

"My apologies." The other vampire nodded. "Hesha Ruhadze at your service."

Beckett had heard of Ruhadze. Another collector of antiquities and a scholar, their paths had almost crossed during an especially violent escape in Ceylon. Ruhadze had uncovered the manuscript Beckett had been searching for and Beckett had had to deal with the leftover monstrosities still upset by the theft.

"So speak."

"Tell me about the Thousand-Faced Goddess, Mr. Beckett."

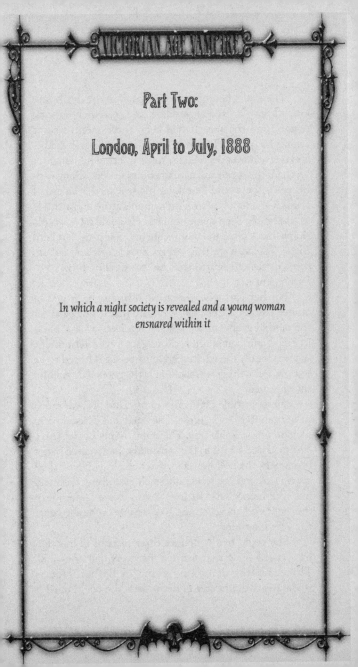

Part Two:

London, April to July, 1888

*In which a night society is revealed and a young woman
ensnared within it*

Chapter Ten

The Blake family arrived in London the day before Good Friday attired all in black and seemingly seeking refuge from the sun. It had been three months since Emma, Lady Blake had been lain to rest—if rest she did—and her widower deemed it proper to bring his daughter south for the social and parliamentary season. Along with his peers, he would be taking his seat in the House of Lords immediately after Easter, but his attire and attitude would be of a deep shade of black. He could have worn a simple black armband to indicate his mourning, but Lord Blake instead wore the darkest broadcloth and coburg suits. Regina imagined that he was looking forward to Parliament not at all.

For her part, the season would have been one of dinner parties, salons and spectacle had it not been for the morbid events of the past winter. Dressed as she was in crepe and bombazine, still forgoing even jet jewelry, she was hardly the excited bride-to-be she'd hoped to be by now. But neither was she simply the bereaved daughter she appeared.

Those terrible nights in County Durham still roiled in her mind. Mary's corpse, discarded and desecrated in such an unspeakable way. The empty tomb. Little Anna. The mad free-for-all in the catacombs, punctuated in her memory by the hollow sound of her Uncle Thomas's skull giving way and the sickening smell of burning flesh and hair. But most of all, the long gashes in the underside of the vault's lid, mute witness to a terrible crime she could not yet understand.

She could hardly believe three months of inaction had passed since that terrible discovery, but they had. Three months of lurking alone in Bernan House, studiously avoiding her father as best she could until it seemed that some of the horror of that winter took on the aspect of a phantasmal dream rather than a blood-chilling memory. But what choice did she have but to wait? With her father's support, perhaps she could have done more, but that had not been her fate.

Lord Blake had been furious when they returned to Bernan House from Lion's Green that January evening. He had banished the three lieutenants from the house immediately, giving them only time to make a splint for Easton's broken arm before sending them off with the promise of divine paternal wrath should they set foot in his house again. Traitors and scallywags, he had called them, these men who had fought with him but had the temerity to aid his daughter in her mad quest.

Regina hadn't escaped his ire either. He had never struck her, but this time she feared he would. His face was a bright crimson and his admonitions fired out of his mouth like cannon shots, practically Elizabethan in their flourish. "Treasonous and foolish girl!" he bellowed. "Fatherless wretch! Benighted changeling! Are you my child, to disobey me so?! To throw yourself in the very pit I'd save you from!"

Any effort at reason had failed. The empty tomb was just some new Slavic rite. The claw marks left there by some previous unfortunate. The dead maid a case of simple murder among the poorer classes. The girl Anna just another victim of a harsh winter. "It's not your place to ask why, daughter! Just trust in your father and obey!"

And so it had gone. Three hours of angry words followed by three months of silence and forced civility. The man Regina had always looked to as guide and guardian was gone, swallowed whole by a chasm of grief and a river of evening brandies that started well before noon. Morris was horsewhipped for his part in bringing the "conspirators" secretly away to Lion's Green and after that was very reluctant to take Regina anywhere without her father's consent, and Lord Blake had stopped giving consent.

Regina did not leave the confines of Bernan House all through the winter. No trips into the nearby villages or to Durham to go to church. No jaunts to the south to escape the cold weather. Not even a single ride in the country. Such were the necessities of mourning, Lord Blake said. For them to travel so soon after Lady Blake's death would have been a breach of etiquette too great to imagine. In late March, finally, her father took her to church at Bishop Auckland, where he sternly watched as she prayed for forgiveness for nigh on two hours. She felt the cold stone of the church floor in her knees for three days after that.

She knew the London season—running from Easter through mid-August—would ultimately end her isolation. Father might have fantasies of cloistering her during this time, but his obligations in Parliament were too significant to avoid. He'd also, in his time as a widower, latched uncharacteristically on to the notion of propriety and social obligations, which was to Regina's benefit. After all, a viscount and his daughter, even in mourning, had to be seen during the season.

Beyond her own liberation and a renewal of her search for whatever dark fate had claimed her mother, Regina also hoped that distancing her father from Bernan House and from the lurking presence of her mother's Hungarian in-laws might lift some of the gloom from his heart. Seeing the house at the end of Arlington Street, however, she despaired anew. This had been their house in London for as long as Regina could remember, and she had bright memories of running about the halls as a girl and returning here when they left Egypt to revisit England. In her mind's eye, the house was perennially full of sunshine and music.

What greeted them that afternoon was anything but. Her father's agent in the city, Mr. Goosehound, had evidently felt Lady Blake's passing strongly himself. Indeed, he had instructed the staff to ready the house for the deepest of mourning, and Regina felt she was entering another somber crypt as she left the coach that had brought them from the train station to St. James. Curtains of bombazet and heavy broadcloth shut out light at every window and the colorful Arab and Indian tapestries and artifacts Colonel Blake had collected were altogether absent. Even the air seemed unnaturally still and stifling. Goosehound and the half-dozen servants who ran the house were lined up in the downstairs parlor to receive their masters for the season, like sentinels in a tomb.

"Welcome back, my lord, Lady Regina," Goosehound said. "Please accept my deepest sympathies, and those of the help."

"Thank you, thank you all." James Blake's voice was devoid of much of his customary energy, but Regina at least could tell he appreciated the concern of those who had served him well. He reserved a special nod for Charlotte, the upstairs maid, who had spent several years with the family in Egypt and helped tend his wife in her first months of sickness there. Never one to break decorum, Charlotte responded only with a slight nod of her own.

Regina spared Charlotte, Mr. Goosehound, and the others a slight smile, but could bring herself to do no more. She only wanted out of this house that had become another testament to a tragedy that ran deeper, she feared, than any of them understood.

Looking for any hint of brightness to grasp on to, her eyes fell on the silver plate atop the mahogany sideboard in the front hall. She could see a visitor's calling card resting there, evidence that someone at least knew they were to arrive today. Once Goosehound dismissed the staff and entered into discussions of household affairs with her father, she slipped into the hall and picked up the card. It read:

Mrs. Joanna Claremont
23 Sydney Mews
Chelsea

Joanna! Regina clasped the card to her breast as if it were the dear friend who had left it. Joanna Claremont, née Seward, was Malcolm's younger sister, a fine woman who had married well in the person of John Claremont, the son of a baronet said to be well on his way toward gentry himself. The two had become fast friends years ago, after Malcolm had first been assigned to the regiment in Egypt. Joanna had come to visit her brother one December and they had all shared a festive Christmas together, sans snowy weather of course, along the Nile. The two girls had been exchanging letters ever since and Regina felt she had Joanna—and her tendency to confide quite separately in both Regina and Malcolm—to thank in large part for her engagement.

She would go see her immediately.

***

"Oh, darling Ginny, I'm so sorry about poor Lady Blake." Joanna Claremont embraced her dear friend and soon-to-be sister and welcomed her into her home. Sydney Mews was tucked at the top of Sydney Street just north of Fulham, where Chelsea bled into the more aristocratic addresses of Kensington. It was a quick walk up to Cromwell Road and the new Royal Albert Hall, Prince's Gate and Hyde Park. The address perfectly suited the successful couple moving up the social ladder of the age. Of course it was only in comparison to Monroe House and the even grander Mayfair homes that Number 23 appeared at all modest. John Claremont had interests in many a shipping venture and provided well for his young bride and their first child, Millicent.

Joanna looked, as always, radiant. The girl's effervescent joy had first bonded her to Colonel Blake's daughter, who showed an enthusiasm for adventure and curiosity that was only amplified under the glass of her delight. Back then, seven years hence now, they had been Ginny and Jo, Gypsies of the Bazaar, in their girlish fancies. Now they were women, one married, the other close to, but their bond remained strong.

"Thank you, Jo." Regina smiled honestly. "It is so good to see you again."

Joanna ushered her into a stylish parlor just off the house's main hall. Although not physically as large as that at Monroe House, the room had an open and fresh air to it, a reflection of the character of the lady of the house. The wallpaper was a subtle pattern of irises and lilies that drew the color out of several pastoral panoramas hung in gilded frames. These were scenes of the Sussex farming country where John Claremont had grown up. Joanna sat in a rocking chair and Regina took the small divan nearest her hostess.

"I feel terrible that John and I could not attend Lady Blake's service." Joanna clasped Regina's hands and, after a slight hesitation, continued. "By the time we even received word…"

"I know, it was already too late." Regina looked down at her own lap for a second. Joanna was a darling friend, soon to be her sister even, but airing familial secrets was still not easy. "It was, well, it was awful, Jo. The funeral service was a shabby makeshift affair and the burial itself was, I think, a sham."

Regina felt the emotion of the previous Christmastide welling up again and fought back the tears, mostly successfully. She wasn't going to be a wilting girl at this late date.

"It's alright, Ginny," Joanna said. "Malcolm wouldn't tell me anything, save that it was best that you be parted from one another for the time being. He puts up a good front, but it's clear to me something terrible has upset him. And you as well, I think. Please, I only want to help in any way I can."

"News of your darling brother would gladden my heart, Jo." Regina managed a smile for her dear friend and for the image of her love.

"He is well, as far as I can tell. He has resigned his commission in the hussars in exchange for another posting yet to be determined, so he is in London all the time now." She smiled as Regina's face lit somewhat. "He stayed with us for almost a month last February, until he found lodging with Lieutenant Pool."

"What of Lieutenant Easton?"

Joanna smiled. "Returned to Egypt, I'm afraid. He could not give up the old regiment."

"And where is Malcolm now, Jo? I so long to see him."

"He— that is…" She lowered her eyes, unable to meet her mourning friend's gaze. "He said it would be best if he stayed away. He mentioned your father…"

Regina felt the tears coming again, and this time couldn't quite stop them. "He's pushed Malcolm away, Jo. Banished him from our home, all because he dared assist me instead of hewing to Father's bullheaded orders!"

Joanna handed her friend a white lace kerchief to catch her tears. "What happened? Malcolm won't say anything for fear of damaging his or your reputation, but something is tearing at him. Please, you can confide in me."

And Regina did, up to a point. Once her few sobs were held back and her stray tears sopped, she launched into an edited rendition of those terrible winter days and nights at Bernan House. She'd intended to tell Jo the whole tale, but didn't. Some instinct told her that on that cold day at Lion's Green, she had entered into a dangerous new world and she didn't want to drag her friend completely into it. So, as she went through her story, she found herself papering over the most terrible things from the list of strange facts and horrible events that she'd spent the last three months compiling and analyzing in her isolation. The strange scars on her mother's flesh, the bloodstains on her carpet, the murders of Mary Bolme and her kin, the final bloody daylight expedition into Lion's Green, they all went unsaid. It became a simpler tale, of an unfortunate death and the strange ways of the Ducheski clan. Joanna seemed more than shocked enough at the account of an un-Christian funeral, occult sigils and a vanished corpse.

"My Lord," said Joanna when her friend had seemingly finished her tale. "Do you think... that is... John's brother is Dr. Harold Claremont, who practices in Kent. He's spoken of cases of such disappearances of cadavers, of body-snatching ne'er-do-wells."

"I suppose it's possible." The image of her mother's corpse dissected in a gruesome medical cabinet in County Durham flashed through Regina's mind. Could that be the case? "If so, though, I think my cousins are complicit. They were so insistent on burying her in their unholy crypt that I have a hard time believing they simply left her to be stolen by a ghoulish medical student or other resurrectionist."

"Have you contacted the coroner? An inquiry might..." Joanna's voice trailed off as the implications of such an investigation played themselves out to her. Coverage in the scandal sheets and whispered words in all the wrong ears would taint Lord Blake and his daughter long before any truths came to light. "No, of course not."

"No," Regina agreed. "I have to find the truth myself."

Joanna's expression froze for a heartbeat, a sign Regina recognized of her weighing options and considering scenarios. An instant later, her decisions made, the respectable Mrs. John Claremont faded before the bright, trouble-seeking Little Jo Seward, gypsy of the bazaar. "Right then, we will help you do just that."

"Oh, Jo." Regina leaned forward and embraced her dearest friend. A lonesome quest suddenly seemed possible with her help. She felt a sudden urge to tell her the rest of the tale, in all its gruesome detail, but she didn't. Thoughts of her father and the damage scandal could do him held her back, along with an acute desire not to betray the confidences Miss Ash and she had shared.

"One thing you can do for me," Regina said after releasing her friend, "is tell me everything you know about a certain Lady Merritt of Park Lane."

Chapter Eleven

"Are you really sure about this, Regina?" Joanna seemed less the excited coconspirator of a few hours ago, and more like an overprotective aunt or chaperone.

"Yes, quite. I simply want to look around." The hansom was waiting outside Number 23. Gerald, the driver who attended the Blakes in the city, was sitting high up above the small cabin and wore a long coat against the cold night air. As always, though, he was a jovial fellow. He'd smiled broadly when he'd seen the two women come from the door.

"But, at night. Even Mayfair isn't wholly safe, you know."

"Stop fretting, darling Jo. We did more dangerous things as girls in Egypt than I could ever find in London at night ."

She was not convinced. "Regina…"

"Oh, my dear. You know I'm hardly serious. Of course there's reason to be careful and be careful I shall. Your brother did not choose a foolish girl to love, after all." Regina walked to the cab and called back to her friend one final time. "I'll be fine, dear. Expect me before dawn."

"To Park Lane, please, Gerald." Regina's confidence was something of a front, of course. She had no real idea where she was going or what she was doing. Joanna's stories of Lady Merritt's were hardly reliable. The hansom headed south and then east from the Claremont home and she watched the night streets, hoping for some inspiration or recollection that would guide her.

There was little or no fog, so she had a good view of the London night. She'd been out many times the year before, coming home after a dinner or dance, but had never spent much time watching the city streets. In comparison to the Cairo of her youth, London's nights were quiet and underpopulated, capital of the Empire or no. But on this night, she saw some of the denizens she hadn't taken note of before.

There were servants going to fetch things for master and mistress, of course. They moved about in little clutches, keeping together for the safety of numbers perhaps. She saw lone gentlemen as well, dressed in evening clothes, even though it was long past the time when one went out in proper company. She wondered if these men were simply late for some rendezvous or up to some form of no good.

Which led her thinking back to Joanna's stories of Lady Merritt. She'd actually blanched when Regina brought up the name and tried suddenly to divert the conversation away from the matter at hand.

"Does Lord Blake know about any of this, Ginny?" Joanna had asked and it had taken Regina almost an hour of discussing matters of familial obligation to bring the topic back around. Joanna, who'd not been terribly well loved by her own father, felt Regina had an obligation to share her suspicions with Lord Blake, or at least to inform him of the missing body of his beloved wife. Regina told her again of the disastrous result of just such a tactic the previous January, but Joanna seemed to hold out hope of a renewed presentation. It took Regina most of the hour to convince her that until she had more facts to bring to him, there was no point. He was only likely to find some makeshift cloister or asylum in which to imprison her, social obligations or no.

Then, at last, Joanna spoke about Lady Merritt. "There's hardly a delicate way for me to put this, darling, but Lady Merritt is a woman of ill repute. John confided in me that a former business partner of his became involved with—or rather with a client of—one of the girls who frequented Lady Merritt's home. He supposedly launched into lewd tales once he'd had enough port. I don't know many details or how she manages to maintain a Park Lane address with her reputation, but supposedly she has friends in very high places." She hadn't shared her feelings about what it might mean that Regina's mother had attended such a place.

"Where on the street, milady?" The driver's question snapped Regina from her recollections and brought me back to the task at hand. Mother.

"I'm not properly sure, actually. Have you heard of a Lady Merritt who inhabits that street? She is said to hold salons at night for the amusement of—"

"That's no proper place for a lady like yourself, ma'am, if you don't mind me saying."

Was Joanna's suspicion thus confirmed? Lady Merritt's was a brothel and that made Regina's mother... a prostitute? But that would hardly explain grave robbery or what had happened in County Durham. No, Regina decided there must be something else to this story. "What do you mean, Gerald? Improper how?"

He stopped the cab, and dropped to the street. Regina looked out at him, and for such a big man, he seemed very sheepish. "That is, ma'am... it's difficult to explain..."

"Just say it, man."

"Well, that is. I brought your mother there last year, and I wouldn't want to tarnish her reputation or your memories of her."

Regina stepped out of the cab to get close to the driver, hoping to create a sense of confidence and discretion with the man. "It's all right. I won't share anything you tell me. I wouldn't even ask, but there are things my mother left unfinished, things that require me to venture here. I'd hoped I could count on your discretion, but if I have thought wrongly..."

He looked sheepish. "No, no ma'am. You must forgive me. Lady Merritt's is at the end of the street, near the corner with Park Lane and Stanhope Gate. She is bound to have guests already, but I'll take you there, Lady Regina."

She caught his arm. "What made you hesitate? I... I need to know, for Mother's sake."

"The lady holds salons and parties almost every night, but they are attended by a strange lot, ma'am. I've only ever been there three times, but each time I felt... it's difficult to explain... *uncomfortable*."

Regina waited for him to continue.

"Don't mistake me ma'am, I was raised in the East End and I know how the rough sort live, but this lady's guests put me on edge, is all. Some look like the finest of peers, but others are wilder. The last time I was there, I saw a syphilitic man walk in all tall an' mighty, as if he owned the place despite the pustules on his face and the scars on his neck." He looked down the street, as if trying to assure himself of privacy. "An' I think there's more to it. I awaited your mother every time and got a chance to talk to the other drivers, and I heard a bit about other houses that welcomed what they called 'the Lyceum.' I thinks it's some sort of society of masons or some such."

"I still don't understand why you hesitated."

"Well, it's your mother, ma'am. She told me once never to talk of all this, especially not to his lordship your father. It would be dangerous, she said. Those were her words."

"I see." Regina reached into the cab to fetch her shawl. Tension bunched in her gut and chest, but she took a long breath and straightened herself. She'd had to know it all, but she couldn't endanger others. "Drop me at Merritt House and then go home. Tell no one of this evening."

"But ma'am—"

"No argument. I'll use a hansom to get back." With that, she climbed into the cab and shut the door behind her. The driver climbed back to his seat high above her and guided the horses to a house on the west side of Park Lane, with its back to the expanse of Hyde Park. The house itself was unlike most others in the area, set back from the street some and detached from its neighbors. It was as if the compacting effect of the crowded capital had left this home untouched. This, Regina knew, was the sign of wealth and power.

When the cab stopped, an unusually tall man—obviously a valet or houseman—stepped forward from his position near the iron gate that marked the entry to the tasteful front yard of Merritt House. He was wearing a severe black and gray outfit, as if he too were in mourning, but Regina knew well dark colors were the style in London. It was possible, she decided as his waistcoat caught the wan light of a nearby gas lamp, that he wore a deep indigo and not black. He stopped after opening the door.

"May I announce you, ma'am?"

"Regina, daughter of James, Lord Blake."

The man didn't move to let her disembark. "May I see your invitation, Lady Regina?"

Regina heard the driver move on his perch above her. He too must sense the threat in the question. "I am here on the invitation of Miss Ash," she said.

The valet hesitated, as if weighing competing interests, and then stepped aside. "Welcome, ma'am. If you'll follow me?"

He led her through the gates and along a short pebbled path through a front yard made of tall rosebushes. Gas lamps set low gave enough light to walk by, but deepened shadows and played tricks with the eyes, making it difficult to judge distance and perspective. The path led down the side of the large house and as they rounded a corner, Regina came closer to an especially large rosebush than she had thought.

"Ouch," she exclaimed. She looked at her forearm, left bare by her gown, and saw a long scratch made by a thorn she hadn't seen. Three or four small beads of blood rose to the surface of her skin. The valet paid her discomfort little heed, so she hurried on.

Around the back of the house was a finely manicured garden, less like a typical tiny private yard than like some hidden square—clearly a social space. Finely cut hedgerows created a small maze and Regina heard both the gurgle of water and the murmur of whispered conversation. Indeed, she could see a good dozen men and women standing about the terrace that dominated the back of the house and a few others scattered around the pebble path that led from it toward the yard. More of the thorn-bushes accented the space and she made sure to keep her distance from them. Such private gardens were almost unknown in claustrophobic London. This Lady Merritt must be wealthy indeed.

"Lady Regina, daughter of James, Lord Blake." At the valet's announcement, several of the people assembled on the terrace turned their attention toward her.

As a child in Cairo, Regina had once stumbled into the women's quarters in a large Arab house her father was visiting. The sense of discovering—and being discovered by—a hidden world was the same at this moment as it had been then. Excitement born of discovery and the dangers it entailed. One of the women on the terrace, a blond dressed in a gown of deep burgundy that featured a corset so tight her waist seemed no wider than her fine, pale neck, pushed past the dark-skinned mountain of a man she had been sharing a word with and locked a hungry gaze on Regina.

"Welcome," she said and flicked her gaze to the valet.

"Upon Miss Ash's invitation, milady." He bowed slightly as he spoke, as if unable to look directly at this stark beauty.

Regina found herself with the opposite problem. She had to force herself not to stare as the wasp-waisted woman walked toward her. Her gait was almost a dance, her tiny waist and flared hips swaying to an unheard but deeply felt rhythm. The fabric of her gown, which caught the pale gaslight and turned it into a crimson sheen, seemed woven into a delicate crepe. It rose to her collarbone, but left her throat and neck bare. Her eyes were two beads of jet set in pearl orbs.

"Milady," Regina said with what she hoped was not too obvious a stammer. She curtsied, and had to consciously stop herself from doing so as deeply as if she had been before the Queen. Something told her that too much deference could be a dangerous thing. "Thank you for having me in your home."

"A friend of Miss Ash is always welcome here." She smiled brightly but her eyes remained solid and hungry. "Victoria has great taste in her companions. Please, join us."

The woman—Lady Merritt, presumably—turned, and free of her gaze, Regina followed. She took the time to get a better sense of the assemblage she was about to join. The man the lady had left to greet Regina was either African or West Indian. His clothes and demeanor, however, spoke of time spent in Paris and London, of a gentleman's life. Along with him was an olive complexioned man, whom Regina took to be Italian or Spanish. His hair, longer and more natural than any British gentleman would allow himself, framed an aquiline face and eyes of the richest brown.

Other small groups of guests were scattered about the terrace and Regina spied still others in the yard and through the large French doors into the house. Compared to the dour styles long dominant among the peerage, these ladies and gentlemen all seemed to flirt with scandal. Women in wasp-waist corsets like Lady Merritt's were the rule rather than the exception here, emphasizing rather than masking their shapes. Regina watched as a redheaded girl took a lanky gentleman by the hand and led him into the gardens. The man, a blond, broad-shouldered type, had lost his tie and seemed addled by the affections of this young thing.

Just before they disappeared into the privacy of the hedge maze, he looked back in Lady Merritt's direction and Regina saw a hunger in his eyes that brought her up short. His lust was such, it seemed ready to swallow the world whole. Regina wondered just who was leading whom in that couple.

"And just who is this fine addition to your fiesta, Doña Merritt?" The question, asked in the lilting tones of Iberia, resolved the question of the origins of the olive skinned man. A Spaniard or perhaps a Portuguese. Regina turned to face him and found her skin tingling anew. His eyes, which she had thought of as just brown on first glance, now revealed themselves as chestnut jewels, hiding flecks of gold. His dark, swarthy features evoked images of secret escapades and seemed to be a rebuff to all the stiff, gray propriety of English manhood.

"This is Regina, a fine exemplar of English womanhood." Lady Merritt let out a polite laugh of impolite mockery. "Please excuse her gaping."

"Don Cerro de León," he said with a bow, grabbing her hand for a kiss that should have been shocking or gauche, but was neither.

"A pleasure…" Regina let out. Somewhere in her heart, she realized that something was amiss. In the space of a few minutes she had found herself lost in Lady Merritt's gaze and then felt her entire body quake for this charming Spaniard. She was like a drunk who realizes her behavior is ludicrous but can do nothing to stop it. She was a mere observer to her body's attendance in this strange gathering.

"Oh," said Cerro as he clasped her arm with one hand. "You have scratched yourself." He used the fingers of his other hand, ungloved, callused and electric, to sop up the still-wet beads of blood that had risen to her skin. She felt a slight burn where he touched her wound, and knew she wanted more.

She didn't even notice Lady Merritt's little snicker or words of excuse as she left to attend to other guests.

"May I introduce my protégé, Theophilus Bell, of the United States of America."

"Ma'am." Bell, the black-skinned man, nodded. He neither bowed nor made any other sign of deferral.

"Mr. Bell had the misfortune to be born in bondage, but had the wherewithal to escape and even seek justice against those who put him in chains. To the plantation owners he was a monster, but to me… a prize student."

Bell said nothing and fixed Cerro with a cold stare. Regina was very glad not to be the subject of that stare.

"Mr. Bell does not enjoy it when I discuss these matters so casually. He finds it crass." Cerro flashed her a quick smile and she took a small step closer to the man. "But he forgets our duty to serve as exemplars to others. His story is a powerful one, don't you think? Triumph over the limitations of race and society?"

Regina had an impression in some distant part of her brain still capable of coherent thought that she was entering into a dangerous game that had gone on between these two men for a very long time. Despite this, she stared deep into the chestnut eyes of the Spaniard and felt herself quiver. He smelled of soft talc, she realized, and that made her want him all the more.

"Excuse me," Bell said. He turned on his heel and walked over into the house through open French doors. He seemed to engage another group in conversation, including a fine-featured brunette who was dressed in a man's tweed suit. For some reason, Regina barely registered that as strange.

"Well, it seems Theophilus has decided to seek other company." Cerro's words brought Regina's attention back to him just in time to see him dab his fingers to his lips. The same fingers with which he'd wiped her scratch clean. "Shall we explore Lady Merritt's garden, perhaps?"

Regina smiled drunkenly. "Yes, of course."

The gardens were a true wonder, a secret and marvelous companion to the great public park further west. Finely tailored hedges twisted into a delicate maze that swallowed Regina and Cerro whole. Every turn seemingly brought a new delight, from night-blooming orchids arranged in special pots to delicate gurgling fountains shaped like Greek nymphs and other figures from mythology. They sat on a small stone bench near one such ornament, a pool overlooked by a finely sculpted miniature marble man. The nude male figure, about eighteen inches long, white and glowing in the wan light cast by lanterns, gazed at his own reflection as if enraptured.

"Narcissus," Regina said.

"Yes, so enchanted by the beauty of his own reflection that he withered away rather than cease his gazing." Cerro laid his hand on her waist, exerting just a touch of pressure to draw her even closer. "Personally I find only the beauty of others so enchanting."

"Yes…" Regina said, agreeing with his statement and his unstated request for her.

He drew her to him, and his lips brushed against hers. The kiss felt like silk and she let out a slight sigh. His hands moved to her neck and undid her cape. It fell to the ground. Without thinking, she raised her chin and let his lips descend to her exposed throat. His gentle kisses barely touched her flesh at first, getting ever-so-slightly harder with each repetition, until they were strong and delicious impacts on her skin. Little jolts of pleasure accompanied the kisses, sending reverberations through her body and threatening to make her swoon. They only grew more intense as he buried his face in the cleft of her neck and shoulders. At some point they ended up on the cool night grass before the fountain of Narcissus. The ecstasy went on seemingly forever and still it wasn't enough.

"I do hope you've had enough, Don Cerro."

The voice was a familiar one and when Cerro looked up from her neck, Regina opened her eyes to see Victoria Ash looking over them, standing upside down. It took her a moment to realize that in fact she was lying on her back and Victoria was standing upright. It was very hard to think straight and she was dimly aware of a warmth spreading on her neck and a cool sensation in her extremities.

"Go away, girl." Cerro's voice was dismissive, distracted.

"I think not. That young lady is under my protection and I would appreciate it so very much if you'd clean up your mess and scurry off to whatever rookery you've chosen to nest in."

"I said go *away!*" This time Cerro's voice was neither dismissive nor distracted. It was an angry bark, full of the promise of violence. His body, which had been so soft and enveloping, became a cold weight of banded iron imprisoning Regina. Icy fingers of animal panic grasped her spine and she began to squirm, fighting to get free.

"Be *still!*" Cerro's anger, now aimed squarely at Regina, felt as if it had stopped her heart. She had the urge to dig her way into the ground, so much she wanted to get away from him. He was like a vise, screwing her into the earth. She barely registered the wet, red smears on his mouth, but clearly saw the inhuman rage burning in his eyes.

"Temper, temper, *señor*." Victoria's tone was mocking, a cut to the quick. "You do your vaunted superiors a disservice by—"

"Can I be of assistance?" The question came from a newcomer. Regina squirmed to see the woman who might just be her savior and found herself looking at what might be a parody of the New Woman—a slight young girl dressed in the tweed of a country gentleman, including tall riding boots and a plaid Inverness cape.

"It would perhaps be best if you mastered yourself, Don Cerro," the girl said with a voice devoid of any coquetry. "For the sake of our traditions, if nothing else."

Cerro didn't answer for a long minute and Regina felt a rumbling in him, like a dog growling before it strikes. Then, he suddenly bent his head to her neck again and she had the thoroughly unpleasant sensation that he was lapping at it. His tongue, cold, wet and devoid of any seduction, ran quickly up and down her like a slimy eel. Disgust curdled her insides. Then Cerro was up and off her. He brushed dirt off his trousers and onto Regina before leaving without a word.

Regina, still lightheaded and nauseous, got herself sitting upright without too many ill effects but feared she wouldn't get any further. She watched the two other women.

"Thank you, Miss Parr." Victoria smiled like a satisfied cat with a belly full of mouse. "I fear what that Spanish cur might have done if not for your intervention."

Parr gave her a cold glance. "You had better be more careful with your companions, Miss Ash. If you do not keep them under watch, others will. Do we understand one another?"

"Surely you don't blame me for Don Cerro's…"

"Do we understand one another, Miss Ash?" Miss Parr took a step forward so that she was between the prone Regina and the standing Victoria.

"Yes. Of course."

"Thank you." Miss Parr then left the same way Don Cerro had.

***

"Foolish girl!"

Victoria's admonition sent a fresh chill down Regina's distinctly unsteady spine. The two had walked in silence through the hedge maze until they found an enclosed gazebo—more of a miniature cottage, really. Victoria had guided her inside, lit a small lantern, and closed the door behind them. The small, intimate space seemed tailor made for a lovers' rendezvous, but to Regina it felt more like a gilded jail cell. Victoria had grasped her by the arms, roughly shaken her and tossed her bodily onto one of the benches—all the while admonishing her in a shrill voice.

"What in the Devil's name are you doing here?"

"I… that is…" Regina's head was still spinning and she couldn't quite get her thoughts to work properly. "I was looking for Mother…" Was that right? "Or the Ducheski…. Her crypt was…"

"Empty, yes. I expected as much. But do you realize what could have happened? To embarrass me in front of Cerro and Miss Parr. I should…" She looked down at Regina with all the care of a physic about to lance a boil.

"You knew?" Regina's voice was small and a lump caught in her throat.

Victoria gaze turned from iron to velvet in a heartbeat. She approached Regina and bent at the knee so she could look the girl in the eyes. Her face was full of concern and even apology.

"Oh, dear girl," she said. "I only suspected."

"The crypt was empty," Regina repeated. "And my cousin Gareth and uncle Thomas, they fought, and the girl Anna…"

"My poor girl," Victoria stroked her and Regina felt warm under her gaze. "Why didn't you simply come to my home? I left you my card for that very purpose."

"I… that is… Thomas had mentioned Lady Merritt and…" Why was she so confused? Where panic and fear had been, embarrassment rose to the fore, sending tingles to her cheeks and beats of sweat to neck.

"I understand, but you have to be careful. These are dangerous circles you are entering into. To wander here without a guide is not advisable."

"What do you mean?"

"We are a very exclusive lot, my dear. Strangers are not welcome and there are those among us who are ready to take drastic measures to maintain our privacy. That ridiculous suffragette Juliet Parr, for example."

"I have to find out what happened to Mother." Regina's resolve was returning, slowly but steadily. She felt safe now.

"Yes, of course, you do." Victoria smiled warmly. "But you'll need a guide."

Regina felt hope swell in her. "Will you…"

"Of course, dear girl." Another smile. "You are in no condition to embark upon this tonight, however. Come, I will bring you to your door and you will sleep. Tomorrow night, you will come to my home and we will discuss matters. Yes?"

Regina nodded, gave a wan smile, and let Victoria guide her out of the gazebo, through the maze—where they recovered her shawl—and out to Queen's Road where a barouche carriage was waiting for them. Regina, fighting fatigue, still managed to direct the driver to Sydney Mews and the Claremont residence. Before she disembarked, Victoria spoke again.

"Remember," she said, "not a word of tonight's events to anyone. Privacy is our most sacred rule."

Regina muttered her assent, then went to the door and knocked. Joanna was there quickly and despite her insistent questions, Regina simply stumbled upstairs to the small guest room. The door closed, she removed her gown and undergarments and crawled, exhausted and naked, into the small bed.

It was only when she woke, well into the next afternoon, that she found the clots of blood in her hair and the red-brown stain on the shoulder of her dress.

Chapter Twelve

"She sleeps like the dead." Joanna Claremont immediately regretted the turn of phrase. Given the torment Regina had undergone this past Christmas, it was ghastly of her. Her brother's expression said that he silently concurred with her appraisal of her own failure of etiquette. "I'm sorry," she whispered.

"It's alright, Joanna," Malcolm Seward said just as quietly. "I'm just glad she is back safe and sound with you."

Joanna led him into a downstairs drawing room, where they could speak somewhat more freely without fear of waking Regina. He'd arrived this morning, paying a casual visit on his sister, only to find her in a state. It was now almost midday, but Regina slept on.

"I do not know what to do, Malcolm. She was gone almost the whole of the night and returned in such a state! And with people I have never seen."

Joanna had told her brother the story twice now, although she'd left out her understanding of Lady Merritt's occupation—she would not risk making her best friend unmarriageable in her own brother's eyes. Still, the late-night departure to follow up on some thread of rumor about her poor deceased mother and the pre-dawn return in the company of a mulatto coachman was more than enough to recount several times.

"I never saw if there was anyone else in the barouche that was outside when she arrived. The coachman just deposited her and turned on his heels without a word."

"One of the women who attended Lady Blake's funeral had a dusky coachman named…" Malcolm searched his memory. He'd only seen Miss Ash's man a few times in those terrible days. "Caesar, was it?"

"What happened last Christmas, Malcolm? Ginny spoke of a terrible body snatching, but I fear even she's holding more back from me. Please, brother, there never were secrets between us."

Malcolm Seward was quiet for a very long time. His baby sister and he had shared many things and these last few months she had been his only avenue of contact, even once removed, with Regina. He owed her more than he could ever repay, but most of all he owed her his protection.

"It was… Well, it was a tragic affair is all I can say. Lord Blake—"

"Oh, that man!" Joanna belatedly covered her mouth as if her hand would somehow muffle her outburst. "He keeps his daughter and his most trusted lieutenant apart when he knows they long to be together. Please, go upstairs and wake her, Malcolm. She misses you so."

"No," Malcolm said and stood up. "I can't betray Lord Blake again. Please take care of her, Joanna."

Before Joanna could protest, he'd grabbed his coat and was out the door.

***

Regina left Number 23 soon after waking in the mid-afternoon and returned to Monroe House and her father. She found him brooding in the library at the back of the house, a glass of whiskey within reach and a pipe smoking. The room was thick with tobacco smoke and she thought at first that her father had fallen asleep in his chair, so silent he was.

"Are you well, daughter?" He took another puff from the pipe after speaking. "You have been gone a full day and night."

"I was with Joanna, Father." She took a seat next to him. "She said to tell you how sorry she felt about Mother and that she and Mr. Claremont would be coming by soon to pay you a visit."

"I'm in no mood for company."

"Father? What is it?"

He put down his pipe in a nearby ashtray and raised the glass of whiskey to his lips. That drained, he rose and walked to the cherry-wood cabinet near the back window of the house. He took out a decanter of amber liquor and gazed out down the alley that ran behind Monroe House beyond the iron gate surrounding its small yard. "It will be night soon."

"Yes, I know." Regina grasped for a way to engage her father. "I know I was gone a while, but Joanna is such a dear friend…" She had the distinct impression her father wasn't even hearing her.

"There are things that live only at night," he said. "I saw them, long ago, when I was young."

Regina remained silent, parched air caught in her throat.

"We burned the thing, Lewis and I. It was utterly destroyed." He took a long draught of the whiskey. "But then in Cairo… what if there are more of the things?"

"Father?" she ventured. "What are you saying?"

"The night. I hate the night," he said in a near whisper. He put one arm against the lintel of the window and bowed his head. To Regina, he looked as if the he bore the weight of the world on his shoulders. He seemed very small then, which made his sudden outburst all the more shocking.

"Promise me," he said, turning to face Regina and suddenly full of desperate energy. "Promise me that you will not go out into the night, Regina. It isn't safe."

"But Father…"

"Promise me!" He took three quick steps and was right in front of her, his cheeks ruddy from drink and a desperate look in his eyes. Those eyes seemed fixed on a space behind or through Regina, and she could see tears welling in them.

"I promise," she said. It was not the first time she'd lied to her father.

***

There were seven of them that night in the India Room of the fashionable Pall Mall address of the Taurus Club for Gentlemen. Malcolm Seward knew there must be others in the club—servants certainly, but he'd seen a naval captain in the main library when he and Pool entered who hadn't joined them. He assumed other Taurine Brothers were elsewhere in the building as well, although his knowledge of the inner workings of the club was still sketchy at best.

This was not his first time at the club. He and Pool had first come here in February, the evening after the *Bartholomew Thomas* had carried Easton off to Egypt. They had shared a brandy with Captain Nathaniel Ellijay, a member of the Horse Guards who was also here tonight. Over the intervening months, he'd come here more and more. Pool was always his chaperone, presumably because he was a full member, and had introduced him to many other brothers. Many of those he had met were in the India Room tonight.

"Brothers," said Ellijay, standing and raising his glass. "The Queen."

"The Queen!" The six others, Seward included, echoed back the toast without hesitation. These were all men who'd risked life and limb for the Empire and its monarch and the toast which in some circles might be seen as aristocratic foppery was no joke to them.

"How are things amongst the guard, Ellijay?" The man asking the question was General Sir Christopher Bartow, a veteran of the Egyptian and Sudanese campaigns of ten years hence. He'd been the subject of much speculation back when Seward served in those same expedition—wagging tongues said he was the common son of a Liverpool stevedore and a seamstress and questioned how he'd ever become a sir, much less a general. This brotherhood seemed to be the answer.

"Well enough, General." Ellijay was wearing a simple gray suit this evening, but his hair was sharply cut and his stance spoke to Seward of a man used to the field of battle. "Ceremonial duties can make it challenging to instill the proper discipline in the men, but they are coming along."

"Good to hear it!" exclaimed Admiral Knowlton, the highest-ranking person in attendance. A barrel-shaped man, he'd regaled Seward on his last visit with tales of his youth on the clippers of the navy before sails were so thoroughly eclipsed by steam. He'd seemingly visited every port from Lagos to Hong Kong and many besides, and despite having retired his commission three years ago, one got the impression that solid land suited him not at all. "Keep those boys sharp. The last thing we need is soft fools guarding the Queen."

Seward smiled and some of the tension flowed out of him with his next breath. He knew this was an important night for him, but he felt a kinship with these men that silenced most of his worries. These were soldiers and seamen, the men who had forged the Empire and kept her in place, and he found none at all of the weak-willed aristocrats who looked to their commission as nothing more than another item to boast of to fine ladies.

"Perhaps," Pool put in, "we might proceed to some of the business at hand."

"Quite, quite." Ellijay moved to the head of the long mahogany table in the center of the India Room. The others deferred to him without question, despite the fact that several of them outranked him. They arranged themselves in chairs along the table in a pattern obviously already agreed upon. Seward, for his part, was guided to the opposite end of the table.

Ellijay stood with the General on one side and Admiral on the other, and a painting of the Viceroy of India in his gilded military garb behind him. The painted potentate, wearing a white turban and holding the curved scimitar of that land, seemed to Seward to be looking over the proceedings like a guardian angel or a demigod from on high, a contemporary Ares or Apollo.

"My fellows," Ellijay said, "we are here to consider the initiation of a new brother. Who proposes the candidate?"

"I do." Pool stood when he spoke. "I have fought side by side with Malcolm Seward and vouch for him."

"Good," said Ellijay, and Pool sat down. "Lieutenant Seward, do you wear a sign of your intent to be in our number?"

"Yes." Seward reached under his collar and brought out the small iron bull-head pendant Pool had given him all those months ago. He thought a second of Regina tossing it aside that night in the coach house, wondering if that would be seen as a weakness on his part among these men. "Lieutenant Pool gifted me with this."

"A bull. What do you know of bulls, Lieutenant?"

"Captain?" The tension in Seward's guts returned. "I'm not sure I understand…"

"No, not yet at least," Ellijay said. "The bull was the sacrifice of choice for the gods in pagan days. For Mars and Apollo in Rome. For Mithras in Persia. For the soldier gods."

"I see."

"You will, Lieutenant. You will."

***

It was easy enough to get out of Monroe House. Her father locked himself in his study shortly before sunset and she could hear him snoring loudly not long afterwards. She then waited until Charlotte was in the back of the house to slip out the front. She'd taken the precaution to don a simple black visiting dress, set her hat with several long pins, and ready her cape in the privacy of her own rooms. She made it to the street unseen, or so she thought.

"Lady Regina?" Gerald was smoking a pipe on the stoop, the doors to the stable open to the street. "Do you want me to take the coach out?"

"No, thank you." She walked over to him, terrified that her father would look out from one of the front-facing windows and see her. "I need to impose upon you the same burden my mother did, Gerald. Please, do not tell anyone that I have gone this evening."

"Milady, that is…" He shifted weight from one foot to another as if his boots suddenly no longer fit right.

"Please. As a favor to me?"

He looked at the cobblestones of the street. "Yes, ma'am."

"You are a fine, fine man!" she exclaimed and ran off to catch a hansom up the street. As the black little buggy carried her north out of St. James and toward Bloomsbury, she hoped that Gerald would keep his word to her better than she had to her father. The ride to Charlotte Place took a good deal longer than the quarter hour it should have because of a terrible lock on Oxford Street where a wagon of goods bound for one of the markets or shops nearby had overturned, attracting a ravenous crowd of the curious and those seeking to liberate some of the spilled goods. Despite the late hour, hansoms, carriages and pedestrians clogged the road. The yelling of merchants, the high-pitched whistles of bobbies, and the braying of one very unhappy mule added to the cacophony. It was well and truly night by the time the cab pulled to a stop before a tall, three-story house at 49 Charlotte Place.

A man Regina recognized as Cedric, Miss Ash's driver from the previous winter, opened the front door and came out. He paid the cabbie, then opened the door for Regina and guided her inside. He never said a word and invited no conversation with his gaze, apparently regarding Regina as just another animal to be herded along for his mistress. He left her in a salon on the middle floor with a view of the tight little yard at the back of the house, and the alleys that wound their way from there. A few minutes later, Victoria Ash entered through another door.

"Good evening, Lady Regina," she said. "I trust that you are recovered from last night's excitement?"

"Good evening to you, Miss Ash. Yes, I'm quite myself again." Regina had eaten like a starving waif when she awoke from her long slumber and felt physically reinvigorated.

The two sat on the plush and gilded chairs that evoked the more extravagant years of the Regency, much like Victoria's choice of clothing. This evening, she wore a silk and taffeta gown with an exposed neck and shoulders cut to emphasize her slight frame. Her underskirts, in a silvery white that contrasted with the emerald of her gown, flared to spread the material like a fan when she sat. Her gown, Regina realized, matched her eyes perfectly.

"Thank you for offering me your help, Miss Ash."

"I only wish we could have spared everyone last night's little display. This is not a game, Regina." Miss Ash's voice had the tone of a scolding mother, something Regina was unprepared for and in no mood to abide by.

"I apologize if I offended, *Victoria*." If Miss Ash was to use Regina's Christian name, then she would use the other woman's as well. "But you need not remind me of that. I am not here to play, but to find answers."

"Asking indiscreet questions is only going to get you hurt." Victoria's hand brushed against Regina's and her tone lost its recriminatory edge. "You've stumbled into a dangerous world, my dear, and you must be careful. This is not County Durham."

"London is not so terrifying as all that."

"That's because you know only a part of it. Little balls and salons, tea services, dances and music recitals. You haven't glimpsed what those things cover."

"Of course I have. Every dance or dinner is an exercise in status and brinkmanship. I know full well that deals are negotiated in those circumstances and that my betrothal to Malcolm was arranged on just such an evening. I am no fool, Victoria, no matter what you might think."

The other woman didn't speak, but her eyes locked onto Regina's. If eyes are indeed windows to the soul, for just a second, Victoria drew back whatever draperies she kept over them and let Regina glimpse the rage within. It reminded her all too much of the fire she'd glimpsed in Don Cerro's gaze upon the interruption of his seduction—a chill ran down Regina's spine and she suddenly felt weary of this woman.

Still Regina held that hard gaze. Whereas the Spaniard's fury had filled her with terrible fear, Victoria's eyes seemed to draw Regina in. In them she glimpsed the price Miss Ash must have paid to climb whatever social ladder she had. Fear gave way to a sort of envy, a desire to harness that same anger in herself, to beat back those who would put her in her supposed place.

"Those are fine observations, but there are other things afoot. Things you must be cautious around." The drapes of civility and concern closed again and Victoria's voice became that of a friend, a sister. "A wrong word can cost you dearly at Merritt House. We rarely forgive mistakes."

"And this mysterious 'we' is the so-called Lyceum?"

Victoria graced Regina with a smile. "In a manner of speaking."

"So what is the truth, then?"

"That is a long and twisted tale, my dear, and not one that can be freely told. If I am to reveal such truths, I must be assured of your discretion. I must have a solemn oath."

"If it will help me find the truth about Mother, I will swear whatever oath you require."

Victoria rose from her chair and crossed to a small, delicate cabinet in the corner. In it was a pair of small crystal glasses and a dark-hued bottle, likely port. She removed the cork and poured a measure of the sweet Portuguese wine into one of the glasses, which she then posed on a small end table between her and Regina, alongside its empty twin. She returned to her seat.

"Drinking to an oath seems a little mannish, Miss Ash," Regina jibbed, "but if it will put your mind at ease…" She reached for the glass, but Victoria's hand, lightning-quick, stopped her.

"One moment, my dear." She reached into her hair and drew out a long, thin hat-pin. It was silver and glinted in the gaslight of the room. "One truth I can convey to you is that we take matters of pedigree, of blood, very seriously. As such, the oath I ask of you is one that must be sealed in blood. Remove your glove and give me your hand."

Regina hesitated, but Victoria's gaze was like a siren's song calling her in. This was clearly a test, to see how far Regina was willing to go for the truth. *The plain truth is the highest of monarchs*, she heard her father say, and removed her glove.

Victoria grasped her hand and lanced her index fingertip deeply with the pin. The pain was sharp and Regina yelped before she could control herself by biting her own lip. Blood welled to the surface in a second and ran down her finger. Victoria guided it to the glasses, letting several drops fall into the port and into the empty glass. She then released her and quickly handed her a kerchief to staunch the bleeding.

The bloodletting was only half-done, though. Victoria then took the needle to her own pale flesh and Regina assumed she had done this many times because she flinched not at all. Blood, noticeably darker than Regina's, rose to Victoria's fingertips and she let several heavy drops fall into the two glasses. She then took up the wineless glass.

Regina took the gruesome mixture of port and blood and raised it toward her lips in emulation of her hostess. Perhaps it was the shock of the pain in her finger, or the memories of Cerro's attempt at molestation, or just the solemnity of this strange rite, but Regina drank the crimson liquid greedily. The port masked most other flavors, but she tasted something warm and strong behind the wine, something that reminded her of Victoria herself.

Miss Ash seemed to have felt the same sensation, for her quick pink tongue darted to the bottom of the upturned glass to collect the least drop of blood therein. A tingling grew on Regina's neck as she imagined that delicate tongue where Cerro's eel-like appendage had been.

"Very good," Victoria said. "By that drink we are bound, to protect one another and to remain in perfect confidence."

That sounded wonderful to Regina. "Yes."

Chapter Thirteen

It was, in the final analysis, a secret society. Victoria's descriptions were sometimes flowery, but Regina understood that there existed in London and elsewhere in the Empire an association of select, well-bred people who conducted their affairs away from the prying eyes of the world at large.

According to Victoria, many of these folk were peers, gentry or—like herself—well-to-do members of the common classes. There were, however, some of their number who had emerged from the most common circles. Regina thought of the dark-skinned Theophilus Bell, supposedly born a slave in America. She marveled that he looked quite young for a man born before their War Between the States, but age was always hard to judge, and she had little experience with Africans.

Regina had heard accounts of the Masonic orders and Theosophist societies that were all the rage in some circles, but Victoria's account seemed more familial than arcane. She referred to others in the society as her cousins, her kindred. It seemed more a hidden aristocracy, bound by ties of blood and precedence, than a society of degrees and gradients bound by common cause.

"That's a fine metaphor for us," Victoria said when Regina commented to that effect. "Like groups of aristocrats, we have a common interest in preserving the Empire and its benefits, but we also have our own squabbles, rivalries and even hatreds. Above all we have an iron law of secrecy."

"Why is that?"

"For the same reason that you or I cannot sit in on the discussions of the Privy Council or read through communiqués at the Admiralty. Secrecy is a key ingredient if one wishes to accomplish anything. We meet and do

A MORBID INITIATION

business exclusively at night as a commitment to that very code of secrecy and to our other values."

"And, if I may ask, just what is your business?"

"You don't ask about our values?"

"It seems prudent to proceed one question at a time."

Victoria smiled. "Quite. You are a gifted interrogator, Lady Regina. You remind me more of your mother every night."

Regina burned to ask another question in that moment but held her tongue. This was a test of her patience, she felt.

"Our collective business is to preserve the Empire, our place within it, and our ability to lead our lives in the manners we deem proper. Individually, we go about much the same types of business your father and his peers do: making sure our property rights and social positions are secure, currying favor with those whom it would be advantageous to know, educating the young when the need arises, and so on."

"Do your kindred hold estates, then?" Land was the core of the gentry's and peerage's positions in the Empire, and its inheritance and sale was very strictly bound by laws to keep estates secure. Just how did this night society fit in?

"Some of us do, yes. But in a broader sense we act more akin to an urban equivalent of the great peers in the country. Just as most residents in Yorkshire live on land owned by a duke or count they never see, most residents in London live along streets that are either the territory of one kindred or considered the property of many."

"But this is done without deeds or the courts, correct?"

"Yes, yes. Perhaps my analogy is a poor one. Instead of a shadowed nobility you could think of us a loose association of clergymen, who subtly tithe a variety of areas to support themselves. Moneys, goods, services and other valuables, drawn lightly from those who do not know we exist, give us the ability to pursue our agendas and support the great work which is the Empire."

"I must say that this all seems a little convenient for you and your kindred, Miss Ash. I wonder if your 'congregations' are pleased by this additional tithe or the fact that you remain distant and hidden from them."

"In return for a powerful, prosperous and beneficent Empire? Very much."

***

For James, Lord Blake the nights since his beloved wife's death had been an unending chore. He had hoped that perhaps he could be satisfied that she was at peace at last, that the fevers and other sufferings she had endured in Egypt and elsewhere were finally gone, erased by the cold comfort of the grave. He still hoped that was the case, but his confidence was failing.

In County Durham it had been Emma's insufferable kin who had caused him pain. The funeral had been a laughable farce, and he still felt like a coward for having surrendered Emma's body to their care. That conversation with the dreadful Eleanor Ducheski weighed on his soul— why had he given in to the old crone? Every time he asked himself that, he felt uneasy. Sweat would come to his brow and he would feel the nausea he associated with his first few days in India, so many years ago. It was as if the mere memory of the woman was enough to make him sick.

The last few weeks in Bernan House had been better, certainly. Regina was in a state, but such was to be expected, and the maid Mary had fallen victim to some terrible accident, which required him to contemplate— though not attend—yet another funeral. Still, that cold, empty house, was at least quiet and free of too many recriminations. He had wanted to stay there through the winter, and would have if not for Regina.

And so, London. If his daughter had found some distraction in the teeming metropolis, as her frequent absences to attend various balls with Joanna Seward attested, he was glad for her, but Lord Blake found only disquiet and despair. The dreams had begun upon their arrival in the city, and this night they were worse than ever.

They all started in the same place, the library at Bernan House. There, he found himself in his favorite chair, comfortable and content, if only for the briefest time. Soon, he became aware of something awry. In that queer way one knows things in dreams, he knew that something terrible lurked in the next chair. Unable to avoid doing so, he peered over to see…

At this point, every iteration of the dream was different, carrying with it a different shade of disgust or violation. First it had been Eleanor Ducheski who sat in that chair, her flesh dry and cracked, her eyes boring into his soul like the mouths of two great worms. Later the same night, when the dream had repeated, it had been Emma who sat there, shockingly nude and wearing a mocking smile. Her bare flesh bore all the marks of her depravity in Cairo and she spoke to him as she had once in those dreadful days. "Did you really think I loved you, James?" she asked with a mocking lilt. "Really, your brain is as useless as your loins."

Another time, Emma had been there, but clearly dead, covered in clotted blood and moist grave dirt. Worms, white and fat, crawled through her skin and fell from the rotted flaps of her skin. With voice cold and distant, like the first cold wind of a November morning, she whispered to him in death. "James…. I miss you…" Suddenly animate, she extended skeletal arms toward him and pulled him toward her putrid breast. "Kiss me…."

That night—which was last night—he'd woken screaming her name.

Thus he had been in no rush to find sleep last evening and had instead poured himself more than enough whiskey for two. Eventually, drunken torpor had replaced natural fatigue and drawn him into Morpheus's arms. And there, tonight, things were much worse than before.

The dream came only in pieces at first, flashes of previous nightmares and memories of moments of dread. The bodies of fallen soldiers from the Egyptian campaign mixed with the usual inhabitants of his dreamscape. Then he was in the library—or was it elsewhere? a bedroom perhaps?—speaking with Emma. She was neither the harlot who shamed him or the ghoulish monster who terrified him this time, but simply his wife. She wore a beautiful blue dress and her hair was skillfully arranged—she reminded him of better days when they had gone to balls and dinners. He smiled at the memory. She didn't.

"I'm so sorry, my darling husband," she said softly. "I never meant to see you suffer."

He moved closer to her—rising from a recline?—and took her hand. "Nothing is the matter, my dear. You are here now. All is well."

She looked away. "No, my darling, I wish it were so…" She lifted her hand to his cheek and he felt how cold her flesh was. "Please take care of yourself."

"But, Emma—"

She quieted him with a kiss and he trembled. Her lips were as cold as slabs of marble, but he felt a longing for her as few times before. She drew away.

"Goodbye, James. Please sleep."

He woke to the sunlight coursing through the open window of his bedchamber. His head felt leaden and he knew a powerful ache would follow that soon enough. He slid out of bed and closed the window, chastising himself for having carelessly left it open. He then went to his dresser and poured water from a jug into a porcelain washbowl. He splashed his face in an effort to shake the wool from his brain. When he went for a second handful, he found the water pink. Then a thick red drop fell from his mouth into the water. He grabbed a hand mirror and stretched his lip to expose it—it was torn and bloody, bitten to the quick.

Chapter Fourteen

Over the ensuing weeks, summer overtook spring at last and London bloomed into the great capital it was. Kensington Gardens and St. James Park filled with the laughter of young ladies and the men who courted them. Barouches and victorias rode the Ring, the leisurely carriage road around Hyde Park that served as the prime avenue of aristocratic socialization. Business flowed along the Thames as freely as water, ships loading with cargo in the East End and barges and ferries plying further upstream. Omnibuses, hansoms and street hawkers crowded the major streets and it seemed that everyone in the capital had something to sell or somewhere to be.

Regina Blake noticed this blossoming not at all. Instead, she saw the family life she'd once treasured wither away in the daylight hours while she stepped further and further into the rich night society of Miss Ash and her kindred. The contrast between the two worlds could not have been greater. Days spent at Monroe House on Arlington Street consisted of watching her father become less and less the vigorous man she had known her entire life. He spent his days in the House of Lords and nights at one or another of his clubs. Doing his duty as a peer, he even hosted a few languid dinner parties, but it was all a morbid pantomime. In unguarded moments, Regina would see him close his eyes against the lethargy that had gripped him, and although few others noticed it, he lost all appetite save for gin and whiskey. His attention wandered and it became ludicrously easy for Regina to invent reasons to spend evenings with the Claremonts or to sleep well into the day. He no longer cared to ask where she was headed, it seemed, but she still took the caution to claim she stayed with Joanna, who acted as her accomplice and alibi.

The night was a rich tapestry through which Victoria guided her. Like the closed-in heat of an opium den or brothel, it always seemed on the verge of overwhelming her, but would instead reward her with some new strange delight. At first it was only one or two nights a week, but by the middle of June, Regina was arriving at Charlotte Place almost every night, precisely a half-hour after dusk, when the last ruddy light faded in the west.

There, she would first shed the blacks of mourning and don the stunning gowns of taffeta and satin that Victoria had especially tailored for her. Miss Ash chose the colors and they were deep, lush ones—wine-stain red, deepest indigo, evergreen emerald. Tight-waisted corsets and low bodices replaced the shape-masking undergarments of Regina's mourning attire. Victoria's maid Theresa took care to prepare her protégée's hair and makeup, transforming the young daughter of a grim viscount into a beautiful courtier among the kindred of London. Regina always completed her costume with the black-rose cameo Victoria had gifted her. This process of transformation took roughly an hour, after which Victoria would greet her with a smile. When she was stuck in some dreary daytime affair or when her father did an especially poor job of hiding his drunkenness and broke her heart, Regina would gird herself with thoughts of that smile.

Evenings with Victoria followed a rough pattern, in that each one involved a social gathering in some relatively exclusive location. There were return visits to Merritt House on Park Lane, which seemed to the site of a running ball throughout the social season. There seemed to be no Lord Merritt and when Regina asked Victoria about this, she discovered he'd died some fifteen years ago. Childless, Lady Merritt had inherited.

"Merritt House and places like it are for mixed company," Victoria explained on their fourth evening there, by which she meant that not all the guests were her kindred in the night society. "Some of the others are like you, friends and protégés who have come into our circle and sworn to abide by its rules. Many of these wear some visible symbol of their association with a kindred."

Indeed, just as she wore Victoria's black rose, Regina noticed that several of the other women in attendance wore wasp-waisted corsets patterned after Lady Merritt's. Every night she attended it was the same, although the pattern they emulated changed. Lady Merritt was the queen bee and her "girls" the drones of the hive. Similarly, she saw men in attendance who wore formal sashes under their jackets, adorned with matching regimental medals. There was an elegance, Regina realized, to these symbols of kindred association. None of them were obvious blazons, but a careful observer could note patterns of attire and determine the groupings in attendance. Then, a second challenge would ensue: determining who among the group was the kindred and who were the associates. While Lady Merritt flaunted her leadership, others seemed to relish being masked by the seconds.

"Then," Victoria continued, "there are others whom we invite into our midst without knowledge of our associations or practices."

"What about the 'iron law' of secrecy?"

Victoria smiled and her green eyes latched onto Regina's soul. "It's something of a game. The challenge is to interact with these unwitting guests without revealing ourselves to them. The closer they come to the truth, the more delicious the play."

"Isn't that dangerous?"

"You will find that we enjoy a certain amount of danger in our nightly gatherings. It keeps the wits sharp."

Lady Merritt's led to other events in mixed company, such as night dances in Kensington Gardens and at St. James Square, evenings at several other lavish houses on Park Lane and Bayswater Road, and special nocturnal concerts at the Royal Albert Hall. The most lavish soirée yet occurred in the first week of June at the British Museum in Bloomsbury.

Regina had been to the museum many times and loved its Egyptian displays, which reminded her of happier days. In the daylight, it was a gorgeous but highly reserved space, filled with antiquities and draped in the silence of libraries and other centers of learning. This night, Regina found the space transformed. Tasteful electric lighting bathed the hallways and display rooms in a low yellow light, accented with occasional candles and lamps. The sound of chamber music echoed gently through the grand building, coming from a small stage set up for the enjoyment of the forty-odd people milling through the displays. Valets and maids moved quietly through the small crowd, carrying a few glasses of drink, but mostly ferrying small tokens Regina could not quite make out to and fro.

"The company tonight is decidedly less mixed," Victoria said, a tone of caution in her voice. "By all means enjoy yourself, but do exercise some degree of discretion."

Regina spent much of that night close by Victoria, watching and observing, trying to get a sense of what was new and different about this gathering. There seemed to be fewer people in her position, for one thing, and although there were distinct cliques forming, there were far fewer symbols of kindred association. Was this evening thus reserved only for those who had fully entered into this strange night society? If so, what was she doing there? And what, she still wondered, did becoming kindred really entail? She continued to observe.

The tokens making their way back and forth on silver platters in the hands of red-coated valets were visiting cards. One manservant brought one to Victoria. It had only three characters printed on it, in a simple script: HRH. *His Royal Highness?* Regina thought. Would the Prince of Wales be here? She awaited an explanation from Victoria.

"Regards from our beloved prince," she said, pronouncing *beloved* as if it were the name of an especially

A MORBID INITIATION

unpleasant palsy. "As is his practice, he lets us know both that he will not attend and that he is well aware of our gathering. Perhaps one of his representatives will be kind enough to grace Dr. Bainbridge's affair."

Regina noted the presence of Theophilus Bell and Don Cerro that evening, neither of whom had reappeared at Lady Merritt's since her first night there. Cerro, still beautiful and charming, now caused a chill in Regina's blood. Memories of the terrible, savage hate he had shown when silencing her bubbled up every time his eyes found her in the crowd. Nevertheless, she did manage to return his gaze. Ultimately he seemed to tire of the game and returned to entertaining the gaggle of kindred who wished to hear about his time in America.

"I'd wager he's going to show off his African's scars again." The speaker was a scholarly man dressed in fine black evening wear. He was standing very near Regina, apparently having approached while she had locked gazes with the Spaniard. "He's done so at every party in London, I hear, and I don't see why mine would be any exception."

"You would be Dr. Bainbridge, then?"

"Yes, yes indeed. Edward Bainbridge, Professor of Antiquities and Egyptology, at your service." He bowed and used one hand in a flourish that was a touch *de trop*, but affable nonetheless. After the stark, overwhelming beauty Regina had come to expect in the these nightly affairs—the wondrous green of Victoria's eyes, the lustrous ebony of Theophilus Bell's skin, the dashing Spanish lines of Don Cerro's face—Bainbridge's utter normality was refreshing. His coat and tails were well-tailored, certainly, but he still was something of a pear-shaped man, with a middle that spoke of good eating and better drinking. He wore round spectacles that briefly reminded Regina of poor Thomas Ducheski, and his well-pomaded hair started significantly higher up his forehead than it had as a younger man. His gentle, pudgy smile only completed the image of a friendly instructor.

"Lady Regina Blake," she answered. She did not curtsy to an untitled man, kindred or no.

"Don Cerro," Bainbridge continued, pronouncing the name with the lisping *c* of Castile, "seems all too anxious to make a spectacle of his American protégé. I hardly see how this is to build confidence in either of their capabilities."

"You'll forgive me, Dr. Bainbridge," Regina said after a minute of observation during which Don Cerro seemed to be attracting a goodly crowd of guests around him, "but I have not quite grasped just what our Spanish friend's position is. If I may be so bold, in what am I to have confidence in him?"

Bainbridge turned to her and she had the distinct impression that he was appraising something, weighing alternatives. She was certain his eyes fell to her black rose cameo at least once. "He is a magistrate—or 'archon' if you prefer the classical terminology. He is charged with the inquiry into happenings among our number. It is through his efforts and those of others like him that we maintain our traditions without recourse to the daylight courts and constabulary."

"I see." Regina had come to understand that since the kindred met only at night, they used the term 'daylight' as a term for the greater body of society. Some also used the term 'kine,' she'd noticed, referring to the 'kindred and kine' in the same way a churchman might speak of the clergy and laity, or the sacred and the profane. "And Mr. Bell is also an archon?"

"No, I believe not. He serves more as Don Cerro's sergeant-at-arms, I would think." He smiled and raised a hand to adjust his spectacles, which seemed very determined to travel down his slightly crooked nose, and Regina glimpsed a silver and pewter ring on his left hand. Meanwhile, Cerro was gathering quite a group, around him, including both men and women who were laughing

A MORBID INITIATION

heartily at whatever *bon mots* he had for them tonight. The gaggle around him made observing the goings-on difficult, so Regina paid attention to those who were keeping away, just as she and Bainbridge were.

It took her several minutes to spot, then recognize Juliet Parr, the woman in man's costume who'd interrupted Victoria and Cerro's argument that first evening at Lady Merritt's. She was hard to recognize because the menswear was totally gone—instead, she wore a light blue silk taffeta gown with a cage crinoline of impressive proportions. Blue sapphires glinted from her throat and ears and her hair was done up in an elaborate construction that added inches to her overall height.

"No fisticuffs tonight, I would hope," Regina said, letting something of snobbish tone of an aristocrat into her voice.

"Oh, no. Certainly not. Miss Parr is no friend of Don Cerro's, but they would not dare spoil this evening."

"Another iron law?" Regina said.

"Call it a traditional understanding to keep rivalries in their place. Your father is a soldier, is he not?"

"Yes." *How did he know that?* she thought. "A colonel in the hussars."

"Well then, I'm sure he could tell you that even in the gravest matters of honor, one does not duel on a dance floor. Certainly not when one is responsible for making sure such things do not occur." He adjusted his glasses again. Regina caught sight of the pattern on his ring, and her throat went dry. The sigil was a square enclosed within a circle, with an adjacent triangle:

She swallowed and her eyes fell on the man's cravat. What she had taken at first glance to be a mundane pattern to the silk suddenly coalesced into alternating rows of tiny triangles and squares. A tie-pin of a perfect circle pierced the cravat.

Memories of the horrors those simple shapes had heralded at Christmastime danced in Regina's head. She wanted to flee from this affable professor who bore the mark of little Anna's heretical Savior. She wanted to lash out at this man revealed to be a part of the inbred tribe of Slavs who had stolen away her mother. Neither would be advisable, however, so she fell back on the charms and etiquette her mother had drilled into her, even in Cairo. *Continue the conversation*, she ordered herself.

"P— Pardon?" Regina hoped her voice hadn't faltered. "Is Miss Parr a magistrate as well?"

"More a constable, the reeve of this particular shire. Where Don Cerro investigates breaches of tradition, Miss Parr keeps the peace as best she can. It's all rather complex, but they very much dislike sharing responsibilities."

Regina left alone the idea of a female constable, which she found intriguing, but hardly as much as her interlocutor's choice of jewelry. "Dr. Bainbridge, may I ask the provenance of that ring? Its craftsmanship seems altogether superior." She took his hand to examine the thing. "Just what is the significance of this symbol?"

"*S'il vous faut demander…*" he said with a slight grin, like a schoolboy with a delicious secret.

"I'm afraid I do indeed have to ask, Doctor. But please, I hope not to have offended." She smiled, a little coyly perhaps. "I understand the value of secrets…."

"Quite, quite." He chuckled. "It really is not a great mystery. Many geometric shapes have special significance in ancient texts, and these happen to be three of the most critical. The squared circle is generally seen as a union of the celestial sphere and the four material elements, a sort of harmony both resulting from and causing the elevation of the will, represented here by the triangle. This last makes of the squared circle a variation on the Phalec, the cabalistic sign of Mars. I belong to a fraternity that uses this 'Elemental Phalec' as a sort of coat of arms—the union of fundamental powers and the enlightened mind, if you will."

She smiled, and said altogether pleasantly, "This sounds like superstition, Doctor, or even witchcraft."

She'd hoped to get a rise out of Bainbridge, to make him forgo his affable mien and perhaps reveal some of the hidden truths she was trying to get at. The nature of this fraternity of his, for example. She was disappointed. Instead of outrage or shock, he responded with good humor.

"Oh, I suppose so," he said, "but we all have our amusements."

***

James, Lord Blake, could feel the first real whispers of summer in the afternoon air while he made his way through the lines of tombstones. He was not alone to visit Highgate Cemetery this warm day exactly a month after they had raised the maypole. The green and granite city of the well-to-do dead was filled with relatives come to pay respects, with poets seeking inspiration from the proximity of the tomb of Coleridge (located at the nearby St. Michael's Church), and others simply enjoying a slightly morbid stroll. As was proper in such surroundings, black was the wardrobe of choice, and Lord Blake felt the sun—still high in the western sky—beating on the broadcloth of his waistcoat. Sweat was rising in little beads from his brow, and he didn't know if they were a symptom of overheating or trepidation.

"I swore I'd never come here again, but here I am." He spoke to a gray slab of granite jutting up from the grass. It was hardly the most prestigious tomb in the cemetery and definitely not the most adorned. Just a simple marker with the words "Capt. Henry Lewis, Esq. — 1825-1869" chiseled into it.

"You probably knew I'd come back eventually," Blake said and kneeled to look at the stone, as if it was a human face he needed to stare in the eyes. "You can stop laughing, you old bugger."

He sat in the grass with his back against the gravestone for a long while, long enough to drain a flask of brandy one swig at a time. The alcohol and the heat of a June afternoon filled his head with cotton and unwelcome memories. The *thing* in the depths of the Borough and its terrible claims about his newly made wife. That mad night's chase through the tight alleys and along the tarred roofs of the dense squalor of that quarter of town just south of the Thames. The thing holding Lewis's body in one hand and his head in another. The fire and the screams of the poor locked in the boarding house along with the creature.

James Blake had spent seventeen years of his life forgetting that terrible evening, loving his wife and children, and serving his monarch. It had not been enough. His son was lost to him and his wife dead. Only Regina remained. Dark tides were rolling in, and had been since Christmas at least.

He tipped his head back to drain the already-empty flask.

***

"She has been out, Eleanor. I do not approve."

The master was upset. Eleanor Ducheski could feel it in her bones. She always got a particular jolt of agony through the twisted vertebrae between her shoulder blades when Master Wellig's murderous rage began to boil. She was thankful for the warning, because he was devilishly good at masking rage under a layer of calm. She'd once seen him extract every bone out of a wayward page—one by one, keeping the boy conscious throughout—when under the grip of just such a calm.

"She'll be under lock and key forevermore, Master." She lowered her head and wondered if he would deliver a deathblow immediately. That would be a terrible waste of all her work, but Anton Wellig had been known to waste materials for the sheer joy of gratification.

"See that you do. She must be perfect for the ritual."

"Yes."

Eleanor left her master's makeshift chamber in the small, well-warded building in Hampstead he had seen fit to use as a makeshift chantry. It certainly wasn't Lion's Green, but it did have several well-insulated cellars, including the room where dear Cousin Emma would now remain.

There were several things to do, of course. First would be the murder of Simon Ducheski Whitehouse, the Londoner cousin who'd thought to make a name for himself in the family by acting as watchdog over Cousin Emma. He'd let himself be convinced to go about the town. Unfortunate, that.

Second, she would send a wire to Gareth. He was as recovered as he could ever be from Thomas's fatal mistake of treason, and she needed a kinsman she could trust. It seemed little Regina had stumbled into the benighted world while in London (at least according to another cousin attending to that foolish Bainbridge). Gareth could watch her and act when the time came.

Yes, he would like that.

***

"How is Doctor Bainbridge connected to the Ducheski?" Regina had waited three nights to bring this question to Victoria, fearful of looking silly. Her patron among the kindred had warned her to observe and she did not want to disappoint, but she was also fatigued by the amount of half-facts and weak inferences she had dancing around her mind. She needed some answers. "Is he a relative of Mother's?"

This particular night, Victoria had suggested leisurely boating along the Serpentine, the lake that snaked its way through the middle of Hyde Park. Regina had taken just such a jaunt the year before—in her first social season in London after the return from Egypt—and found it very pleasant. A bucolic, sunlit escape from the metropolis. It was a different experience at night, however. The cool night air was laced with yellow-white fog, threatening to become the dreaded, blinding "pea soup" for which the city was infamous. The dense banks seemed to float just above the surface of the water, swallowing the gaslit shore and diffusing the moonlight into a pale, uniform whiteness. Occasionally other skiffs would appear as ghostly silhouettes, only to vanish back into the haze. Regina could well imagine Charon guiding his charge of the damned to Hades across just such waters.

Even Victoria, sitting facing Regina in the skiff, while Cedric rowed for their benefit, seemed ethereal with the few feet of mist between them. Only her eyes seemed to punch through the veil, never leaving Regina's.

"Perhaps, but I rather think not."

Regina hoped that Victoria would say more, but all the kindred did was give her a slight smile. It was enough to quicken Regina's pulse. *I must figure this out for myself*, she thought, only dimly aware that she had given her own thoughts Victoria's melodious voice.

"So he is not a relative, but he displayed some of the same symbols as were all over Lion's Green… And hidden in Mother's bedchamber and at the cottage on Gables Moor." She pushed the sudden image of Mary's desecrated corpse from her mind. This was not the time for panicked thinking and girlish squeamishness. "Bainbridge mentioned a fraternity. Could the Ducheski be members as well? Even Eleanor? Or perhaps simply associated...."

Victoria smiled. "*Hermetica Aedicula ex Tremere*," she said in a Latin worthy of Ovid. "The Hermetic House of Tremere, just one of the clannish little cliques that divide our society."

"Are you a member of that house, then?"

"Me?" Victoria seemed ready to laugh. "My goodness, no. Dr. Bainbridge and his associates are interested in matters far more esoteric than I. They are very studious, but not a great deal of fun, to be frank."

"So if the Ducheski are somehow associated with these Tremarians—"

"Just 'Tremere,' I believe."

"Pardon." Regina nodded. "These Tremere, how did you come to know my mother?" She'd waited a long time to ask that particular question and she had an instinct that she was somehow pushing the limits of Victoria's tolerance, but her patron did seem to be in a answering mood this evening, so it was worth the risk.

"To the heart of the matter at last, then." Victoria had removed one glove and let her bare hand trail along the surface of the water. Crystal ripples formed along its night-black surface. "What can you tell me about Dr. Bainbridge's general social position in the capital, dear Regina? Among our kindred, I mean, of course."

Regina thought about it for a long moment. She'd only met the man once, but if Victoria was asking, then there was something to see. "He is trying to make amends, I think." He'd seemed a very friendly, well-mannered sort, and she'd thought that hosting a ball at the British Museum must certainly have been a coup, but now she had a tickle of doubt. She followed that instinct. "He spent a great deal of time with me—a guest with little status—making jibes at others with status. And he never seemed to be in the midst of all the interesting people, despite being the host. He was an outsider at his own affair."

"So why not think him a complete outcast?"

"If I am to believe his account of the guests, both Miss Parr and Don Cerro have some special status, and I presume some of the other kindred in attendance did as well."

"True."

"Then, he cannot be an outcast, or else they would not have attended the ball at all. That they did, but chose to largely ignore him, would seem to indicate he is in a probationary social space. If forced to guess, I'd postulate that he committed some grave faux-pas that is only partially forgiven."

Victoria raised her hand out of the water and brought it together with its mate in a gentle clap. "Very well done, dear girl. You have a keen eye and a keener mind."

Miss Ash's praise meant more to Regina than she had expected, and she felt herself flush with a mixture of embarrassment and excitement. *Where was the reasonable observer of a moment ago?* Hoping to keep her mind focused on the task at hand, she took another risk.

"The card from the Prince of Wales also seemed to indicate reprimand rather than acceptance. Was Dr. Bainbridge's offense to do with the Royal Family?"

Victoria tossed her head back and let out a light, pleasant laugh that somehow sunk Regina's spirits. "Oh, no. Prince Edward is not the author of that card, but that is a matter for another evening."

Regina feared Victoria would end the conversation there as punishment for her false inference—*Who was HRH if not the Prince Royal?*—but Miss Ash kept speaking.

"Other than that slight misconception, your deductions are quite accurate. Dr. Bainbridge is indeed in something of a delicate situation among my kindred, and the Tremere as a whole are something less than enthusiastically received in London. This was not always the case, however.

"Before you were born, the Tremere were very much a part of the social scene, and although some were less than dazzling conversationalists, there were others among their number who did contribute to the liveliness of our gatherings. Even more so, some of their companions were especially well-received, including Emma.

"To answer your question most directly: I met her at Merritt House and other such mixed gatherings. We were friends and confidantes—even sisters of a sort—much as I hope the two of us are becoming."

Victoria leaned back and returned her hand to the water, a subtle but clear signal that she had answered enough questions for one evening. Regina bit her tongue and looked at this beautiful mysterious woman. Her skin was flawless, her body lithe and her face young; Regina could not conceive of Victoria being more than twenty-five years of age, and even that seemed silly. And yet she claimed to have been Mother's friend, confidante and sister twenty years ago. Was she lying? Why would she?

Some instinct told Regina that this was no lie—and that scared her a great deal more.

***

A hansom cab, one of thousands in the city, turned the corner of Sydney Mews in Chelsea, headed to Fulham Road and then perhaps south toward King's Road and its population of lesser gentry and common professionals who, unable to maintain their own carriages, were the mainstay of its business. The driver, a Welshman who'd murdered his baby sister in her crib and then fled to London, had no recollection of just why he had come to this particular street, but it never occurred to him to find that strange. If he ever took a moment to really think about it, he'd realize that he'd had many such memory lapses over the last three years, ranging in duration from a few minutes to entire nights. He'd once suddenly realized that he was guiding his cab through the pastoral streets of Whitstable, Kent, looking out over the sea toward the Isle of Sheppey and the mouth of the Thames. If he had thought about it then, he'd have realized his last memory was of picking up a young girl in Covent Garden, some fifty odd miles away and some three days before, that in fact every one of his lapses began with picking up this same girl, and that this was very strange indeed. Fortunately for his continued health, this particular Welshman was like the dozen or so other London cabbies with similar memory lapses and homicidal incidents in their past—he never really thought about such things. His horse gave an uncomfortable whinny as he rounded the corner and he paid that no heed, either.

Miss Juliet Parr smiled from a convenient shadow as the cab pulled away. She was the young girl in question— although "young" could only refer to her outward appearance, given that she'd popped from her mother's loins during the reign of mad King George, some six score years before. There were a few other people on the street despite the late hour, but they were only aware of Miss Parr's presence in the way club-footed boys and old sea captains are aware that somewhere, a storm is brewing. Mostly servants, men and women well trained to keep their heads down and go about their business, they quickened their steps and moved to the safety of anywhere save Juliet's path.

They didn't see her because she didn't wish to be seen. A very convenient benefit of being an undead thing, that.

Number 23 Sydney Mews was a simple house, well-appointed and highly presentable, but no more or less than most homes on the street or any of its neighboring avenues. Yet it was, like all of them, a link in an elaborate social chain that wove its way through London and, ultimately, the Empire. In dinner parties, morning visits, tea services and other events held in it, news passed from mouth to ear. Rumor gestated in these middle echelons of proper society before becoming the grand scandals of Mayfair and St. James, or percolating down to the common classes thanks to the *bavardise* of maids and menservants. Chelsea was where the stories *everyone* knew were born, and Juliet spent an inordinate amount of time dealing with the place.

She'd traced a few worrisome stories to Number 23, from a drunken cabby's lewd warnings about the "Whores of Lyceum" to a duchess whispering about blood pacts between a certain (ill-defined) breed of lady. Someone was speaking out of turn.

Juliet paused at the door to Number 23. She did not take a deep breath, having forgone the need for air a hundred years before. Her hands did not shake in anticipation. Still, she went through a meticulous preparatory routine, making sure that every article was in place, from her clothes to her hair to her tools.

Clothes: Dressed as a man ready for the hunt. Tall leather boots, tweed suit and cap. Had anyone actually been able to see her, she'd have seemed very eccentric indeed. But no one did.

Hair: Tucked under her cap, every strand—no, wait, one brow lock had come out from its imprisonment and fallen down behind her left ear. She tucked it under the cap. Every strand in place.

Tools: The well-oiled leather folding case was three by eight inches, six by eight when opened to reveal its contents. On the left were three scalpels of varying sizes. On the right a pearl-handled straight razor she had spent two entire nights sharpening.

Juliet Parr took out the razor, stowed her folding case in her tweed jacket, and walked into the house.

Chapter Fifteen

The summer continued to bloom and the days to lengthen. Water carts did their work to keep the dust of industry off the busy streets, or least out of the air, but as the winds shifted the smoke of factories in the East End would deposit soot on even the fanciest address. Regina felt increasingly that the entire daylight world was choking on the grime and dirt that seemed to simply ignore Miss Ash and her associates. Without word from Malcolm for over a half-year now, she did her best to lock up that tender part of her heart. Her father too was a source of sorrow, seeming as anxious to remain ensconced in his study in Monroe House as she was to flee the home for the night-world.

Even Joanna, her accomplice and confidante, was hardly the pillar of security she might have hoped for. The web of half-truths and partial secrets that ran through any conversation Regina had with her was eroding the trust between the two women. Regina found herself believing her friend might be somehow seeking to usurp her place in the night society, or to prevent her from exploring it further. Or could she be holding back news of her brother? It took real effort to shake off these doubts, and still a lingering odor of mistrust seemed to have infused itself on Sydney Mews.

And of course there was the vexing question of Regina's mother. For all that she had uncovered among the kindred in the three months since her arrival in London, she felt little closer to uncovering the truth of her mother's fate. In the daylight hours, when she could sleep at all, she chastised herself for this failing. Where was the iron resolve of that long-past December day when she and the lieutenants had braved the dangers of Lion's Green? But come nightfall another expedition in the company of her nocturnal guide would inevitably eclipse such recriminations—after all perhaps it was this night that she would find another clue.

This particular day, not long after the summer solstice, when the nights were especially short, Regina forced herself to list the scant facts about her mother's fate. Emma Ducheski, it seemed, had been involved in the kindred society of London some twenty years ago, before her marriage. It seemed that the entire Ducheski clan was linked thusly, and were either members or associates of the Hermetic House of Tremere. Just what the nature of the Tremere was, she was unsure. Some research determined that "hermetic" referred to Hermes Trismegistos, an ancient mystic believed to be the founder of alchemy, and much admired by the Theosophists and other occultists who were rampant in London that summer. This would provide some explanation for the Ducheski funeral practices.

Were the Tremere seekers after the Philosopher's Stone? Theosophists? She had a difficult time imagining Dr. Bainbridge as an alchemist turning lead to gold, but he might fit the pattern of those gentlemen seeking ancient wisdom in arcane texts. She did know, or at least Victoria had led her to understand, that the Tremere were something of outsiders among their kindred, and anxious to be let in. Minor gentry at the grand ball, as it were.

None of this added up to an answer about Emma Blake's ultimate fate, of course. She put down her pen, folded up the paper she'd used for her notes, and locked them in the trousseau in her bedroom. It was still hours before sunset and she was too restless to wait patiently, so she wandered through Monroe House.

In the entry hall, sitting next to the silver calling card tray—bare, for the viscount had few visitors these days—was a paper folded in three upon itself. Curious, she opened it and recognized her father's precise printing, learned from some time in the Army's cartographer's office as a young lieutenant. It was long his habit to prepare messages for the mail or for cables, that servants or army orderlies would bring to the appropriate offices. This was the text for a telegram, one to be cabled to Cairo, it seemed. She did not recognize the receiving address, but the message read:

OTHMAN—AM GOING MAD—HAUNTED BY
IMAGES OF EMMA AND FEELING OF
IMPENDING DISASTER—FEAR FOR MY
SOUL AND MY DAUGHTER—PLEASE HELP

Othman? Who is this Othman?

Regina had an urge to destroy this message before it could be sent. Her father's "fear" for her sounded more like another reason to cloister her away as he had in Bernan House for the winter. The freedom she'd managed to find in London would *not* be taken away from her! She'd do anything to stop that!

Her hands were shaking with sudden rage and the piece of letter rustled like dried leaves in an autumnal breeze. She carefully folded it up again, put it back near the silver tray, her hands still trembling and beads of sweat rising to her brow.

She ducked into the downstairs sitting room, which should have been the center of the house's social life but had seen little use under the pall of mourning and Father's drink. Choosing the divan furthest from doors and windows, she sat down, laid her face in her hands, and wept.

Her mother was vanished, her father was spiraling into despair, and she was responding with rage at them and longing for a benighted world of elaborate soirées and secret hermetic houses. *What kind of daughter am I? What have I become?*

A MORBID INITIATION

***

The girls who worked the alleys between Marshal Sea Road and London Bridge Station in Southwark were used to a rough sort. They were a motley crew of orphans, runaways and other women who had somehow been cut off from the support of family. More than a few had been summarily expelled from a warm home when they refused to service an uncle or father's perversities, and the more jaded of them reflected on the irony of their current profession. Others had spent their childhoods as match and orange girls selling wares on the street or door to door, or even as mudlarks, walking barefoot through the muck left when the tide brought the Thames low, trying to collect bones, pieces of iron or other treasures. They'd ultimately found that the only commodity they had to sell with anything resembling reliable marketability was their own flesh.

That they worked this crowded, impoverished part of town and not the somewhat more lucrative West End theater district spoke of the harsh life they had grown accustomed to. Their fancy men were not even glorified thugs—they were thugs pure and simple, men for whom the only reason not to break a bottle off inside an uppity tart was because good glass was worth more than a bad whore. So, "Big Lucy" Meadows was fairly certain she'd seen it all, but she'd never seen anything like Scabby Gary.

Lucy thought "Old Blister-Arse" might be a better name, but the other girls went for Scabby Gary and it stuck. The man caught his appellation because most of his flesh was a twisted mass of scar tissue and weeping sores. Lucy's little sister Mary had died when a boiler burst and doused her with scalding steam. Scabby Gary looked like that, skin all cooked and peeling, except he was walking around and looking for a girl to play with.

He had money, which forgave his appearance for the most part. And he usually brought his girl of the moment to a little room in a workhouse or inn. Lucy usually didn't follow men into places—she liked to do her business right proper up against the alley wall, where she could scream and run if she needed to. But then, it wasn't as if someone so hurt as Scabby Gary could really be very much to handle, could it?

As it turned out, it could.

"You see," he said that last night, after he'd secured her to the rusted iron bed frame, "I've had problems with fire. Yes, problems."

Lucy would have screamed then, not that it would have done much good given the bribe Scabby Gary had given the operator of the workhouse to overlook his own work therein. She *would* have screamed if Scabby Garry hadn't removed her tongue with pliers and a pair of large tailor's shears. As it was, she had to keep her head sideways so as not to choke on her own blood and the only thing preventing her from fainting was the large nail he'd hammered into her left kneecap. Every time she passed out he knocked the nail to return her to attention.

"Yes, but I can't afford to have problems. It's just not done in my family." He smiled, his raw lips parting to reveal blackened teeth. "So I have to see my fears up close. Just what did the fire do to me? Just what would it have done had it burned longer?"

That's when he placed the matches on the rickety nightstand and started smearing her with whale oil.

***

"I have news!"

Lieutenant Anthony Pool burst into the small apartment in Covent Garden that he shared with his once-regimental brother Malcolm Seward. The latter had been reading through the morning edition of *The Times*, staving off the boredom of this interminable summer with the latest dispatches from the colonies and the continent. The untimely death of the German Emperor Fredrick, a mere three months after ascending to the throne, was having repercussions on the international scene and there were already questions about what moves Iron Chancellor Bismarck would take with a new monarch on the German throne. The details of the agreements between Germany and Austria were coming to light and seemed to be worrying the Foreign Office. Meanwhile in Africa, a certain Cecil Rhodes was assuming mining rights in the Matabele and large-scale colonization seemed a reasonable next step—if only to prevent another situation as that with the Boers in the Transvaal.

All in all, Seward thought, this was not a summer to be dallying about London. He should be in the colonies making his fortune, not reading rumors in the press about Mr. William Gilbert's and Sir Arthur Sullivan's latest comic operetta at the Savoy Theatre, set to open in the autumn. It was to be titled *The Yeoman of the Guard,* they said, and Seward took that as another depressing sign of his own suddenly stagnant career. Thus he was ready for any news Pool might have for him.

"The date is set, my friend." Pool gave a broad smile, and sat in the chair opposite Seward. "I have spoken with Captain Ellijay and he is ready to authorize your initiation as a full brother. Your patience is finally rewarded."

Seward dropped his paper. "When?"

"Ahem, yes, well, it won't be for a little while still." He raised his hands in a somewhat apologetic gesture.

"Blast it, Tony! I'm wasting away in this apartment while other men make the Empire!" He shook the newspaper at Pool, folded it and pointed toward the news of southern Africa. "New colonies! That's where I should be!"

"Patience, my boy, it's just another month more."

"A month? More like a lifetime!" He dropped the paper to the ground as if the weight of it was too much.

"Well, if you truly can't wait, then perhaps you *should* find another colonial posting. I'll just tell Captain Ellijay that he'll have to find another lieutenant for the old Oxford Blues."

"What?" Seward's jaw dropped and his mouth gaped open like a child who, thinking to find a box of candies, instead uncovers an entire sweetshop. "But…"

"That's right, Lieutenant Seward," Pool said, suddenly standing at attention, "as of August 1st, you are to report to the garrison of Her Majesty's Own Horse Guards to begin duty therein."

"Ha ha!" Seward exclaimed, elation overcoming shock. The 1st Horse Guards were the elite of the elite, the cavalry regiment who guarded the Queen under the purported leadership of her son Edward, Prince of Wales. This was hardly a simple ceremonial posting—the so-called Oxford Blues had distinguished themselves in Egypt along with Colonel Blake's 12th Hussars—but the Horse Guards were nevertheless stationed in Westminster proper and membership was a fast-track to even greater things. "Ha ha!" he exclaimed again.

"Indeed," said Pool. "Indeed."

***

"God bless them and keep them." Regina was looking across the Thames at the Southwark Bankside and Borough, the compacted knot of squalor pushed up against the river's south bank directly opposite the prosperity of The City and Westminster. The tenements and workhouses, stacked too high and too tight, were a blightful reminder of the contrasts in Imperial society.

One usually could only see the silhouettes of the buildings at night. She'd walked the great stone Embankment along the north shore of the Thames on several evenings and paid little attention to the twisting alleys and lost lives she could just glimpse across the water. Perhaps there had been fog those other nights, or her eyes had been drawn to the buildings, churches and centers of state that stood like soldiers at attention just north of the Embankment. Either way, she'd blinded herself to the realities of Southwark. Tonight that wasn't possible, not because it was one of London's rare clear evenings (which it was), but because a fire was spreading through the Borough.

One of the buildings ablaze was right on the water, a warehouse or manufacturing floor of some sort. It projected a huge billow of black-brown smoke tinged red by the flames still feeding off its wooden timbers and whatever goods had been within. As with all fires in tightly packed places, of course, this one had spread, driven by the breeze back into the Borough proper. An eerie orange light emanated from unseen blazes deeper in the warren of buildings. The screams of the victims, the clanging bells of the poorly equipped fire-brigade, and the crashing of damaged structures—not especially stable to begin with—giving way echoed across the water. London was no stranger to fire, Regina knew, and in the overcrowded popular neighborhoods, where construction was shoddy and gas lighting rarer, people relied on candles for light to see by—which meant, inevitably, fire. Nevertheless, she had never seen a blaze like this, not at night, and it tore at her defenses. Young and old would be consumed and standing here, just a few hundred yards away, she wondered if the blaze was going to eat Southwark whole.

"It's terrible," she said.

"Yes, although it has a certain horrific beauty to it." Victoria was with her that night on the Embankment, as she had been every other time Regina had visited the great stone walkway under the stars and moon. The promenade had been commission by Her Majesty to beautify the riverbank and provide a suitable axis of pedestrian communication from the centers of commerce in The City and those of state in Westminster. At night, it became an unofficial domain of the kindred, who walked along it the same way the daughters of dukes rode their gigs through Hyde Park in the afternoon. It was a place to meet, to chat, to get a sense of happenings in the secret benighted world. The uninitiated—the kine—were never completely absent and Regina had seen how the tradition of secrecy played itself out. To those who could not yet recognize the patterns of secret precedence and allegiance, the Embankment was just the site of the nightly promenades of certain well-to-do folk with difficulty sleeping.

"I'm sorry," Regina said, "but I can't see anything beautiful in destruction, Miss Ash." She wondered if her benefactor's surname might indicate some traditional bond with fires, but that seemed unlikely.

"It's not so much the destruction, darling girl. It is the reaction to it." Victoria's voice was a soft monotone, a whisper one uses at the opera or theater to avoid disturbing the patrons. It was, Regina realized, a tone of reverence. "The pressed mass of humanity struggling to survive despite the harsh hand of fate. I find that beautiful."

"I can see that. Cairo had much of that quality when I was a girl. But still, it seems tactless of us to only admire that beauty when tragedy strikes."

Victoria turned away from the destruction to face her protégée. Regina was surprised to see that her alabaster flesh was flush and her green eyes shone with the beginnings of tears, red in the firelight carried across the Thames. "That," she said, "is a lesson for you, darling girl."

They continued their stroll toward Westminster, the bend in the river and ultimately Waterloo Bridge hiding the bulk of the fire, although the pillar of smoke caught in a southward wind remained to remind them. The

Embankment seemed well inhabited this night. It was now past midnight and the two women had crossed paths with a dozen other gaggles of people. Some Regina recognized from previous evenings in Victoria's company. Several of the corseted girls from Lady Merritt's were out this evening, each in the company of a different man—including at least one famously lecherous actor from the Savoy Theatre—which only added to Regina's perception that the women were especially exclusive prostitutes.

They reached Westminster Pier to find a larger grouping of folk gathered on a terrace designed to give the best view of the river and the south bank. The squalor of the Borough was long gone and Regina could see across the Thames, the gaslights along the edge of Lambeth Palace, the official residence of the Archbishop of Canterbury. The grounds of the palace were shrouded in darkness, but the steady light of gas flames was visible in several of the windows. Perhaps the archbishop could not sleep.

The gathering on the lookout seemed to Regina like a microcosm of the Imperial power concentrated in the buildings immediately to the north: Buckingham Palace, Westminster Hall (the seat of Parliament), the Admiralty, and the rest of the Whitehall power structure. For each there seemed to be an equivalent in the kindred crowd below the structures. Most of them were male, it seemed, including a goodly number of soldiers dressed in regimentals.

"Do you remember what I told you after we met at Lady Merritt's in April last?" Victoria's question was *sotto vocce*, as if she were worried about being overheard even though the grouping was a good fifty yards away still and clearly engaged in their own conversations.

"I believe you called me a silly girl, Victoria." The reprimand, already three months past, still stung and Regina's tone was curt.

"Do not prove my hasty judgment correct, Regina. After that."

"You warned me that these were dangerous circles."
Regina's voice dropped to a whisper matching Victoria's.

"Precisely. I'd advise you to remember that once we cover the distance to the outlook."

"But who—"

But Victoria was already heading toward the group, somehow matching careful grace and surprising alacrity, and Regina had to hurry to catch up. She felt her pulse quicken as they reached the outer edge of the grouping. There must have been twenty or more people, and Victoria dived in with the grace of a veteran socialite. "Good evening, Captain," she said to one man dressed in the regimental uniform of the 1st Life Guards, "a pleasure to see you again." She was past the man before he could do more than bow.

Regina got the distinct impression that the gathering was organized in circles of influence. She had noted this before, both in the crowd who had watched Don Cerro pontificate about Theophilus Bell in late April and at other functions since then. It was, as far as she could tell, the kindred society's version of the laws of precedence at dinner parties. Although she was hardly the fainting viscount's daughter she could have been, she did know that the rules of etiquette imposed a precise order in which dinner guests entered the dining room and a precise diagram for their seating. It was the mark of a great London hostess to flawlessly seat a Knight of the Garter ahead of a viscount, but both after an archdeacon of the Church, for example.

The kindred seemed to have their own unspoken (at least within Regina's earshot) rules of precedence. Their night-time habits seemed to preclude the centrality of a great repast, so the matter of seating was replaced by these implicit orbits of status. Over the course of any evening, the most prominent kindred would form the center of gravity of the social event, with those in lesser positions spending their time at progressively greater removes. No one was immobile, of course, and Regina felt a certain pride in her growing ability to decode the social cues that seemed to govern movement through kindred gatherings.

Her brother Daniel had been fascinated by the heavens and the two of them had scoured a variety of astronomical texts to pass the time in Egypt. Thus, Regina was able to conceive of kindred social precedence not as a static set of rings, but as a highly complex orrery with each object following multiple paths. Prominent kindred, for example, could spend much of an evening near or even in conversation with the preeminent person that evening and bring with them (as "satellites") members of their entourage. Regina herself had spent much time close to prominent kindred as a moon to Victoria's planet. She had noticed that even those who seemed banished to the periphery of an evening could occasionally momentarily approach the most preeminent kindred before returning to the edge of the crowd. She thought of these people as social comets, rushing in unannounced for a brief moment of recognition.

This analysis had taken months of observations and was hardly perfect. Most notably, it could take hours to puzzle out the order of precedence in any new gathering. Because of the constant movement of all the parties, it was impossible to get more than a rough estimate of the social space from a single moment.

Nevertheless, when Victoria guided her past the bemused captain and a few other soldiers, she had to do just that. There were several kindred within the inner space of the gathering, which seemed defined by the best viewing position of the outlook. Victoria, clearly familiar with all the players, was striding forward into the social fray, and her warning to Regina seemed to echo in the young woman's mind. There was a palpable undercurrent of tension here, which reminded Regina of the times a representative of the Egyptian Viceroy had visited her father in Cairo—civility masking hatred and always the unsaid threat of violence. It was key, she knew, to establish who the preeminent kindred was here.

Don Cerro? He was indeed here again, although Mr. Bell seemed not to be. Instead the Spaniard was chatting with a short man with heavy blond sideburns wearing the suit of a merchant. Regina noted that he glanced over his shoulder and to his left, as if scanning for a threat. There. Juliet Parr, his "jurisdictional" rival, to believe Dr. Bainbridge, was that way and made no secret of staring daggers into the Spaniard's back.

One of the guiding principles of the social orrery Regina conceived of, was that rival kindred tended to stake out opposite positions. They would spend entire evenings making sure the most preeminent guest was always between them, thus avoiding the necessity of a confrontation (Regina assumed). So if Cerro and Parr were opposed, then the center of all orbits should be right between them. Regina looked the group there.

There were three people standing in a small group roughly between Parr and Cerro, but Regina assumed two of them to be satellites of the third. She and Victoria headed for the group and it parted as they approached. Regina's eyes were instantly drawn to the figure whom she was sure was the axis upon which this entire evening turned: a woman, somewhere between Regina and her mother's age, dressed in one of the finest gowns she had ever seen. Deep indigo fabric embroidered with a beautiful pattern, spread wide by an impressive cage crinoline underneath. Jewels of lapis and diamond framed her delicate throat and their color matched her eyes. The woman's chestnut hair framed a fine-featured face, and although not a match for Victoria's intoxicating beauty, she exuded the confidence of a woman ruling over men.

Regina's mind returned to that instant when she had seen past Victoria's curtain of civility and glimpsed the anger and determination beneath it. In this woman's case, the curtains were thrown wide and Regina saw in her a bottomless will. She approached the woman, but was a few steps ahead of Victoria and could hardly turn around to get a cue from her guide (as she had in most previous encounters).

Going purely on instinct she dropped into a deep curtsey worthy of the Queen herself. "Your Grace."

In her peripheral vision she saw Victoria curtsey to a similar, but not quite as profound, depth, and felt she had made the right estimation of this slight but potent woman's worth. *Is she the mysterious HRH of the British Museum soirée? Is it Her Royal Highness?*

The great difficulty of the curtsey (and a deep bow for that matter) is that one ends up looking squarely away from the worthy one is submitting to. Regina thus could not judge, even peripherally, the reaction of the blue-eyed woman, and a slight panic that she had stayed head-bowed too long overtook her—but wouldn't raising her gaze too soon be far worse? Then, as soon as it had come, the worries were gone and she raised herself out of the position of submission. She couldn't quite explain, even to herself, why she knew it was right, but she did, and it was.

"This is the young companion I have heard so much about, is it not, Miss Ash." The woman's voice was crisp and with slightly archaic tones, reminiscent of a monarch but with a hint Warwickshire. She did not use the royal "we," Regina noted.

"Yes, Your Grace. May I present Lady Regina, the daughter of Viscount James Blake and my protégée. Lady Regina, Her Grace Lady Anne Bowesely, Seneschal of His Royal Highness our prince and protector."

"Well met, Lady Regina. You account well for yourself."

"Thank you, Your Grace." She curtseyed anew, although this time only slightly to acknowledge her better's attention. Her mind, meanwhile, was racing. *Seneschal? Prince and Protector?* Could it be Prince Edward after all? Regina understood that he was somewhat isolated from the affairs of state, but could this entire night society be his venue for authority? A secret society to beat all secret societies, then?

Lady Anne's blue eyes flicked over to Victoria, releasing Regina to get a quick sense of who the two men flanking the seneschal were. One wore the characteristic blue uniform of the Horse Guards, the markings of a captain, the insignia of the Order of the Garter, and several other decorations. The other was Lieutenant Pool.

Regina almost blurted something out and it was clear Pool recognized her as well from the events of last winter. She bit her tongue, however, keeping Victoria's warning in mind.

"Captain Ellijay and I were discussing plans for the upcoming ball, Miss Ash, and I wondered if you might be so kind as to carry word to your associates. We shall feast the third anniversary of His Royal Highness's return to the capital from his travels. I would hope that you would inform Lady Merritt and the rest of your extended entourage that the prince will receive them August 9th at Sydenham Palace."

"Of course, Your Grace, although I cannot hope to speak for anyone but myself and my charge, I will happily carry word to the others."

Ellijay, Regina noted, took on a more aggressive stance, obviously displeased with Victoria's polite dance around Anne's orders. The medal that hung from a ribbon at his collar, a golden disc emblazoned with the head of a bull, seemed to gleam with the same rage as his eyes. The seneschal herself, however, seemed to take it in stride. "Thank you, Miss Ash, Lady Regina."

And with that, the two women were swung out of the tight orbit around Lady Anne, as she and the two soldiers turned to address another gaggle of kindred. Regina gaped after Pool, who spun around on his heels daintily just long enough to give her a simple, roguish smile. He was wearing a taurine medallion as well, this one a silver bull's head on a black ribbon around his neck.

Regina recognized that medallion.

Chapter Sixteen

"The truth can be a painful thing, Regina." Victoria was sitting in the small courtyard of her Bloomsbury home. "Are you sure you wish to know everything about your Malcolm?"

The little yard of Victoria's three-story home hid behind high walls, isolating it from the bustle of life outside. Bloomsbury was hardly the warren of sins of St. Giles, the bastard child of the West End, but neither was it Mayfair or St. James. Many of the members of the night society Victoria had introduced Regina to lived in those posh addresses. She found Victoria's choice to haunt a more common corner of London refreshing.

"Captain Ellijay is kindred in your society?" The question was largely rhetorical, the interrogation almost absent from Regina's tone.

"As you say."

"Then I have to believe Pool is a protégé of his. He bears his mark." She fingered the black-rose cameo on her neck, the sign of her own association. "The bull's head isn't used in any recognized military decorations. I checked."

"I believe we've established your keen eye for matters of association in our little society, my dear." She leaned down to examine the rosebushes that lined the north wall of the garden. The blooms were closed for the night, resembling dark ruby confections. "That one person is associated with the night society does not mean that all his friends are, however. I would hardly call your dear Mrs. Claremont a protégée."

Regina swallowed and wondered if there was a threat implicit in bringing up Joanna. "Malcolm had a similar medallion, though of baser metal than Pool's. I saw it last Christmastime."

"On the first evening we met, I assume. I'm doubly impressed that you remember such details given your state of distraction at the time." Victoria smiled and Regina felt her pulse quicken. Her nocturnal guide hadn't brought up that night in the coach house at Bernan House so directly all season. She'd alluded a few times to "understandable passions"-but now it sounded like another threat. Regina felt herself being reined in after having learned to run during her encounter with Lady Anne.

"Yes, well I do remember it. Quite precisely. Malcolm is involved in these affairs as well."

"And is that truly your business?" Victoria's her green eyes caught the light of coming in from the house. "You are only to be his wife."

Regina flushed, sensing some scorn in the comment. "What do you mean?"

"That he is a man with a man's life that will always exist away from you. Do you think your father's occasional allowances for your girlish precociousness can translate into something more with Malcolm? He wants you for his wife, my dear, a woman to bear children, keep house, and ask few questions."

"You know him not at all, Miss Ash!" Regina stood from the wooden lawn bench she'd been sitting on, ready to storm from this strange woman's world once and for all. "We have an uncommon bond."

"Perhaps." Victoria stood as well and approached her protégée. "But you know as well as I that we all have our secrets, especially in your family."

Regina felt her heart racing and when Victoria' hands came to Regina's shoulders, she felt the heat of that forbidden kiss wash over her again. "Yes, but I must know…"

"Knowledge is a valuable thing, dear girl." She came closer still to Regina, so that their bodies touched. "It always has a price."

"I…" She was having a very difficult time thinking and instinctively looked away from the taller woman's eyes. "I'll pay whatever price I have to. The hidden workings of the kindred seem already to have cost me my mother. I cannot lose my lover as well."

"Then I will help you." Victoria's voice was no more than a whisper.

"Thank you." Regina felt a tear well in her eye, a sadness for some ill-defined innocence being lost, and then Victoria's lips touched her throat. There was a sudden moment of hypersensation, like after pricking a finger on a needle but before the pain comes. But there was no pain, just a pleasure Regina knew she would surrender herself to forever.

***

"What," Captain Ellijay asked, "is the soldier's creed?"

"Duty." Malcolm Seward had been practicing these words almost incessantly over the last seventy-two hours, ever since Pool had told him his initiation into the Brotherhood of Taurus had been accepted. He knew the questions he would be asked and the answers he would give.

"And what is the soldier's purpose?"

"Victory." Sitting alone in his sister's home, whispering the words to no one, all this had seemed a little silly. Reminiscent of the drilling of his days in the field but without the obvious need to quickly assume firing position or to master a horse. Now, however, standing in a large room in the basement of the brotherhood's clubhouse on Pall Mall, it seemed deadly serious.

The room itself was called the Surgery and it lived up to its appellation. It had all the signs of having started its life as an operating theatre. The main room was a large octagonal shape currently kept almost totally dark. The ceiling rose to the ground level of the club, where adjoining rooms served as galleries for observers. Captain Ellijay stood in one these galleries, this one brightly lit. Other figures stood or sat in the other, darkened galleries.

"For whom does the soldier bring victory?"

"For his brothers, his commander, his monarch, and his God." Seward felt a bead of sweat working its way down his spine, under the woolen jacket and cotton shirt of his hussar's uniform.

"What is the soldier's lot?"

"Sacrifice." Seward stepped forward into the deeper shadows of the room. "Of life, of blood, of health, of all."

"And what is his reward?"

"The respect of his brothers. The lands and plunder of his enemies." That was the last of the words. The ceremony he'd practiced was almost over. Next would come the act.

The light changed as more gas was pumped through the lamps set high above his head. The illumination was scant but it revealed a large table in the middle of the surgery, set slightly higher than the floor where he stood. It was covered with a rich dark cloth that had a circular pattern woven into it. It draped all the way to the floor. As Malcolm walked up the few steps to the center of the room, he realized that this was no table. It was an altar.

On it were the three items he had expected, but they still made his heart race. In the center was a silver bull-head pendant, the more beautiful cousin of the simple iron one that had hung at his neck for nearly a year. It would be his once the ceremony was over and he became a full initiate, a Brother of Taurus. To the right was a short broad blade, a sword he knew was modeled on those carried by the legionnaires of Rome. It would be a second sign of his initiation. And to the left was a golden bowl full of a blackish tincture, the ox-blood that would anoint him.

"Drink."

Without hesitation, he did. He grasped the bowl with both hands and brought it to his lips. He tilted it none too gently and the still-warm humor poured into his mouth. It was partially clotted and trails of blood-jelly streamed out of his lips and down his face, but he swallowed hungrily until the bowl was empty.

His head swimming—had there been a drug in the blood, he wondered—he put the bowl back down and waited for the signal to take up the blade and pendant of his new station. He was aware of the gore drying on his face and dripping on his chest, but it felt holy somehow.

"Know, Brother Malcolm, that you are preparing to join the ranks of an army that stretches to the dawn of time. Wherever man has built for the glory of God and pushed back the barbarians, we have been. In Rome, we knelt with Caesar before the altars of Jupiter and Mars. In Persia, we slit the throat of the bull in honor of Mithras and take our name from that act. In Jerusalem, we bore the cross and freed the city from the Saracen." There was a long moment of silence and then Ellijay spoke in unison with at least ten other voices from the shadows. "Are you a brother in arms, Malcolm Seward? Are you ready to act as a true soldier?"

He swallowed and his mouth felt dry. "Yes. Yes, I am."

"Then a conqueror's wages are yours." Stark electric lights sparked to life and threw glaring spots of luminescence on a series of objects in time with Ellijay's enumeration. "Rank,"—a uniform with captain's bars— "land,"—a series of legal papers Seward recognized as a land deed—"plunder,"—a stack of ingots large enough to guarantee his wealth—"and woman."

At the last, all the lights in the gallery were extinguished and the Surgery itself returned to the wan luminescence of low gas lighting. A door in the far wall, directly opposite from the one through which Malcolm had entered and now across the altar from him, swung open with a faint creak. Out of the room or hallway beyond strode a woman with the head of a bull.

Seward swallowed. The animal head was a mask of some sort, but it was a fine one, covered in black luminescent hairs that caught the faint light. She wore a cloak of matching color but her movements were unmistakably female, as were the long shadowy legs that swept out of the cloak with her every step.

She reached for the clasp on her neck and undid it. With a shrug the fabric fell from her shoulders to the ground. A corset covered in that same black horsehair bound her waist, pushing her hips out and her bare bosom up. Stockings of faint black gauze were tied to straps that descended from the corset's bottom, and these covered her thin legs from mid-thigh down.

Seward's gaze descended her body slowly, his pulse accelerating and his britches tightening with every moment. The corset supported but did not cover small pear-like breasts, shockingly white compared to the dark fabric below them. They culminated in dark aureoles and hard buds for nipples. Her hips flared seductively from the bound corset-waist, framing the swirls of black hair that grew around her sex. Her legs were long and strong, but he noticed that she was trembling.

"The bull-woman," Ellijay said from above. "The harlot of heaven. To be a brother-in-arms, you must face her and make her yours."

He walked around the altar, feeling the tight constriction of his own bulging sex and smelling the odor of the ox-blood on her chin and lips. A sledgehammer pounded in his chest, driving railway spikes of envy through his heart and out of his crotch. When he got around and close to the bull-woman, she flinched.

He hesitated and he could see gooseflesh rise on her chest, fine, invisible hairs standing erect on her breasts. He reached out and touched the left one, and she yelped slightly. She was weak. He moved his hand along her pale flesh and felt the hard bud of her nipple slip between his fingers. A soft gasp escaped from her lips. She was enjoying this.

He looked up into the dark galleries. Were they still watching? Surely. What did they expect? He knew the answer to that: conquest.

He moved his hands from her breast, out to her arms and up to her shoulders. She writhed slightly under his gentle touch, but flinched again when he grasped her there with sudden force. She screamed when he spun her around and threw her bodily onto the altar. The bowl went flying, sending drops of blood flying a across the Surgery.

She looked up at him with her huge bull head and its empty glass bull eyes, and he knew she was scared no longer. She was his. He walked forward and removed his white shirt, now stained with ox-blood. He put his hands on her knees and pulled them up and apart, until her heels were on the altar top and her sex was open for him. It was a tight pink slit of flesh. He bent down to bite and lick at it, leaving a smear of dried blood there.

She yelped and writhed and the rank odor of animal copulation came from her. He breathed it in deeply, savoring it like the finest of perfumes. Her hand reached for his chest and first one, then the other leg curled around his back to draw him in. He bent down and took her right nipple in his mouth, first sucking it, then biting it. Her fingers ran through his hair.

He pushed back slightly and undid his belt, and shed the remainder of his clothing until he stood naked over her. His manhood stood erect and swollen, its head fully out of the fleshy sheath. She reached hungrily for it, and he felt fire in her touch as she wrapped her fingers around him. He moved forward and removed her hand, and pushed her left leg straight up with his right hand on her calf. With his left hand he reached down and positioned himself, then slipped it around to her right thigh.

With a powerful grunt, he thrust into her. She yelled out and he felt the tight constriction, the blockage of her tearing hymen, and he knew he was deflowering the whore of heaven just as he had both of Harold Dunn's daughters. It made it that much better.

Pain and pleasure melded in the bull-woman as she continued to yell out, but met each thrust with one of her own. He felt the fire building in his loins and she threw her head backward over the back edge of the altar, unable to support the weight of the mask any longer. He knew what to do next.

He released her left leg and reached to the altar with his right hand. Guided by instinct, it found the short sword's hilt and closed around it in a firm grip. He raised the blade and, at the very same moment that his loins emptied their seed into the woman, he sliced her throat to complete the sacrifice of the bull.

***

Regina was certain she was dying. Malcolm—her beloved Malcolm!—had sliced open her throat at the same time he deflowered her. Her hands went to the wound and found a crimson wetness there. Her head swam and she felt a terrible chill growing within her as her lifeblood ran to the floor of the room in great dark rivulets. Her head, weighed down by the bull-mask, lolled over the edge of the altar and the blood ran over her jaw line and down her face. She could see it dripping out of the holes in the snout of the mask, falling onto the overturned golden bowl on the ground.

There were sounds, but she couldn't hear them. She was dimly aware of the slithering withdrawal of her lover-murderer's sex from within her, but even that was distant. A moment or an eternity later she felt herself being moved, dragged or carried from the altar, but that could have been a dream. The world closed around her and darkness reached up to swallow her whole.

Victoria had said the truth would be costly, but death seemed too dear a price by far. Memories filled the void of darkness through which she floated: Victoria, her guide in the night society, taking her to the Taurus Club on Pall Mall, where they went in through the servant's entrance and descended to a subterranean chamber. A woman waiting there, a prostitute whom Victoria knew. Her guide dismissing the woman and telling Regina to take her place.

"I told you it would be difficult," she said in the memory.

"I'm ready," Regina remembered herself saying, "for anything." She boldly disrobed then, not even waiting for the prostitute to leave. Standing naked, trying to hide her fear, she had Victoria affix her corset, stockings, and finally the mask.

Malcolm was a different man when she saw him. Oxblood was smeared on his face and shirt and he looked at her for the first time without love. He couldn't know it was her under the mask, of course, and she saw his lust stripped of all romantic garlands for the first time. It both terrified and excited her. His hungry ravishing was painful and wonderful, her deflowering a savage, wanton act that tore down all her inhibitions. It was like the night last winter in the coach house, amplified a thousandfold. Sprawled on the altar, she moved her pelvis to meet his manhood thrust for thrust and longed to feel his seed in her. She was his, conquered absolutely.

And then came the knife and her lover was her death.

"There is always a price." Victoria's voice again, but stronger this time, closer. The numb darkness gave way to a blurry expanse and the sensation of her throat full of a heavy liquid. She smelled copper and tulips and couldn't understand why.

"You only have to decide if you can pay it," Victoria said as her face resolved itself in the blur. It was sideways— or perhaps Regina was lying down, she couldn't tell. Regina heard a rough gurgle and thought it just might be her.

Victoria, who was seated opposite Regina, removed the long silk glove on her right hand and arm, carefully folding it and putting it on the seat beside her. Using her left hand, she reached behind her head and drew out a long hatpin. It glinted silver in the light of a swaying lantern. She clasped it tightly in her left hand, her index finger firmly pressed almost at the needle-sharp tip. She placed that tip on the soft flesh on the inside of her right elbow and drew it slowly down her forearm, all the way to the wrist.

The alabaster flesh parted into a pink, puckered, bloodless gash. Then, the hatpin set aside, she extended the maimed arm toward Regina. Thick black arterial blood, like week-old pudding made from afterbirth, welled from the wound and flowed in a rich stream down Victoria's arm to pool in her cupped palm.

"Chose," she said and placed her hand at Regina's lips.

The girl had barely the strength to part her lips or extend her tongue, but barely was still enough. Her own blood, red and hot, spilled out of her mouth, but it refused to mix with its darker cousin and just ran over the pool of Victoria's hand like oil over water. Regina's tongue found the rich contents of that pool and lapped it up. It was cold and sickly sweet, and it seemed to run up her tongue and down her wounded throat of its own volition.

Regina drank the hand dry and moved her thirsty lips to Victoria's wrist, where her artery was split open like a ripe fruit. She sucked at that fruit like a babe at its mother's teat.

By the time they arrived at the house on Charlotte Court, Regina could walk of her own power. She didn't want to be far from Victoria, though, and clung to her. The night air was cold on her naked flesh, but she didn't seem to mind. Neither did she even consider it strange that the wound on her neck wasn't bothering her anymore.

In fact, it seemed to have closed altogether.

Once inside the house, Victoria removed her own cape and walked up the stairs, toward her private chamber.

Every few steps, she shed another article of clothing. At the top of the stairs she stepped out of her red satin gown. By the time she was up the second flight of stairs, most of her undergarments were gone as well. When she walked into her bedchambers, Regina only a few steps behind, she was entirely and fabulously nude.

Regina had never seen anything so beautiful. Once again she remembered their first meeting in the coach house in December and it paled before the spectacle of Victoria's graceful nakedness. Like an ancient Aphrodite come to life, she crawled slowly onto the four-poster bed in the center of the windowless room. A cat finding a place in the sun, she extended her body until she lay on the cream-colored satin bedcover and then turned over. Regina was transfixed at the threshold of this most sacred of chambers.

Victoria lifted her head to gaze at Regina, but didn't say a word. Her meaning was clear, like a message sent directly to the young woman's soul: *Come to me*.

Regina entered the lush bed chamber and felt the Persian carpet under her feet. She made it to the bed and crawled onto it and on top of this animate goddess. She straddled Victoria, edging herself forward until her pubis was resting on the other woman's stomach. She looked down, hoping for a way to please her.

Victoria reached for the pin in her hair anew—she'd discarded the hat early, but left the pin in her hair—and handed it to Regina. Again, no words, just wants made thought: *Feed me*.

Regina took the pin and simultaneously shifted up onto her knees—she felt, without thinking about it, that Victoria wanted a touch more freedom of movement. She looked down into the deep wells of those emerald eyes before moving to the task at hand. The needle in her right hand, she cupped her left breast much as Malcolm had done, moving her fingers to the root of the nipple and pinching it so it stood erect. With only a heartbeat of hesitation, she lanced that bud with the long silver needle.

The sharp, hot pain was wholly erased by the enraptured look on Victoria's face.

Regina removed the needle and released the pressure on her nipple. Red warm blood welled out of the puncture wound, and fell from her breast in heavy drops. She leaned forward so these would fall on Victoria's face and watched happily as the goddess let them slip down her tongue.

The next second was a blur of hunger and motion. Victoria lunged upright, her mouth closing on the bloody nipple as she lifted Regina bodily off the bed and threw her to the ground. Regina was dimly aware that such strength shouldn't be possible in a slender woman like Victoria, and that she herself should crash against the Persian carpet and the hard floor beneath it with enough force to split her skull, but none of that seemed to matter. Somehow, in that flurry of motion so sudden it was invisible, Victoria was able to extend an arm to arrest their fall a few inches above the ground. Instead of crashing like a dead weight, Regina felt she was diving into Victoria's embrace.

All the while, she felt the blood draining from her breast. It was like heaven.

Hours later, she fell asleep on the bed curled against Victoria. They were both fully nude and Regina savored the contact between their flesh.

***

The cat that lived in the cluster of trees and the small drain pipe midway up Arlington Street, St. James had once been a ratcatcher's pet. They had shared "a taste for the death of vermin," the illiterate ratcatcher once said. That was before he fell down drunk in the street and got his arm and leg crushed under the wheels of an omnibus, of course. The man was begging for scraps in Limehouse now, but the cat had left him as soon as the steady supply of vermin ended.

Arlington Street, home to spacious aristocratic manors and near several large parks, had its share of rats, birds and other things to eat. Trash in the sewers was sometimes worth eating as well, and the cat regularly made off with parts of meals eaten in gardens or left by open kitchen windows. So it was a happy arrangement, but that did not mean the feline was unwilling to accept food from the Burned Man. This newcomer to this little corner of Arlington Street had flesh that smelled of tar and disease, but he also left out scraps of food for the cat while he watched the comings and goings at the large house where the cat had once stolen an entire blood sausage. (The residents called it Monroe House, but to the cat it would forevermore be The Sausage House.)

After several days and nights of the Burned Man coming and going, always bringing the scraps to share, the cat rewarded him with a purr and a rub. The ratcatcher had liked that and it usually got the cat an extra treat. This time it did as well: three especially tasty bits of lard flavored with something the cat did not recognize.

The cat never quite understood where the pain in its tummy came from, or just why the stuff it vomited mere moments before its death smelled so much like blood. It did register the smile of pleasure on the Burned Man's features.

***

She woke still curled against Victoria, whose pale skin had turned icy cold. There were no window, and very little light, but Regina knew somehow the sun was rising. Victoria was a slab of marble—cold, unmoving, dead.

Regina screamed.

Chapter Seventeen

John Claremont had left at first light to catch the first train toward Eton, where a new client was to meet him. He'd peeked in on Joanna as he left, touching her gently to wake her. She'd smiled, accepted his gentle kiss, and wished him well on his trip. She'd allowed herself a bit more time in her bed, but hadn't slept.

An hour later and she was up, had done her toilet and was dressed for the morning. The maid served breakfast and the two women chatted slightly about the rain that had lasted all night and into the day. Both hoped Mr. Claremont would be able to stay dry. She spent the rest of the day at the business of a lady hoping for social advancement, visiting well-born friends in the morning and leaving cards at the homes of those whom she'd yet to see this season. She also dedicated much time to her dear Millicent, the daughter who'd brought her and John so much joy. She knew he had wanted a son—and still did, of course—but he'd been a caring father for the babe's now eight months of life and that meant a great deal to Joanna. Her own wastrel of a father had done very little for her, concentrating the tiny bit of affection he had on Malcolm, and even that had been hardly worth mentioning. She was determined that her children would have it better.

At quarter to eight that night, right after dinner, a sopping, sobbing, terrified Regina Blake appeared on the doorstep of 23 Sydney Mews.

"Oh dear, Ginny, come out of the rain!" Joanna ushered her friend in while the maid fetched a towel to wrap around the girl. "Where did you come from?"

"Bloomsbury." Regina's voice was a tiny thing. The rain had matted her hair to her scalp and shoulders and she wore no shawl or cape, just a cream-colored muslin morning dress, devoid of the taffeta underskirts and petticoats that would give it its shape. The cloth was soaked through and the hem stained with mud.

"Did you *walk?*"

Regina nodded. Her boots, at the end of unstockinged feet, were clotted with road mud. She was shivering.

"My God, let's get you out of these clothes and into bed. Then you can tell me everything."

"I… I've seen such things…."

"Shh. In a moment." Taking the towel from the maid, Joanna wrapped it around Regina. "Everything is all right—"

"*No!*"

Regina pushed Joanna off her with a sudden burst of prodigious strength. The lady of the house fell back onto the floor with an exclamation, feeling as though she had just been manhandled by a stevedore.

"Nothing is all right!" Regina screamed, a wild look in her eyes. "They're out there right now, Joanna!"

"Who…?" Joanna felt a dull ache building where her left elbow had impacted the floor. Her left hand felt numb. "Who are you talking about?"

Regina paced, seemingly dimly aware of the question asked her. "They drink blood, always blood. And they gather at night, in grand balls and soirées." She suddenly locked Joanna with her gaze. "And Mother. I think Mother…"

"Lady Blake is alive?" Joanna felt a thrill of joy at the news. It was short-lived.

"Yes! Or no." Regina collapsed into the divan. "I think she's among them…. They are living one minute, dead the next…. Undead."

Joanna got to her feet and approached her troubled friend, although with care. Her left arm had developed a shooting pain between the elbow and wrist and she feared a serious injury might be lurking there. Concern for her darling friend overcame caution, however, and was rewarded. As soon as Joanna sat in the divan, Regina melted into her like a child.

She muttered incomprehensible things while Joanna guided her up the stairs and into her own bed. She fell asleep immediately, still dressed in sopping clothes. Joanna stripped her of the garments and she barely stirred. She had no underclothes and the dress was inexpertly buttoned closed, so it came loose with a minimum of moving her about. Joanna managed to slip a nightdress on her, tucked her under a heavy blanket, and left her to sleep.

The condition of Regina's clothing raised at least as many questions as her rambling speech, of course, but that could wait for morning. For the time being Joanna would sleep in John's bed in the next room and periodically check in on her.

When she did so at around eleven o'clock that night, Regina was gone.

***

The ritual chamber had taken months to construct. Working from notes recovered from the Parisian chantry of heretics within his own order, Anton Wellig had carefully reproduced the symbolic conditions favorable to the transformation of the vampiric form. In the hoary nights of the Middle Ages, he knew, Tremere himself had used just such a ritual to steal the gift of vampirism from the petty monsters of Hungary. Others of the order had used derivative rites to birth a variety of monstrous servitors over the ensuing years, from animate gargoyles to homunculi made from the recovered ash of vampiric enemies. The Ducheski family, who existed under Wellig's patronage, had provided more insight into the necessities of vampiric transmutation, and he had already spent two centuries experimenting with selective breeding among that extended family.

Emma Blake (née Emiliana Ducheski) was the result of just such experimental breeding. She displayed none of the congenital deformities of her relatives—no curved spine, no fused toes, no albinism, no cranial malformation—but also seemed not to have the familial gifts. For the Ducheski were a special family, whose living bodies produced minute quantities of unliving blood. This granted them the merest fraction of a true kindred's gifts, but it did make them useful aides and agents. Emma, however, had no such gifts, or so Wellig had long thought.

The Parisian notes, however, added a whole other element to the equation. The heretics had apparently conducted a long examination of the effects of vampiric transmutation on different types of mortal shells, with a specific eye toward the use of these subjects in blood rites. If Wellig's calculations were correct, Emma had the potential to be a perfect receptacle for certain rites of blood poisoning. Those who consumed her blood would be brought low, sooner or later.

The road from theory to practice was, as ever, no easy course. The proper transformations first required Emma to leave mortality behind and rise as a vampire near the winter solstice. Then she had to be subjected to the proper rites at midnight, precisely forty-three days after the summer solstice, so that her humors could be properly aligned. Tonight was the night for that second stage.

The chamber was a perfect square aligned so that the corners pointed at the cardinal directions. Bainbridge's contacts among the city's masons (the mundane builders rather than the muddled occultists and political old boys) had permitted the construction of the chamber near the town of Greenwich, east of London. That Greenwich was also home to the base meridian for modern longitudinal calculations was not a major factor in the choice, but Wellig happily worked that into his astrological calculations.

In the center of the square was a near-perfect hemispherical pool, approximately nineteen feet, three inches in radius (it was quite precisely twelve cubits in radius, using the length from Wellig's elbow to middle finger tip as the base measurement). The pool was three-quarters full of ritually prepared blood, taken from human victims of plague, influenza and even malaria, and mixed with the venom of thirteen varieties of serpents. This, of course, made of the pool a huge ritual cup, or a corrupted grail.

Facing the northeast wall was the one irregularity in the inversed hemisphere of the pool: a large triangular groove. This flaw inversed the healing power of the circular bath and transformed it into the Phalec of Mars, a symbol implying both the dominance of will and the necessity of bloodshed. Not coincidentally, a variant thereof was also the symbol of House Tremere.

Assembling all the ingredients and readying the ritual space had taken months. Emma had been less than cooperative at times, testing Wellig's patience. But now she was ready. She floated in the gore-filled pool, awaiting the precise moment of midnight, when Wellig would begin the invocation.

Then she would be ready at last, ready to poison a god.

***

The morning after Regina's strange arrival and departure, Joanna Claremont took a hansom to the local post office and mailed three letters, each expressing varying degrees of concern. The first was addressed to the Right Honorable Viscount Blake, Monroe House, Arlington Street, Mayfair. It read:

My Lord,

It is with a heavy heart that I must write you to express my concern over the health of Lady Regina, your daughter.

As you surely know, Lady Regina and I have been the dearest of friends for many years and she has spent much time with me this season. However, I fear she may have fallen in with a bad sort and I believe she has need of all her loved ones at this time.

I realize that the loss of Lady Blake, may God keep and guard her soul, has weighed heavily on your family and I hope you know that my thoughts and those of Mr. John Claremont, my husband, are with you in your grief. I fear that in your understandable sorrow, you may have pushed dear Regina away from your own bosom and simultaneously cut her off from the support of the only other male figure truly dear to her since her brother's inopportune decision.

I beg you to reconsider your banishment of my brother from your home.

Yours truly,

Mrs. Joanna Claremont

The second letter went out to Lieutenant Malcolm Seward, Taurus Club, Pall Mall, Mayfair. She had no idea if Malcolm would get it soon, but that was the only address she had for him. It read:

Dear Malcolm,

Terrible news! Darling Ginny appeared at my home yesterday soaked through and raving about terrible things. She then vanished with the fall of the night. I am at wits' end. Please, you must help!

Your sister,

Jo.

The third letter had a special quality and her hand moved mechanically across the paper. Indeed, she began only with the vague sense that there was someone else to whom she must write, some other person who deserved— no, who *must* know of Regina's condition. Until she took her pen to the envelope and wrote *Miss Juliet Parr, in care of The Highgate Society for Women's Suffrage, Gordon House Road, Highgate* across it, she had no precise idea to whom this urgent letter had to go. As soon as she finished the trailing cursive *e* on the last word of the address, the information vanished from her mind once again.

Each word of the letter itself was the same. At the time, she felt as if she were moving in a dream, where necessary information seems to appear in the mind when it is needed and vanish when its usefulness is past. She found this strange, worrisome even, but this did not stop her from writing the letter. For the briefest instant she had the image of a brown-haired girl with unblinking eyes and a strangely mannish fashion sense, a girl who had visited pain upon her with a razor, had ordered her to write this letter and then forget it all—but the next moment that memory was gone as well.

The letter read:

Miss Parr,

As per your request, it is my duty to inform you that Lady Regina, daughter of Viscount Blake, has appeared at the home of my husband and I in a terrible state. She seemed utterly confused and raved about the consumption of blood by people or peoples unknown, whom she termed "undead." She also reported her belief that her mother, the late Viscountess Emma Blake, who died this past Christmas at the Blakes' manor house in County Durham, was somehow still living. Regina then disappeared last night.

I trust you will find this note useful.

In confidence,

Mrs. Joanna Claremont

The closing courtesy was largely unnecessary since Joanna forgot about the letter entirely an instant after depositing all three letters, exiting the post office, and turning up the Brompton Road. The following week she would chastise herself for having somehow lost her last penny stamp, but by then she would have other matters to concern her.

This morning she followed the road a few hundred yards, spared a glance at the Museum of Manufactures where she and John had spent a happy afternoon in March admiring the products of the latest industrial technologies, and then headed to the Holy Trinity Church. She spent the next two hours kneeling on a hassock in one of the back pews, praying the Lord God, Blessed Christ, and the Holy Spirit to save the soul of her dearest friend from whatever devils had besieged her.

Part Three:

Sydenham & Points South, August, 1888

In which a dance macabre is held and reunions lead to further incidents

Chapter Eighteen

"My lord, I must demand that you desist from this behavior immediately."

John Claremont had done very well for himself over the course of his twenty-eight years. A cobbler's son, he'd managed to claw his way up into the higher ranks of the middle classes and become a partner in a successful trust owning several small manufactures in Essex, London and elsewhere. He had married the daughter of a gentleman farmer and made several important friends in the gentry. He had hopes of someday achieving those ranks of society himself, and he saw his home on Sydney Mews in Chelsea as a step in that direction.

One of the great secrets of his success, he felt, was being affable with his betters. Although the quality had a traditional distaste for industry and commerce, they recognized the growth of those sectors and their importance to the Empire. Through friendly relations and well-designed financial partnerships, he'd convinced a few that he could sully himself with the unpleasant aspects of industry and return their estates a tidy profit on their investments. He prided himself on always remaining calm and deferential when in the company of his social betters. Thus, it was highly uncharacteristic of him to make demands of a viscount with important colonial and military connections. Add to this the fact that this particular viscount was very likely to become a relation of his—the father of Joanna's brother's bride—and his demands were all the more unusual.

But then, it was hardly usual for him to return from investigating a new business opportunity in Leeds to find James, Lord Blake berating Joanna in the small salon on Sydney Mews. Not usual at all, in fact.

"Where is my daughter!?" The viscount seemed not to have heard John Claremont's demand. Joanna was recoiling as best as possible, pressing herself against the back rest of the divan as Lord Blake leaned over her, his face only a few inches from hers. John, standing in the doorway several yards away, could still smell the brandy on his breath. "Tell me, woman!"

"My lord, please…"

"Colonel!" Lieutenant Seward—Joanna's elder brother—was in the salon as well, dressed in regimentals, and his military burst seemed to snap Lord Blake out of his rage. Despite his concern for his wife, John Claremont did not fail to notice that his wife's brother was wearing the blues of the Horse Guards, a regiment he had thought limited to peers.

Lord Blake took a step back and Joanna, freed from the shock of the man's attack, burst into tears. "Oh," she sobbed, "I don't know, Lord Blake. I swear I don't."

John moved to comfort the mother of his child, but her brother held out a hand to signal him to stay. Seward then knelt before Joanna and took out a sheet of ivory paper. John recognized it as his wife's favorite writing bond.

"You wrote us these letters, and mailed them either last night or more likely this morning. We both received them in the afternoon. I recognize your handwriting, Jo."

John listened, trying to uncover just what madness had suddenly gripped his home. If the letters had arrived in the afternoon, she must have mailed them in the morning. The London two-penny post was one of the great marvels of the age.

"I… It is," Joanna said, after looking at the letter in question, "but I swear I don't remember what I was worried about…." More sobs.

"Who is this 'bad sort'?" Lord Blake brandished his own letter on the same bond and in the same handwriting. "You say here my daughter has fallen in with?"

"Please, Joanna," Seward said, "we can't locate Regina. She hasn't been to Monroe House in several days now."

"I… I can't…" Joanna fought back more tears and closed her eyes, concentrating. "I feel as if I've woken from a dream, Malcolm. I feel like Regina's in terrible danger, but I can't remember why or how…"

"Blast it!" Lord Blake's blood was up again and he seemed about to resume yelling at Joanna as if she were an especially stubborn mule.

John found himself not paying attention to that, however. Instead he noticed a strangely cold feeling in his chest and looked down to see another strange sight. There was a bloody blade-tip sticking out of his chest. He made a small noise that sounded like "Ulp!"

"Hello," Gareth Ducheski said once John Claremont collapsed.

***

Cedric hadn't said a word in the hour since Regina had returned to Charlotte Place. The coachman had let her in, followed her through the house and out the back door into the garden. Regina was sure she'd intended to rush up the stairs to the bedchamber, to follow the route she'd been drawn through on the previous terrible night. (A *wonderful night*, a voice deep inside her exclaimed.) Yet, when she'd reached the base of the stairs it had become clear, without any outward sign of why, that to climb them would be wrong. Of course she wanted instead to head into the garden to await Miss Ash.

She heard the whirring of a nightjar somewhere in the trees and stared into Cedric's unblinking eyes. There was only the dim luminescence of the city's gaslit streets reflected off the low clouds and the glow of the half-shrouded face of the Moon. No torches were scattered about the garden tonight and the closed buds of the rosebushes seemed like black, dead things. The coachman's face was shrouded in deep black and his eyes were like spots of coal.

Somehow she knew he hated her, just as she hated him. Hated him for knowing the truth of this terrible world she had found herself in, for being calm and impeccably dressed while she shivered in the wet shift of a dress she'd run out of here in this very dawn, for his proximity to the she-thing who had done this to her.

Hated him for being closer to Victoria than she was.

"Good evening, Regina."

Victoria, suddenly behind Regina, placed her hand on the young girl's neck. It sent shivers down her spine as it caressed the tender flesh under Regina's jaw line. It took the girl a few seconds to realize that Victoria's hand was cool.

"Thank you, Cedric."

The coachman left with a last silent hateful glare and Regina oriented herself to Victoria, who sat on the stone bench beside her. She was magnificent, of course, dressed in a black satin gown that shimmered in the non-light of the August night. Her pale alabaster skin seemed to glow and her lips appeared deep purple-black. Regina collapsed into her waiting arms, tucking her face into the crook of her bare shoulder and wrapping her hands around her waist like a child returned to her mother.

Her mother, she thought, and realized the skin against which she pressed her brow was colder than the night air—as cold as the grave.

"No!" Regina exclaimed and pushed herself away from the Victoria-creature. She fell off the bench and the gravel of the garden path dug into her thigh. She scurried back, sharp rocks finding her palms. "No... what..."

Victoria smoothed out her grown and looked on Regina with the confident concern of a houndmaster whose favorite pup is misbehaving.

"What... What are you?" Regina's voice quavered with the sobs she was suppressing. Tears ran down her face.

"You have spent the season with me, darling girl. Surely you know me by now."

"I... I drank your blood..."

"Quite so."

Regina's hand went to her neck. It was smooth, but she felt sure there was a faint white line remaining of the fatal gash that had been cut there. "I... died."

"Oh, my girl." Victoria waved to the bench on which Cedric had been seated. "Please, pick yourself up off the ground. Surely we can have a conversation without you cowering like a child. You've come so far."

The reprimand was like a splash of cold water on Regina and she felt a sob die in her throat. She moved to the chair and took a deep breath. *Mother*, she thought. *Remember Mother.*

"I have never seen you eat," Regina said, fighting back panic with analysis. Forging ahead through the bog lest she be sucked down. "No food. No drink, save for..."

Save for my blood, her mind completed, remembering with sudden clarity red droplets trickling off her own breast into Victoria's beautiful waiting mouth. The same mouth that had drunk down her blood in a small brandy glass—without brandy—and had kissed her neck last month, causing delicious pinpricks there. It had been like—

"Don Cerro. Don Cerro as well," Regina whispered, her mind making a lightning-tree of connections: His attempted ravishing, the sensation of first his kisses and then something else at her throat, the blood in her hair. She'd thought it from his rough handling of her! She had been *food* for him!

"You are all…" she began, but stopped without completing her thought. No, histrionics were absolutely not what was called for. Panic tried again to grab at her, sending a sudden wave of nausea rushing through her. She tasted bile in her throat.

"Yes? What, pray tell, are we all?" Victoria seemed amused.

Regina's mind raced, remembering suddenly the apoplectic fear she had felt at Cerro's reprimand of her and the awe at Lady Anne's endless will. She also recalled the dance of status and association in which she'd seen all Victoria's so-called kindred partake. The bawdy girls who imitated the wasp-waisted corsets of Lady Merritt. The men who all wore the exact same cut of suit based on the pattern set by their preeminent member. The protégés and mentors.

"There are degrees," she said at last and was rewarded by a slight smile from Victoria. "Degrees of initiation. Some are your kindred and others are just protégés, like Lieutenant Pool is to Captain Ellijay, and…"

Victoria smiled and waited.

"I am to you."

Regina felt her head swimming and heard the shudder in her own voice. "Your night society feeds off the day, drinking the... the blood of the 'kine' and existing at night. Drawing the living in, like you did me."

"If I recall, I found you in Don Cerro's care," Victoria said, like one sister chatting happily to another, "and very much drawn in already."

Regina looked down at her bare, bloodied hands. "Yes, you're right. I came looking for Mother." *Who was drawn in herself. Who is still out there, somewhere.* "Tell me more about the Tremere, and about the Ducheski."

"Of course, darling girl." Victoria patted the space on the bench next to her.

Regina stood up and moved there, caught as she had been all season in a conflict of emotions. She remembered the statue of Narcissus and felt empathy for him, unable to draw himself away from the terrible beauty of his reflection despite the agony of his own starvation. She returned her cheek to Victoria's neck and was unsurprised to find neither warmth nor pulse of life there, just the cold pleasure of touch and texture.

It was enough.

***

The woman's scream was the best part. Well, not so much the scream as the emotional scent of panic, of a heretofore predictable world collapsing in upon itself. Gareth breathed in deeply as John Claremont died at his feet and his woman screamed and screamed and screamed.

The first of the other two men bellowed with rage and charged him. The little salon was hardly big enough for the old man—for it was the old colonel who moved first—to gain much momentum, but neither could Gareth move out of the way very easily. Even if he'd had the room to move, he might not have. The scar tissue that now covered his frame was not terribly flexible and it hampered his movements. So instead he simply let the old man run into him and pivoted as they fell.

The black blood within him, although it could not heal his burns as well as it had knife wounds and gunshots in the past, still gave him tremendous strength. Thus he quickly pinned the old colonel down. He'd hoped to have the tiresome aristocrat impale himself on the stiletto, but the bastard was lucky enough to avoid the blade in the initial tussle. No matter. Gareth held him down with his right hand and raised his left with the knife held high. He permitted himself a little flourish, reversing grip on the blade one-handed to better plunge it into the old colonel's windpipe.

Then the other man struck. Gareth got just a whiff of young Lieutenant Seward's intention but couldn't react quickly enough. A powerful blow took him on the back of the head and he lost his grip on his blade. He rolled over onto his back, only to see Seward brandishing a fireplace poker and already readying another blow. He kicked the fool in the groin.

"You still smell of your little tart, Lieutenant," Gareth said after getting to his feet. "You've been in her for real this time, eh?"

"Bastard!" The colonel again. He was determined to reuse the same tactic and barreled into Gareth, carrying him back into the salon. They both ended up stepping on John Claremont's prone form and Gareth smiled through scarred lips to hear the colonel's own footfall push the man's death rattle out of his chest. He then used his superior strength to pivot again and allow the old colonel to take the brunt of the fashionable armoire into which they careened.

It made a terrible ruckus, of course, something Gareth liked quite a bit. That the woman screamed again and ran from the room was an added pleasure. He imagined she would head to the nursery upstairs and the infant girl he could smell up there. An idle thought came to his mind as he clasped the colonel's windpipe in his right hand: perhaps he would bake the child into a pie and feed it to the mother.

The lieutenant made another attempt, but foolishly came in close. Gareth's left hand snaked out and caught his throat. He then lifted both men off the ground, so their feet dangled and he could feel them choking. "Your women are more trouble than they are worth, my fine military gentlemen. You, Colonel, with a wife discontent with the greatest gift of all. And you, lieutenant, with a whore who asks too many questions." He smiled. "Come to think of it, Colonel, isn't young Seward's whore your daught—"

The pain in his back took the wind out of Gareth's lungs and sapped the strength from his limbs. He dropped the men and reached to fish whatever was causing such agony out of his kidney. When he turned around he saw that the screaming woman wasn't screaming any more. Instead, she was holding his own stiletto in her hands. It was covered with his own blood.

His sacred blood would heal the knife wound given time, but then Lieutenant Seward found the poker again and there was only oblivion.

***

Dr. Bainbridge's *Hermetica Aedicula ex Tremere* was more than a simple association, as it turned out. In a society of monsters—and that was what these so-called "kindred" were, beauty or no—they were a special case.

"If you believe the legends they promulgate about themselves," Victoria said when she finally deigned to answer Regina in full a few nights after their discussion in the garden, "they were once a cabal of medieval heretics and warlocks. The stories of black arts and the evil eye, of witches to be burned at the stake, grew out their activities and activities of people of their ilk."

Regina caught the glimmer of a shiver in Victoria's voice at the words *burned at the stake* and she wondered just who or what else had fallen to the attention of witchfinders and inquisitors in past eras. *And how did they fool them into stopping their trials?*

"The cabal forsook the day and remade itself into kindred and from there initiated others into their house." They were riding in Victoria's barouche along the Rotten Road running along the southern edge of Hyde Park, a fashionable place for women in good society to be seen in the morning and afternoon—and their monstrous kin to wander at night. "They further claim to still know those black arts."

That shiver again, this time clearly not in Victoria's voice—which remained as melodious as ever—but in something else, something deeper. Just as she had known to wait for Victoria in the garden, she now knew through some connection with her kindred guide that that these claims of black arts were no mere boasts. Miss Ash had seen—and felt—them used before. She was wary of them, almost fearful.

What could cause fear in a creature such as she? What scares a devil? A saint? Or a devil of another sort? Saints, Regina guessed, would be hard to find in this new world.

"And Dr. Bainbridge is still trying to make amends, to be fully accepted."

"Essentially, yes. You understand, darling girl, that all this happened a long time ago." She waved off her discomfort like a countess would an inappropriate suitor. "We do have a tendency toward long memories, however."

More connections led to more questions. Victoria had befriended Emma Blake two decades ago, but seemed to be a young woman. Theophilus Bell also seemed a young man, but bore the scars of an adult slave from before America's Civil War. Were the kindred immortal? And, having drunk their blood, was she?

She wanted desperately to voice these questions and demand answers from the creature in woman's form who'd seduced her, but she dared not. That same unspoken connection between them told her that discretion was the key, and she had been following that motto ever since that night in the garden. She had to peel back the layers of secrecy and horror one by one, deducing and decoding as she had all season long. Victoria confirmed suspicions and sometimes provided further answers, but eschewed direct questioning.

"The social sanction Bainbridge is striving to overcome is more recent then." Regina searched her mind for other clues. Who had been there at the British Museum? Cerro and Juliet Parr, that she could remember, both officials of some sort. But not Lady Anne the seneschal and quite pointedly not the unnamed and unseen HRH. "Lady Anne mentioned the return of the prince from abroad. Bainbridge and the Tremere had it easy in his absence, yes? They took some liberty and have been reprimanded upon the prince's return."

Victoria's ruby lips parted in that smile which managed to simultaneously thrill Regina's heart and chill her soul. "Oh, my darling girl, you are truly gifted! Such an acute sense of the unspoken and the unseen."

Regina risked a more direct question. "If the Tremere are excluded from kindred circles, how am I ever going to find mother? That's assuming the Ducheski have even brought her to them."

Victoria lifted a red-tinted eyebrow in indulgent reprimand. "Your Ducheski relations are just another Tremere façade, child, and if you want to find your mother you must be able to move among their kindred."

"Of course. I'm sorry." Regina's stomach tied itself in a tight knot, ashamed to have upset Victoria and alarmed to be apologizing to a creature such as her.

"If Emma is in London, someone at the ball will know." She called out in a louder voice to the coachman, who was guiding the carriage from his seat ahead of the two women. "To the house, Cedric. We have to make ready for tomorrow's evening train."

***

"Dover."

Getting Gareth Ducheski to talk was, in the end, a problem in two parts. The first, and most time-consuming, was to discover just how to ask the questions they wanted to put to him. Lord Blake had spent the first twenty-four hours relying on a mundane series of incentives to cooperation, centered mostly around increasing amounts of pain with the understanding that such pain would stop only in the event of Gareth's full cooperation.

The first few hours after Gareth had recovered consciousness had consisted of a series of beatings, starting with a few bare-handed slaps, punches and kicks, and progressing through the use of belts, the iron fireplace poker and whatever else came to hand. The rest of that day and all the subsequent night, Lord Blake dedicated himself to extractions using the late John Claremont's sturdy set of tools. Most aristocrats disdained physical labor, but Blake was a colonial man and had gained a love of doing things himself. He thus approached this task with gusto, using the pliers on Gareth's teeth, fingernails and toenails. A sturdy pair of garden clippers allowed him to remove whole toes and the man's left ear. The opposite eye he dug out with a spoon.

This all was harder than it should have been because of Ducheski's cursed ability to heal. They'd watched the deep wound in his kidney stitch itself into a pinkish mass of scar tissue (largely indistinguishable from the other scar tissue that covered his flesh) and despaired that no incentives would have an effect. Thankfully, Lord Blake's persistence outlasted whatever witchery healed the man and after the first few extractions, his body stopped its devilish regeneration. Still, he did not bleed as profusely as he should and there remained the issue of his own stamina. The man seemed ready to suffer huge amounts of pain and even derived some perverse pleasure from it. Lord Blake could never be sure, but the scabbed nub between the man's thighs seemed to swell with pleasure at one point in the evening. Lord Blake promptly removed the offending organ with the clippers.

Fire ended up being the solution to this first major quandary. Judicious applications of a poker heated in the fireplace, of lamp oil and other flammables loosened the man's tongue in only a few hours. Blake had almost set Mrs. Claremont's salon—where he did his work—alight more than once, but the result was worth it. The man started talking.

There remained, however, the problem of just what questions to ask. He had only vague answers as to Regina's whereabouts. In his words, she was "where she doesn't belong" and at a "gathering of her betters." Hardly helpful. Lieutenant Seward had hit upon the idea of asking about Emma Blake and the other Ducheski, and this proved a more fruitful—if more horrifying—avenue. Seward had shied away from the necessities of Blake's techniques, but his resolve improved with every revelation from their guest's lips. The men and women of the Ducheski family, it seemed, were cursed or blessed (it seemed unclear which) with the "blood of the Savior." This "black ambrosia" (Gareth's words) twisted their bodies but granted them dark gifts, such as unholy stamina and strength. A select few, it seemed, merited to receive greater amounts of this black blood, some to the point of what Gareth called "transfiguration."

Lord Blake did not greet this news happily and Seward had to hold him back from using the fireplace poker to crack open the man's skull and scoop out his brains. His reaction grew worse when he learned that Emma, his departed wife, was one of those chosen for this heathen process. Gareth seemed very upset about it as well and ranted about a woman such as she, who had not been marred by the deformities her kinsmen suffered, not deserving such an honor.

Blake demanded to know who had chosen Emma for such an honor and Gareth was happy to answer. "The Master Regent," he said. "Anton Wellig." Some sort of high priest of their heretical savior was this Wellig.

"And where can we find this Master Regent Wellig?"

"Dover," Gareth coughed. "I'm to meet him and Aunt Eleanor on the first vessel for Calais on the thirteenth of this month."

It was late into the evening of August 12th. If they were to make it to Dover they had to leave immediately. They did.

Chapter Nineteen

Several private trains left Victoria Station for Sydenham in the hours between twilight and midnight on August 12th. The ball was to start at the strike of twelve—the witching hour, Regina realized—and none of the city's kindred wanted to be late, it seemed.

The trip was a short one, Sydenham lying not far to the south of the Thames and London proper. It had once been a quiet country village, but that ended in the years after the Great Exhibition of 1851. The center of that great fair had been the Crystal Palace, a huge glass and steel edifice built in Hyde Park and used to house the collection of marvels gathered from around the Empire and the world at large. In the years after the exhibition, the palace's collection came to be housed in the Museum of Manufactures in South Kensington, and the Crystal Palace itself came to Sydenham.

Victoria described the process of moving the edifice those miles as if she'd witnessed it herself, and Regina realized she probably had. "You have to understand that the city came of age with the Exhibition. Before then, despite the Empire and the growth of industry, we were still the city of Mad King George, a medieval and Elizabethan city trying to accommodate the needs of the new age. With the Exhibition, we threw off the old and became the center of the world. All eyes turned to London and hearts soon followed." Her eyes filled with the haze of nostalgia, as if remembering a golden age. "To see the Palace brought low seemed like a step backwards to most of us. It was the symbol of the Exhibition and we had yet to see the rise of the House of Commons or its clock tower, St. Pancras Station, Royal Albert Hall or many of the other locales we now think of as emblematic of modern, Imperial London. There were tears when the great edifice came down."

The train south took them across the Grosvenor Rail Bridge, past Battersea Park and into South London. These very rail lines, now just one part of the network that tied the capital to the nation and the empire, were part of the post-Exhibition developments Victoria was describing. London truly had transformed itself since then.

"When the Palace reopened in Sydenham some three years after the Exhibition," Victoria continued, "it was as a phoenix rising from its ashes. The structure seemed expanded and an enormous park grew around its new home. For the kine, it became a center of amusement and distraction."

"And for the kindred?" Regina was unclear just when she had realized that Victoria used *kindred* not so much to indicate relation directly to her, but as a code for whatever type of creature she and the others had become. That Regina was not yet deserving of the term was both reassuring and vexing.

"For us it became a site for great affairs. The prince-regent had foresight at the time and arranged it to be available for our private use on many nights of the season. The beauty of its design is only truly revealed at night."

As if on cue, the palace appeared around a bend as the train headed down toward Sydenham Station. A combination of gas and new electrical lighting gave the massive edifice the appearance of being made of light rather than steel, glass or the more prosaic crystal. It was a vast long affair, like a massive cathedral with not one but three transepts intersecting it. Glass walls rose five or six stories into the night, with giant steel superstructures forming arcades at the ends of the lateral sections. At the base of these, Regina could see columns lit with bright electrical light, appearing as the solid shoulder of Atlas upon which the heavens themselves rested. The great park surrounding the edifice was dark save for paths marked by gaslights, creating chains of glowing pearls that seemed to snake toward the palace through a sea of night.

Hidden in that sea, Regina had once heard, was the largest hedge maze in London. Little did the daily papers know, that a far more torturous maze, of monsters masquerading as men, of social conventions perverted by blood rites and devilish undeath, also extended from this spot across London and the entire Empire. Somewhere in that Minoan maze lay her mother, like Daedalus trapped in his own labyrinth. Which, of course, made her the maze-maker's child Icarus, ready to fly too close to the light.

That image reinforced itself when they left the train station and rode in a well-appointed barouche to the palace proper, heading through the dark toward the light. There were drivers and cabs waiting, but Cedric rode up with the driver as if he did not trust another to guide his mistress. He kept a long valise—like the one Regina's father used to carry his grouse-hunting gun— nearby and its presence only accentuated the subtext of danger.

If the Crystal Palace had been enticing from a distance, it was overwhelming up close. The cathedral of the industrial age, its thin steel trellises and scaffolds did nothing to take away from its jewel-like appearance. The walls of glass and curving arches of steel rose high into the night and Regina had the distinct impression of entering some ensorcelled world. It just happened that the sorcery in question was very black.

The assemblage was far and away the largest she

had seen in her season of nocturnal gatherings. Lady Merritt had held soirees with thirty guests, all attendants and protégés included, but here the number was at least four times that, and more cabs were still arriving. The crowd spread through a huge ballroom under the high crystal roof. Terraces supported by steel and iron scaffolds overlooked the main room, giving those who wanted some privacy (or a better view) some options. Other private rooms, blocked off by low walls or curtains, beckoned deeper inside the sprawling complex.

The crowd itself had the appearance of a masquerade ball, so diverse were the costumes of the guests. There certainly were a goodly number who wore the traditional eveningwear of the quality—fine silk gowns for the women, black swallowtail suits and white ties for the men—but at least half the crowd bore some remarkable affectation. Lady Merritt's bawdy girls, for example, had outdone themselves in the wasp-like size of their corsets' waists, some of them taking on truly inhuman proportions. Regina felt a cold shiver at that observation, and at the thought that inhumanity was not figurative in this assemblage.

Many guests seemed to have taken a step out of another era, much as Victoria had seemed that first night in the coach house of Bernan House. Men in tights and breeches—now only seen among the daylit crowd in cavalry uniforms—seemed as something out of mid-century. Several men sported their hair long, in the manner fashionable before the reign of Her Majesty Queen Victoria. Some others wore the simpler dress of the middle and even lower classes—tweed suits or canvas work clothing.

The dance of introductions and greetings started as soon as Victoria entered the palace. Cedric remained outside—his hunting valise apparently beyond the pale of evening etiquette for a protégé—and joined a smaller group of other protégés and seconds similarly waiting to be called. Regina remained with Victoria, curtseying and nodding as need be, listening with one ear to the various greetings and social niceties, trying to get a sense of the dynamics of this gathering. The social "orbits" she had learned to identify were in play here, but the scale was such that it was much harder to grasp them in any detail.

Lady Merritt was there, her girls surrounding her like little satellites, flying off to capture other guests. Regina caught a glimpse off Don Cerro and Theophilus, deep in a conversation with a broad-shouldered blond man. There were plenty of faces she had never seen, of course, and she had a strange impression of dissimulation as she played her deadly serious game of identifying the various groupings here. There seemed to be additional levels of complexity at play this night. For one thing, kindred themselves seemed to gather together by certain affinities, much in the same way Lady Merritt and Victoria sometimes did. If the Tremere were an extended brotherhood among the kindred, she wondered if there were other such clannish associations. Lady Anne and Captain Ellijay, who were together again, seemed to share a certain bearing, for example.

"What do you see?" Victoria asked when they had sailed once through the main ballroom and found a private corner.

"There's a third social level tonight." It had been just a suspicion, more instinct at work, but Regina felt satisfaction in Victoria and knew she was right. "The kindred and protégés are here, but there are others, something like servants." If protégés like Regina were not quite full participants in the evening's affairs—she was always in her mentor's shadow, as were the others—

then this third class was almost totally excluded. Like servants in an aristocratic house, they seemed to be part of the furnishings. Instead of providing trays of food and drink, however, they seemed to exist to provide added beauty, like walking tapestries. Indeed, she saw these guests flit from group to group, laughing when appropriate, and following certain kindred around when beckoned. They never spoke save when spoken to. "Are they prostitutes?"

Victoria didn't answer.

***

"My lords and ladies, the prince."

It was Lady Anne who spoke, her voice somehow carrying across the ballroom from her position on the gallery without being a scream or shout. In the same way a gentle soprano can reach to the very back of the opera house, Anne's announcement reached the assembled kindred, protégés and others seemingly effortlessly and called for their attention and silence. Gossips left off their banter mid-quip and sycophants stopped their preening, all turning to face what had clearly become the head of the great room.

Tall black curtains, spread to block off some interior chambers of the palace and suspended from trellises thirty feet in the air, parted thanks to an unseen mechanism. They revealed a further gallery connected to the ballroom by a broad staircase. A deep red carpet lined the stairs and charted a pathway from their base into the ballroom proper. And at the very top of the stairs, stood a god.

"His Royal Highness, Prince Mithras of London," Lady Anne said.

Regina was quite certain she did not have the best view in the room, but it hardly seemed to matter. The man—if such a word sufficed to describe him—at the top of the stairs felt as if he were standing mere inches away from her instead of dozens and dozens of yards. His black-as-night hair was longer than the current fashion and it perfectly framed his ashen-skinned face. His eyes were of that same depthless black, rimmed with the thinnest circlet of silver-gray. His lips were thin and pale, appearing to have been chiseled out of stone rather than fashioned of flesh. In fact, much about this being suggested to Regina the work of the Italian masters of past centuries. To see Prince Mithras was to see Michelangelo's David made animate in his minutest detail of male perfection. To call his physique superb barely touched on its superior nature. Muscle rippled under flesh and his every movement spoke of power unimaginable. Regina felt drunk and had the silly idea that the prince was looking directly at her.

The assemblage, most apparently similarly affected, bowed and curtseyed as one. They then assumed positions to receive the prince's notice once he descended the stairway. Regina and the other lesser guests found themselves subtly but surely left behind as the kindred advanced to receive their monarch's attentions. Like called to like, and Mithras, Regina knew, had no interest in daylit creatures who worried about such petty things as breath and food.

A few steps from the bottom of the stairs, Mithras shed the long, regal cape he had wrapped around his shoulders. It was lined in ermine, the fur of royalty, and three servants rushed to take it from the prince. He wore the uniform of a grenadier guard, although of no regiment Regina recognized—a jacket of the deepest forest green with buttons and tassels of gold. A large bull's-head emblem was pinned to his chest and Regina understood it to be his personal symbol, his seal of office.

Malcolm? She thought of the night in the Taurus Club, of the invocations of Mithras and the slaughter of the bull-woman in the person of Regina herself. *Is Malcolm his slave? Is this truly a god of Persia?* Victoria had hinted at the longevity of undeath, of the benighted existence of the kindred, but the sheer scale here seemed impossible save for the palpably ancient power of the man-shaped thing before her. Regina knew she stood before a millennial creature and she trembled.

Chapter Twenty

With the prince's arrival, at precisely midnight, the evening began in earnest. It seemed divided into three major activities, as far as Regina could tell. The first was presentation before the prince, who was always attended to by his seneschal the Lady Anne. Mithras took position on a throne near the base of the stairs he had descended and a long line of kindred waited his leave to approach him. Just what they discussed was unclear—at times the supplicants seemed to carry news of important business and Regina had the impression that the prince was sitting in judgment, but others seemed there only to make obeisance to one so clearly their superior. Regina had heard stories of the Emperor of China, who demanded that his subjects kowtow before him, kneeling so their heads met the ground three times in abject submission to the leader they saw as a god. This had much the same character.

The dance was the other major activity. A sizeable orchestra played waltzes and other dances and much of the assembled crowd partook. Much as Victoria's breast was devoid of breath, the dance seemed to Regina to be devoid of the joy that usually accompanies such activity. It was a macabre parody of life, a distraction for those not busy meeting the prince or doing their own business.

The third major activity was more of a mystery, and Regina decided it bore investigation. The enigmatic third class of guests continued to follow or lead kindred into the curtained chambers deeper in the palace. There were few regular pairings, and if these men and women were prostitutes, then the kindred were truly voracious lovers. When she noticed Dr. Bainbridge catch the eye of one of these perhaps-bawdy girls, she decided to follow them in. When she noted that instead of proceeding with his chosen girl, Bainbridge simply pointed her toward one of the curtained rooms and then returned to some heated discussion with Lady Anne, she grew all the more curious. When the girl, a buxom redhead dressed in a yellow muslin gown, passed through the wine-red curtain, Regina waited a few minutes to allow her to feel safe and then followed.

What she found left her breathless.

"Mo…Mother?"

Lady Emma Blake looked up from the redheaded girl who was swooning in her lap. Long, needle-sharp teeth extended from her gums and her lips were ruby with the blood of the girl upon whom she'd been feeding. More blood was seeping from the girl's neck, staining her yellow gown. "Regina?"

Terror and relief fought a pitched battle in Regina's breast. Emma Blake bent over the redhead again. When she looked up a second time, the fangs were gone and the wound on the girl's neck had healed itself. Regina ran to her suddenly less monstrous mother.

"Oh, Mother! At long last! If you only knew what hell I have traversed to find you!" She clung to her mother as she hadn't since she was a child, her head buried against the maternal breast. She felt the hot flush of life there, but not its pulse or the heave of breath. "Oh no…"

"Shhhh, my dear girl." Emma Blake stroked her daughter's hair and felt the first crimson tear of blood streak down her cheek. "I'm sorry. So sorry."

"They've made you kindred." Regina didn't know what else to say, looking at the red streaks on her mother's face.

"It was always my fate, darling girl. I thought I could escape it…"

"You still can. Please, come with me. We can make it to London, or…"

"There's no turning back for me, my darling." She nodded toward the unconscious girl still lying on the ground. "I am transformed."

"I've drunk kindred blood too, Mother, surely—"

"You have to forget all of this, Regina." She looked to the heavens, visible through the curving glass ceiling of the palace, far above. "You can still escape with your soul, but it is too late for me. I survive on the blood of the living, my darling girl. The sun burns my flesh. I am…" She closed her eyes and another bead of bloody tear squeezed out between her lashes.

"Undead," Regina completed for her mother.

"Yes, undead. Please, go. I will be in Calais by dawn and you should forget this evening ever took place. Please, for your sake and your father's, leave me buried in County Durham."

"I'm afraid it is altogether too late for that." The new voice was like a cold wind from an empty grave, chill and redolent with humors best unidentified.

Regina turned around to find the new speaker. He stood in the entrance through which she had come, just letting the velvet curtain fall back behind him. Shadows hugged the fabric of his fine suit. He was a tall man, at least six feet, and his top hat only added to the effect. His collar, taller and stiffer than any Regina had seen, framed his long, bony neck and gave the impression of supporting his head by its lonesome. His smile, what there was of it, was thin-lipped and perfunctory. His eyes were hazel, but had an unhealthy jaundiced aspect to them. She recognized him as the dark man who had presided over her mother's funeral.

"I have been looking forward to our meeting, Lady Regina," he continued.

"You have me at a disadvantage, sir."

"In that case, allow me to introduce myself formally: I am Regent Anton Wellig of Lion's Green, Magus of House Tremere, and it seems you already have an intimate familiarity with my dear childe, Emma." As he spoke, Regina caught a glimpse of teeth worn by age or disease into graying stumps.

"Child? You are my grandfather?" Regina knew it wasn't that simple as soon as she said it and spoke again before he could answer. "No—you… you made Mother what she is. You are the person I have been looking for…"

"It is always good to be wanted, I suppose. Although not always good to be found."

"Well, we have found one another, sir, so the time for regrets is past."

"It always is, my dear. Fools indulge in regrets, which are failures from which one does not draw the needed lesson. They are thus bound to be repeated forever more."

"You are a philosopher then, Mr. Wellig?"

"At times. Like the philosophers, I learn from the time I have on Earth and use it to divine the machinations of Heaven." He glanced up at the night sky visible through the glass panes of the great edifice given over to this midnight gala. As he did so, he exposed his neck and Regina understood why his collar was so high and his cravat so full: his skin, gray and wrinkled, bore the marks of some terrible chastisement. Pink scars looped in patterns burned there by hot pokers, while other purplish marks testified to inked scars like those of some African and Polynesian tribes.

Regina glanced down at his hands, curious to see if other marks could be seen on them or on his wrists. Both were well gloved and covered, but she noted that his left hand remained at his side while the right held a medical bag.

"That… that is ambitious, sir." She returned her attention to his face, devoid of terrible marks but still ashen and lined. "Some would call such ambitions hubris. Heaven holds its own counsel."

"Bah!" He seemed genuinely taken aback. "You sound like a relic of past centuries. This is the time of industry and ingenuity. The gates of knowledge have been thrown wide and the bold have the chance to grasp the truth at last."

"Mr. Wellig, I must say that you are a passionate and well-spoken advocate for that position, but I wonder how my mother's fate relates to it. Enslavement and kidnapping hardly seem in line with your enlightened quest."

"Freedom exists only for those with the will to take it, Lady Regina." He smiled his rotten-toothed smile. "And I must commend you on your persistence and resourcefulness. I dare say that few others would have survived your journeys of the last few months, much less found themselves in the presence of dear Emma. You have many admirable qualities, and under other circumstances, I would think we could have been associates."

Regina took a step forward, unintimidated. "And under these circumstances, Mr. Wellig?"

"I'm afraid you have become a troublesome liability." He smiled again and looked all the way into Regina's soul.

She wanted to protest but suddenly couldn't say or do anything. Even blinking or looking away from those sunken beads of hazel he called eyes was inconceivable.

"The prince has seen fit to ban violence on these premises and I do not care to risk his ire just yet, but I fear I could not trust you were I to let you out of my sight at this sensitive time."

Regina was dimly aware of her mother saying something, pleading perhaps, but words coming from anyone save Wellig seemed so unimportant that she couldn't pay attention. Instead, she idly wondered if her mother was still the woman she had known or if the transformation to undeath meant she was wholly different. It should have been a critically important thought, but it was just an idle rumination.

The important thoughts were the ones echoing through her mind, in a voice that was hers but not hers: *Of course, I will stay with Mr. Wellig until his business is concluded. Of course, I will forget all that is said. Of course, I will then return to London and await Dr. Bainbridge's visit. Of course, I understand that the good doctor would mean me no harm, and I will thus offer him no resistance.* It all seemed too obvious.

A small voice that was wholly hers screamed itself hoarse, pleading with Regina not to listen to these thoughts. But the screams were so faint, they surely could not be terribly important.

"Please sit, Emma dear." Once her mother had done so, Wellig turned to address Regina. "Dr. Bainbridge tells me that you have found your way in the company of Miss Ash. This is true, yes?"

"Yes." Answering truthfully seemed utterly reasonable. Still, the smaller voice inside her started at the sound of her patron's name. There was some thought, there, just out of reach.

"Victoria?" Emma Blake looked at her daughter.

"Ah, you know the lady in question, Emma?" Wellig seemed amused. "I suppose I should not be surprised. Our world is a highly incestuous one. Please remove your left glove, dear. Oh, and do be quiet."

Emma Blake did as she was told, stripping off one of the long cream-colored gloves that rose to the short sleeves of her gown. She closed her eyes and sat perfectly still.

"Were we afforded more time, I'd happily investigate the details of these convoluted parallels between mother and daughter, but time is unfortunately of the essence." Wellig set his bag down and opened it. He then reached in—always with his right arm, his left staying at his side—and withdrew several instruments. "Has Miss Ash told something of the House of Tremere, darling girl?"

"Yes." An automatic response again.

"Surely stories of black magic and pagan rituals." He smiled. "Well, there is *some* truth to all that, I suppose. The full truth, however, has more to do with the binding of elemental forces through will."

"The Elemental Phalec." Less automatic this time. Regina felt that he was inviting conversation, enjoying the chance to give a lesson.

"Yes, yes. You are quite perceptive, darling girl." He held up a large syringe filled with a night-black tincture. "The sign of Mars, but deconstructed into its component parts, representing the Will binding Earth and Sky. The calling of miracles."

"The black arts."

He gave her a reproachful look, but more akin to a schoolmaster with a wayward student than that of an unliving warlock who had subjugated her will. "The proper term is *thaumaturgy*, actually. And setting aside religious hyperbole for a moment, I would point out that given our condition, the arts are far more red than black."

At this he lifted up the syringe so it caught some of the soft light. It was a deep red, and Regina knew without a doubt what it was. "Blood."

"Yes, blood. *Vitae*. The superior humor in man and the dominant force among kindred. Blood, in fact, is the perfect element, the union of all fundamental forces into a single substance able to hold back true death. The alchemists never understood this and they have been eclipsed by industry. We understood and we endure."

"Immortal."

"Quite. Would it surprise you to know I have been a thaumaturge for three hundred and fifty years? Immortality indeed, and in that time I have learned many things about this prime element. Most important is the law of sympathy."

"Like affects like."

"Oh, very good dear girl! Yes, thus if you wanted to affect an ancient tyrant who fancied himself a god, for example, it would be very beneficial to have access to a certain quantity of his blood." He plunged the needle of the syringe into the muscular tissue of Emma Blake's arm. She barely reacted. "But when dealing with our kind, blood consumption is the most powerful means of delivery. Thus it would be of great benefit to also have a ritually prepared vessel through which to deliver this blood to said tyrant.

"Fortunately," he continued, "I happen to have both those things." He depressed the plunger and Emma Blake opened her mouth in a silent scream.

"I'm sure you're quite confused, dear girl," Wellig said, continuing his running lecture purportedly aimed at Regina. "Fear not, you will forget all this soon enough, but I do relish the chance to discuss the work to which I've dedicated several decades. So, with the proper blood and the proper vessel, we have all the ingredients. The final step for the rite to be complete, for the Phalec to be drawn, is to add the directing will."

He knelt down to look directly in Emma Blake's eyes. "Emma: *Ego expeto hic, ergo usu venit.*"

Regina barely noticed her mother pitch back her head in another silent scream, or the fine sheen of blood seeping out of her pores like a fevered woman's night-sweat. There was a fine coppery smell, but she ignored that too. Her attention had turned inside, because that faraway voice was saying something, paraphrasing Wellig: *Like blood calls to like blood.*

Now, why was that important?

Wellig led her behind one of the many curtains and they watched as less than a minute later, Prince Mithras entered. His attention fell immediately on Emma, still swooning from the effects of Wellig's thaumaturgic injection.

Regina felt herself caught in the penumbra of that white-hot stare. The chiseled perfection of the prince's gaze swallowed her as well and her mother's experience echoed in her own head. This was a mind so ancient it had forgotten more than Regina could ever hope to know. A soul for whom the sun, the time between dawn and dusk, and the petty concerns of the breathing, were not only insignificant, they did not exist. A will that had challenged the laws of God and usurped the benighted heavens. A hunger that would consume all of creation. And the entirety of this being focused itself on Emma Blake.

He must have moved, but Regina was not aware of it. She simply realized that her mother was now in his arms. His perfect, ashen lips parted to reveal dagger-sharp canines that plunged into Emma Blake's throat. The consumption of her blood made little sound, but her already pale flesh grew ashen gray as it drained away.

"Yes. Perfect." The pleasure exuded from Wellig like a cloud of flies disturbed from feasting on a piece of rotting meat. "His blood calls to him. Even in the body of another, even transformed, it calls."

Even in the body of... And then Regina knew. *Victoria!*

She ignored the signs that her mother, undead or no, was literally being consumed, and looked for the cold feeling inside herself. She'd felt the instinct before, that less-than-natural feeling for Victoria's mood and meaning. The blood. The blood she had drunk from Victoria's veins, that had healed the gash in her throat, that seemed to be center of everything. Victoria's blood.

Images of that wonderful terrible night on Charlotte Place rose from the depths of her memory. The feeling of the needle piercing her flesh to draw forth her own blood for Victoria. The coppery-cold taste of the black arterial flow she had lapped from Victoria's own slit wrist. The rush of pleasure. The desperate connection. The feel of her own naked flesh against Victoria's cold, dead body. The burning need to experience that all again.

"No!" The voice that wasn't hers, the "obvious" decisions placed in her very mind by Anton Wellig, weakened before the connection with Victoria and she stumbled through the curtain. Her legs didn't seem quite in synch and she still felt the urge to just wait idly by while this god-prince consumed her mother whole, but she kept on and pounded on his rock hard flesh. "Stop! Stop!"

He did. Dropping Emma Blake to the ground, he turned to face this newcomer and looked right into her. His infinite will, charged with animalistic hunger, shattered the barriers Anton Wellig had placed in Regina's psyche and he went looking for an answer.

"Regina!" Victoria Ash burst into the room, parting the furthest of the velvet curtains. "My prince..."

A palpable destructive urge rose from Mithras. His fangs were exposed and his hands curled as if they were an animal's talons. He crouched and his nose flared, scenting like a beast. Regina was convinced this moment would be her last, and her final thought was not of the mother she had searched for and whose existence she had just saved, but for Victoria, whose blood was still in her veins. Victoria, whom she—

It stopped. The overwhelming sense of impending violence suddenly stopped and Mithras stood erect once again. Looking into his eyes, Regina saw his limitless will return to the fore, chaining the terrible beast that lurked within him. But just barely.

Regina lowered her eyes at last, and noticed her mother was gone. "No!" She turned to see Wellig dragging Emma Blake through the curtains. The thaumaturge spared a glance behind him and Regina thought she saw real fear in him. That was gratifying. She ran after him, Victoria right on her heels.

They had almost caught him when he grabbed one of the wine-red curtains with his good hand and mouthed a phrase Regina could not hear. The same green flame Thomas Ducheski had summoned up months ago in the Lion's Green crypt to engulf his cousin Gareth, leapt from Wellig's hands and ran up the fabric. It spread with unnatural swiftness, turning the drapery into a massive banner of fire in mere moments.

Regina felt a panic like she had never known course through her veins, and it froze her in place. It took her a moment to realize this terrible, apoplectic fear was not coming from her, but from Victoria. Her kindred mentor fled from the flames as if their sole purpose in existence were to destroy her, and the fear was contagious.

Fire, Regina suddenly understood, was anathema to the undead. In a palatial space filled with kindred, the result was sheer chaos.

***

In the end, the fire did relatively little damage. Lady Anne, one of the few who managed to maintain her composure, had taken the liberty of preparing a dedicated fire brigade for the event. Fires were just too common an occurrence in London to risk such a gathering without taking safety precautions.

Some of the living had perished in the fire, mostly those whom Regina overheard one indelicate kindred refer to as "food stock." Several kindred were also unaccounted for, including the prince himself. Rumors began to circulate among those who gathered at a safe distance to take stock that he was off hunting for the culprits or that he had returned to London proper already. No one entertained the idea that he had perished.

Regina overheard Lady Merritt and several other gossipmongers blame the conflagration on something they called the "Sabbat," but she could not quite grasp what that was. Lady Anne had harsh words for Doctor Bainbridge and Regina wondered if she should perhaps tell the seneschal about Anton Wellig and his thaumaturgic trickery. She was more concerned with other matters, however.

"Emma is gone," Victoria said once Regina finally found her. She was sitting on a bench near the entrance to the park's massive hedge maze and there were streaks of red on her dress. Regina wondered just who had paid the price in blood to restore Victoria's calm. "She and that Tremere, gone in the chaos. To who knows where."

"Calais," Regina said without thinking. Her memories of the evening were confused, a jumble of terror, blood and voices. But her mother had said something about Calais, the French port town closest to England.

Victoria and Regina looked at each other and spoke in unison. "Dover!"

Chapter Twenty-One

Victoria and Regina made it to Dover with only a few minutes to spare. Running down from the train station located on high ground to the docks below and ways from the city's famed white cliffs, Regina felt as if sands were slipping past her down an hourglass. The eastern sky had the first hint of pale, ruddy dawn in it and sunlight was perhaps a half-hour off.

Making their way down the path from the city proper toward the beach, they could see the first ferry of the morning sitting in the docks. Stevedores were loading the last of the baggage bound for Calais and the continent. Smoke rose from the small steamship's stacks and Regina felt sure that at any second she would hear the departure whistle—sounded precisely at 5:15 a.m.—that would signal her mother's disappearance into a world even more treacherous than the maze of London's kindred society.

There had been relatively few people on the special night train from Sydenham (arranged to accommodate any kindred who might depart for the coast after the evening's festivities) and she expected that the ferry, the first of the day, was likewise bound to be largely empty. That it left so early was only to pick up people early in the morning in Calais for the return journey, Regina supposed.

They were getting close now and still no whistle. Regina felt hope swell in her breast. *We can make it!* She turned around a bend in the trail downward and put on an extra burst of speed. Victoria was just behind her.

Almost there! Down some stairs and to the quay. She saw the ferry's first gangplank pulling up, but there was still time. A group of dockworkers, one holding a lantern in the predawn dark, was moving along the quay but she'd just run past them—

Then one of the men tackled her to the ground. Women's boots are hardly the most stable things in the world, of course, and Regina went sprawling with the man over her. She struggled to get some purchase, some leverage to push the brute off her before it was too late. *Who is this madman?*

"Regina! Stop!" The man's voice was familiar, she realized, but she still pushed him off her. He let out a groan as he hit the quay and she turned to glare at her attacker. It was Malcolm.

"Stop, darling," he said, panting. "You have to stop."

Confused, her head spun with relief at finally seeing her lover after so many months and the panic of knowing her mother was mere seconds from being lost again. She looked around and saw her father holding the lantern in one hand and a revolver in the other. "Father?" she whispered.

"It's time to come home, Ginny," Malcolm said, approaching her again.

"I'm afraid it's too late for that, Lieutenant." *Victoria!* She appeared at the bottom of the stairs and advanced toward the others. "Regina has other business to—"

"Stop!" James Blake's face was red with rage as he raised his weapon and pointed it directly at Victoria. "Stay back!"

Victoria smiled, her hard emerald eyes focusing on the retired officer who was threatening her. "You are playing a dangerous game, Colonel. It didn't suit you as a young man and it does so no better now." She took another step.

"I said stop!"

"Father, no!" Regina leaped to her feet, but didn't quite dare to get between Victoria and her father. "Mother is on that ferry. She's—"

"My Emma is dead. These beasts murdered her."

"No," Regina said, trying to keep the panic out of her voice, "I saw her—"

"Regina…" Malcolm began and he too had drawn a weapon.

"You saw nothing!" Blake's rage was making his gun-hand shake. "A devil, a changeling wearing Emma's flesh but without her soul."

Regina took in air to power another argument when chaos and anarchy erupted on the quay. It started with the sound she had been dreading: the high lone whistle signaling the ferry was about to get underway. All heads glanced toward the ship about to pull away, save her father's. And when Victoria glanced that way, looking away from Blake for the merest second, he went on the attack.

Regina would have expected her father to fire his pistol, of course, although she had seen worse wounds healed by kindred blood. Instead, he threw the oil lantern at Victoria and it exploded when it hit the ground where she had been a mere instant before.

The very moment the flaming projectile left her father's hand, Regina felt the dark alien blood within her quicken with something akin to excitement (in the way an eagle is akin to a sparrow). Feeling more than seeing, she sensed Victoria's cold limbs suddenly rush with energy and felt her move with inhuman speed away from the point of fiery impact.

Any normal man or woman would have been engulfed in a sticky, oily inferno. Victoria, so much more than ordinary, should have escaped it altogether, but did not. Indeed, a heavy lethargy was making its way into her soul, and Regina understood without knowing how that it had to do with the dawn threatening in the east. Thus she reacted faster than Lord Blake had any right to expect, but just slowly enough for a tongue of flaming oil to catch the taffeta and crinoline of her gown.

She leaped back toward the steps up the cliffs and emitted a growl like a lioness. She tore at her skirts, ripping the flaming garments off and tossing them aside. Regina saw her fully then, torn gown's bodice and singed stockings covering her, her body crouched at the top of the stairs, her fingers curled so they seemed like vicious talons. Her mouth opened wide to reveal fangs more terrible than any wolf's. She growled anew and Regina felt her rage at the fire and these men reverberating within her own breast.

"My God and Savior," Malcolm said and took a step back. "What... that is..."

"A devil!" James Blake screamed and ran to get around the oil still burning between him and his prey. He stopped short when a rifle shot rang out and tore through his thigh, sending him to the ground.

It took Regina a second to locate the rifleman higher up the path that snaked up toward the cliffs. She saw him silhouetted against the white stone, his billowing black coachman's coat and hat giving him the look of a huge bat perched on the cliff. *Cedric!*

"Quickly!" Cedric called out. "The dawn!"

Victoria's rictus of hate took a few seconds to fade. Her lips, drawn back like a savage thing's, closed over fangs that seemed to sheath into her delicate mouth. She stood up, turned and headed up the stairs. She moved with a long leaping gait, ascending far more like a lynx or panther than woman.

"Thank Christ…" Malcolm said and lowered his weapon. He moved toward Regina, extending his empty hand to her. "Thank Christ."

She looked into his blue eyes and saw not a sign of the man who'd slit her throat in the basement of the Taurus Club. She saw the young officer who'd captured her heart and who would protect her from all the ugliness in the world, from the horror of colonial war to the labyrinthine perversity of the benighted world that had swallowed her mother whole. "I'm sorry," she said and ran up the stairs after Victoria.

Malcolm stood dumbfounded listening to his fiancée's fading footfalls, the moans of James Blake on the ground beside him, and the sound of the ferry steaming into the Dover Strait.

***

The stagecoach Cedric had appropriated was waiting at the top of the path and Victoria was in the back, completely covered in several layers of woolen blankets to block out even the faintest hint of the sunlight just peeking over the horizon. Regina felt in her that lethargy had given way to a death-like slumber.

"Back to London, Cedric," she said with the same voice of command she'd heard Victoria employ. The trip by coach would take much of the day, but that was all right. Once Victoria had woken for the night and was back at her home, they could make ready for the trip to the Continent.

Mr. Wellig had not seen the last of them, she was quite certain.

Epilogue
Cairo, August, 1888

In which the scene of past crimes is revisited

The cursed house in Bab al-Khalq where Anwar al-Beshi had attempted his ritual had finally collapsed in upon itself during the early months of 1887. The British officials now supervising certain aspects of national policy in Egypt authorized a work crew to spend several months dismantling the old home and then building a hospice for the city's Arab poor. The hospice had now been in operation for a full year and local officials had yet to note just how many of the patients who received treatment there walked away with a new ailment. Contagion would be a problem in Bab al-Khalq and the surrounding neighborhoods for many years to come.

The basement of the hospital was where the doctors kept the bodies of the dead. These doctors were British missionaries with delusions of saving souls and flesh at once, for the most part, and they saw no harm in violating Muslim burial practices to conduct autopsies and other anatomical explorations using the corpses of the poor. The dead men and women rarely had family to complain, after all, and why wouldn't they wish to contribute to the battle against disease?

Fahd had served first as a worker in the demolition of the old Mameluke house, then in construction of the hospice, and finally as one of its custodians. A one-armed weakling, he could do very little but always ingratiated himself by running messages and carrying objects for those in charge. He spent a lot of time in the basement with the bodies, often sleeping the night away there. It reminded him of the glorious times when he had served in the temple here, as a slave to Master Anwar. That service had ended terribly, but Fahd took as a sign of his continued worth that he had survived the terrible gashes through his shoulder that had ultimately required the arm's amputation. Still he waited, for somehow he knew his new master would come for him here. He was right.

"It seems your compatriots have left us little to investigate, Mr. Beckett." The man's ironic smile was a sliver of white in his dark face. He stood in the shadows of the stairwell leading from the ground floor into the basement. "A shame, that."

"I'd have been surprised if the temple was still standing, Mr. Ruhadze." The second man came down the stairs. He was a European, paler skin and foreign dress. "But the mural of your Thousand-Faced Goddess was here."

Fahd's addled mind—for the years since the master's destruction had not been kind to him—finally registered recognition. This was the intruder! One of the men who had undone the great ritual that fateful night years hence! The man who had cost him his arm! The new master! He did his best to remain silent in the little corner in which he slept.

"And the ritualist Anwar al-Beshi did not survive your encounter with him?"

"No, he didn't." The European pointed directly at Fahd's hiding place. "But his ghouls apparently did."

"Ah, yes," the Arab Ruhadze said, suddenly looming over Fahd. His golden eyes had the same holy gleam the master's had, Fahd realized. This could mean only one thing.

"Oh, *effendi*!" Fahd prostrated himself before the two men. "I have awaited your holy return! Lead me in worship."

The European smiled.

***

Hesha Ruhadze had done a good job of making the sycophantic Fahd his new best friend. Beckett had little patience for blood slaves and other thralls, but he did admit that they could provide valuable information. Fahd was very forthcoming. He had only recently become a servant of Anwar al-Beshi when the ritual was interrupted. He remembered very well the depiction of the Lady of a Thousand Faces, she was the goddess to which the master had always prayed. He could not, however, provide any details as to how al-Beshi had come to worship this particular deity.

"Master's Britisher concubine was with him longer and he led her in rites to the goddess. Perhaps she would know the answers you seek, *effendi*."

"And what," Hesha had asked, "was her name?"

"Blake, *effendi*. Lady Emma Blake."

It seemed they would be paying Lady Blake a visit.

About the Author

Philippe Boulle is the managing editor of White Wolf Fiction, and thus spends far too much time thinking about vampires and other things that go bump in the night. He is the author of a variety of roleplaying games, **Tribe Novel: Red Talons**, and the science fiction novellas *Heavy Gear: Crisis of Faith* and *Heavy Gear: Blood on the Wind*. He lives in Atlanta, Georgia.

Acknowledgments

My thanks to Tim Dedopulos, Chris Hartford, and Adam Tinworth for doing their best to weed out my plentiful Americanisms; to Myranda Kalis for help with Latin terminology; and to Sara Forsting for encouragement and tolerance in equal parts.

It sent shivers down my spine."
—Tim Dedopulos, author of
Hunter: Apocrypha

Victorian Age Vampire™ Trilogy
Book Two:
The Madness of Priests™
by Philippe Boulle

Regina Blake races from London across Europe to save her mother from the clutches of the Tremere blood-sorcerers. But with every step, she enters further into the benighted world of the Kindred. Her only guides are the seductive Victoria Ash and the mad priest Anatole, but each seems more interested in making her theirs than freeing her mother.

WW11191   ISBN 1-58846-829-1

On Sale in January

Dark Ages™
Clan Novel Series

The War of Princes begins here.

It is a time of War and Faith, of Shadow and Fire.
Constantinople burns, crusaders ride and the Inquisition
rises. For the immortal monsters who have spent
centuries in the shadows, the time has come to strike out.

This epic 13-part series chronicles a vast conflict
among the vampires of the Middle Ages,
covering 30 years of turmoil and change.

BOOK ONE
NOSFERATU
available now!

BOOK TWO
ASSAMITE
available now!

BOOK THREE
CAPPADOCIAN
available in november!

LUCIFER'S SHADOW™

Tales of Fallen Angels
Edited by Philippe Boulle

At the dawn of creation, Lucifer ignited the fires of rebellion. Now, after an eternity, the gates of Hell are broken and the angels of the abyss walk the Earth once more. In the so-called City of Angels, a terrible earthquake sparks three days and nights of rioting, and tales of the end of the world. The Devil himself walks the burning streets of Los Angeles.

In the ten tales of horror and apocalypse in this anthology, demons answer the clarion call and congregate in the modern Babylon, searching for answers and for blood.

WW11904; ISBN 1-58846-824-0